MY PRESENT AGE

MY PRESENT AGE

A novel by

Guy Vanderhaeghe

Macmillan of Canada
A Division of Gage Publishing Limited
TORONTO, CANADA

Canadian Cataloguing in Publication Data

Vanderhaeghe, Guy, date.
  My present age

ISBN 0-7715-9814-9

I. Title.

PS8593.A52M9 1984   C813'.54   C84-098925-3
PR9199.3.V37M9 1984

Design: Don Fernley

Macmillan of Canada
A Division of Gage Publishing Limited

Printed in Canada

This book is dedicated to
Adrian, Karen M.,
Danny, Marie, Gerry,
Karen B., and Steve.

ACKNOWLEDGEMENTS

I would like to thank the Canada Council for a grant, without which it would have been impossible for me to complete this book.

I would also like to thank my editor, Anne Holloway, for her invaluable advice during the writing of *My Present Age*.

"But the present generation, wearied by its chimerical efforts, relapses into complete indolence. Its condition is that of a man who has only fallen asleep towards morning: first of all come great dreams, then a feeling of laziness, and finally a witty or clever excuse for remaining in bed."

Soren Kierkegaard, *The Present Age* (1846)

"No mistaking them for people of these parts, even if I hadn't remembered their faces. Both of them are obvious dwellers in the valley of the shadow of books."

George Gissing, *New Grub Street* (1891)

ONE

The Beast destroyed my brief peace. Before him I could live without guilt, unwatched; for the first time in my life I found myself in the unfamiliar situation of having no one to disappoint. My wife Victoria had walked out on me months before, and although I wished she hadn't, her departure meant I could do more or less as I liked. My father, recently retired, had removed himself and my mother to a mobile-home park near Brownsville, Texas, a sprawling anthill of pensioned worker ants, thousands of miles away. That meant Pop no longer had his eye on me. There was no one left to offend, no one to despair of me and my misdemeanors. After a fashion, I was free.

Free to do what? To give up selling china in a department store and to spend luxurious mornings in bed, rereading *The Last of the Mohicans, Shane, Kidnapped,* or *The Adventures of Huckleberry Finn.* My father, if he'd known what I was up to, would have disapproved most severely of the former, my wife of the latter. Not that they would have cared for either. It's merely a question of emphasis. Pop's preference is for successful and dutiful; Victoria's for the successful and intellectual.

Which is why I've been such a thorough disappointment to both, and why I resent so much The Beast calling public attention to my failings. I suppose I ought to forgive him by reminding myself it isn't his fault that he lacks the imagination to see what he is doing. But I can't. Particularly when I look back on those glorious, innocent mornings, that *paradis perdu*, before the Great Persecution began.

1

Now, lying on my side, comforter tucked securely under my chin, I struggle to dampen my rage while the February morning sunshine leaks into my bedroom. The thick glaze of ice and frost on the windowpane filters this winter light of all warmth and color. The scarred dresser with one jammed drawer, the cardboard wardrobe with Allied Van Lines stencilled on its side, the shoulder-high smudges on the wall plaster, the books heaped in the corners of the room or cracked open on the floor so that they rise in wedges, spines lifted to the ceiling, all look discolored and neglected in this spent, tired sunshine. It is difficult to read the titles of the books from my horizontal position. Cheek pressed into the mattress, one eye narrowed in a squint, I can decipher only one. *The Heart of Midlothian.*

The sound of The Beast's voice has given me a headache. Downstairs, in the apartment directly below mine, old McMurtry has his radio tuned to the local open-line show. I can imagine McMurtry seated beside the set, his angular old shoulders raised in a buzzard's hunch, hairy ear cocked to capture every wrathful syllable spurting from The Beast's lips. The old man's devotion to the *homo horribilis* who "hosts" this Roman circus of the airwaves is fervent, complete. I am regularly treated to a tinny harangue rising up through my floorboards, the words fantastically distorted by the demands McMurtry's deafness places on the speaker of his cheap transistor.

Between the two of them, The Beast and McMurtry, I have almost been driven from my apartment. I would have been gone long ago if this building weren't old enough to fall under rent controls. There is nowhere else I could find to live as cheaply, and given my circumstances, living cheaply is necessary.

So, one might ask, why not make the best of it? Why should I desire to deny a gentleman in his declining years the grisly pleasure of feasting on the carrion The Beast serves up to his audience as Food For Thought? I have never considered myself a particularly illiberal man, a man who would wish to dim the joy of a fellow adrift in the sunset days of a long and blissfully cantankerous life.

Because The Beast and McMurtry *talk about me* on the radio. That's why.

It's an old joke. The madman is informed by the psychiatrist that he is paranoid. "That may be," he replies, "but that doesn't stop people from plotting against me." My point exactly.

I *have* heard them. To be specific, on six occasions in the last two months. They started slandering me some time after I quit my job as a salesman in the china department of Eaton's. No, not delusions. I *heard* them.

The first time was at breakfast. There I was, hung over but still manfully shovelling home the Cocoa Puffs, my radio blaring away keeping me company, when the intro music for The Beast's program began. Even at that early date I had a pronounced loathing for The Beast and all his works, a loathing so strong that the mere sound of those gruesome strains would have ordinarily sent me clattering and clawing my way to the radio to switch stations before The Beast began to bay. But that morning I was so dolefully and deeply sunk in the post-alcoholic whim-whams that I just kept mechanically spooning home my sodden puffies while the dirge played on.

There was to be no guest that day, The Beast informed us. Instead, we were to be treated to two hours of "Brickbats and Bouquets". From his description of this dark festival I gathered that anyone with a compliment to hand out or a grievance to vent was being encouraged to phone in. Human nature being what it is, one could be sure that the air would be thick with brickbats, and not at all fragrant with flowers. The Beast, of course, was counting on this. Oh, he knew he would have to put up with the common run of do-gooder: some dear mom arguing in the face of all experience and evidence that *most teenagers are pretty good kids*. That sort. But that was a small yet necessary risk one ran to land the real bona fide carpet-chewers, foamers at the mouth, and public breast-beaters. Yes sir, it was from their ranks that one got real entertainment value. Give The Beast a crusading lacto-vegetarian, a One World Governmenter, a British Israelite, a bimetallist, or a confirmed pothole-watcher and his heart is glad.

He knew he had a show. The reservoir of unarticulated misery, craziness, and loneliness out there is inexhaustible. No matter how many times The Beast goes to these particular wells the bucket never comes up dry.

The very first caller captured my complete attention.

" 'Brickbats and Bouquets', Tom Rollins here," trumpeted The Beast. "Speak now or forever hold your peace."

"Hello? Hello?"

"Sir, you'll have to turn your radio down."

"Hello? Tom?"

"Sir, you'll have to turn your radio down. We have a ten-second delay. That's what's causing your confusion. Just turn your radio down."

"What?"

"Turn your radio down!"

An earlier instruction must have penetrated. I heard a clunk, as if a phone had been dropped to dangle. Nothing. The Beast began to scold into the sudden silence. Dead air was anathema. "Please, folks, if you want to call in, turn your radios down first. I don't know how many times I've said it. It's very important. Especially for you seniors out there who might be a little hard of — "

"Hello, Tom? Is that you?"

"None other. In the flesh, sir. We hear you loud and clear. Fire away. We're all ears, I assure you."

"Am I on?"

"Indeed you are. Let 'er rip."

There was a pause, then, "You know what really gets me, Tom?"

The Beast gave Radioland a knowing chuckle. "No, I don't, sir. And I guess I won't until you let me in on the secret." Rollins is such a dink.

"These guys who won't work get me is what. We got one of them in our building here. Just a young guy. If he was crippled or simple or something that would be one thing. I mean now they even put the simple ones in those workshops and make them do *something*, don't they now?"

"Retarded," said The Beast.

"What?"

"We say retarded on *this* program, sir."

"Yeah, well, whatever. Now you tell me, Tom, how does the government allow this guy, this guy in particular I'm talking about, not to work?"

"Well," said The Beast, "I don't know, sir. I'd be the last person to explain this so-called government of ours. It allows a lot of things which make no sense to me. But then you and I are just taxpayers, what do we know? They put child molesters in fancy hospitals and feed murderers steak in jail. Have you seen the price of steak lately? I don't get fed half the steak your average murderer does. My wife's got *me* on bread and water." He chortled.

"It's a damn crime, Tom. That's what I used to say to the wife, I used to say, 'It's a damn crime.' No wonder this country is in such a mess. Two months now and that guy hasn't hardly stirred out of his apartment. Like I say, it isn't that he can't work. I seen him working once before, downtown in Eaton's — "

Somebody in the studio hit the cut button; the tirade was scissored off. I froze, cheeks bulging with Cocoa Puffs. Two months? Eaton's?

"Whoa there," admonished The Beast. "Steady as she goes. We don't want to get personal here. Let's keep our comments non-specific."

"Well, anyway, what I mean to say," the caller suddenly continued, brought back from the void, penitent, "is I seen him working once." He sounded chastened by The Beast's displeasure. For the huddled, wretched, and nutty the man is a tin god, I swear. "And he's not working now," said the caller, "so you got to figure he's on the unemployment. What gripes me is how come I'm paying taxes to keep him sitting on his fat rear end up there, God only knows what he does all day, and I'm a pensioner?"

Sitting up there? Fat rear end? Pensioner? McMurtry. It had to be McMurtry. He had had it in for me ever since our quarrel over the parking stalls. Since that time I had occasionally caught sight of him peeking out from behind his curtains, watching me as I scraped frost off my windshield — or I've glimpsed a faded blue eye studying me through the gap between doorframe and door while I toiled up the staircase panting and puffing, lugging home the week's groceries.

It all began innocently enough. I had been patient. I had been as understanding of human foibles as only Ed can be. He's old, I told myself, perhaps his eyesight is failing.

But his fifteen-year-old Chrysler New Yorker kept slowly creeping to the right, week by week inching into my space until Leviathan one day firmly and triumphantly straddled both our parking stalls. McMurtry had finally shut me out.

I had no choice but to knock on his door and ask him to move his car. When he answered, an old man in khaki work pants, suspenders, and yellowed T-shirt, I caught a whiff of pungent socks and boiled turnips from inside his apartment. Past one bony shoulder I could see a shabby chesterfield pocked with old bum hollows; a blackened china cabinet festooned with family portraits; some dirty braided rugs; and a black felt pennant thumbtacked to the wall. In letters formed of silver sparkle the pennant recommended a visit to the Reptile Gardens in Montana.

"Yeah?"

"Excuse me, Mr. McMurtry. My name is Ed. I live upstairs. I was wondering if you could move your car. You see, the thing is, er . . ." Polite hesitation. "The thing is, I can't quite get into my parking space."

God, McMurtry looks old. There are wattles on his neck and canyons in his facescape that hold little white bristles he's missed shaving. His ears are enormous. Years ago I read somewhere that as you grow older your kidneys shrink and your ears get bigger. If that implies some transfer of matter, McMurtry's kidneys have dwindled to the size of raisins. At the time, his mouth was hanging open the way an old person's often does. It was interesting to note it was no longer pink inside but the color of raw liver.

"You the character drives that little yellow Jap thing?"

"That's right. That's me. Well, actually it's Italian. That little yellow thing is — ''

"You don't need all that room for a car like that," he said.

This claim took me aback. "Well, maybe not, but you see I need some room. I've got to get into my space."

"You got room." A pall of obstinacy had settled on his face. I was not sure what I had done. Had I annoyed him by implying he was an incompetent driver? I hadn't meant to do that.

"This time of year," I said, "with the snow and everything it's hard to see those darn white lines." Ed mending fences.

"I ain't blind. I can see them fine. And I seen you got lots of room for that Jap car of yours."

To understand all is to forgive all, as Madame de Staël was so kind as to remind us. Had he been taken prisoner at Hong Kong in '42? He looked a little old to have seen active service. Still, work on the Burma Railway would put years on a man and indignation at things Japanese in his heart.

"If I could get my car in my parking space I wouldn't bother you. But I can't. I'm very sorry but you'll have to move your car."

"Don't put the blame on me for your lousy driving."

I flared. "Lousy driving has got nothing to do with it. You couldn't park a coffin in the space you left me. I defy anyone to get my car in there."

"Huh!"

"I defy *anyone* to get my car into that space." I was repeating myself, never a good sign.

"I'll get her in," he said.

"Well . . ."

"Singing a different tune now, eh?"

"I'm not singing a different tune."

"Just lemme get my coat, Mr. Wiseguy."

Jesus, I'm stupid, I thought as I watched him strike off down the hallway, struggling into his coat. He strutted with the deliberate jerkiness of the barnyard cock, head pecking forward, eyes frozen to glittering glass by his anger.

I sighed and trudged off after him.

Of course, if he was going to err he was going to err on the side of the garbage bin, not his precious New Yorker. Still, I am convinced he did it on purpose. While I shouted and frantically waved my arms trying to catch his attention, McMurtry kept gunning the engine as metal shrieked and a three-foot strip of paint was flayed off my car by the corner of a Sanuway Disposal Unit.

When I finally did get him halted, his crusty, malevolent old face betrayed not a flicker of contrition. He sat behind the wheel, stolid, his peaked cap pulled down level with his eyebrows in a futile attempt to get the flaps on his hat to cover more than half his enormous ears.

I must admit I lost control. "You stupid old fart!" I bellowed, beating the car roof with my fist. "Get out of my car! Get out of my car! Take a look at what you've done. This is an atrocity. This is carnage. I'll never get a paint match. Never. Look at what you've done, you fucking, antiquated vandal!"

"There's something wrong with your steering linkage," he informed me, unperturbed.

"There's something wrong with *your* steering linkage! Yours. Upstairs. Understand?" Picture this: I was actually jabbing myself in the temple with a stiff forefinger. "Get out and look! Look!"

He obliged me. McMurtry carefully eased himself out from behind the wheel, tottered around the car, and peered at the gleaming strip of exposed metal.

"I'll never get a paint match," I said. "Never. I'll have to repaint the entire car."

"You ask me," said McMurtry, "I done you a favor. That yellow there you got looks like dog piss on snow."

In a saner moment I would have had to agree with him. The yellow had been Victoria's choice. Victoria, my estranged wife. She had read in *Consumer Report* that yellow was a highly visible color and for reasons of safety was an excellent choice for a car. That's why yellow was replacing red on fire engines. She had insisted on yellow.

"Dog piss on snow! Dog piss on snow! That's my car you're referring to, you superannuated Hun!"

"That ain't a car," he said, glancing up at me from under his duck-bill cap, "that's a sewing machine with tires."

I let that pass. "What did I ever do to you?" I asked, trying to get a grip on myself. "What? For God's sake, tell me!"

McMurtry pointed to my automobile. "Dinky Toy," he said. He made a contemptuous putt-putt noise with his dry old lips.

Something snapped in my head. I lunged at his New Yorker. The terrible crack of cold metal breaking was succeeded by a silence wide and vast enough for me to realize what I'd done. I had a radio antenna in my mittened hand.

McMurtry's eyes narrowed. "I'm calling the cops," he said, creaked round on his heel, and began to shuffle for the apartment building as fast as his decrepit pins would carry him.

Cops. I saw immediately this was big trouble. You can't wrench the radio antenna off a senior citizen's mode of transportation without having society turn on you like a mad dog. And there's no point in pleading provocation. I was hip deep in shit on this one.

It took a half an hour of abject pleading and spectacular self-abasement outside his apartment door to get him to accept thirty dollars' damages. Thirty goddamn dollars! He never did bother to get the antenna replaced, either. He just wound a wire clothes-hanger around the stump.

Now McMurtry had the effrontery to go public with his vendetta. Mouth crammed with Cocoa Puffs, spoon suspended in mid-air, I had heard him tattle on Ed to The Beast.

"I mean, Tom," McMurtry said, "what can be done about these bums? I mean to say, is there somewhere I could call to have this here character looked into?"

"Far be it for me to suggest anybody report anybody else to the proper authorities," said The Beast. "But doggone it, the fact remains there's just too many freeloaders in this so-called country of ours. If I've said it once, I've said it a thousand times. There are just too many unemployment benefits and welfare rip-off artists getting away with blue murder. Anybody that tunes in to my program knows that Tom Rollins isn't afraid to use plain language. My motto is, call a spade a spade. I want to give a name to what your young friend is doing. Let's call it fraud. Fraud pure and simple. And fraud's just a high-falutin name for stealing. Stealing hard-earned money out of your pocket, sir, out of my pocket, out of our neighbor's pocket, out of poor old John Doe Taxpayer's pocket.

"Now the last thing I want to say on this matter is this. If we saw some guy ripping off our neighbor, stealing his color TV, say, what do you think we'd do?"

"I know what I'd do. I'd call the cops." He certainly would. The merest hint of the illicit had his dialling finger poised and quivering. I could testify to that. The old fart was just crazy keen to call the cops.

"And so would any other John Q. Decent Citizen," said The Beast stoutly. "But please, sir, don't misunderstand what I'm saying. It isn't my job to tell you what to do. My role is that of communicator. Tom Rollins's program exists only to facilitate an exchange of ideas. Which reminds me, by the by," he said, "all my lines are lit up. You wouldn't want me to deny an equal chance to all those folks out there to exercise their God-given democratic right to speak their minds on the issues of the day, would you? So . . ."

"So maybe I ought to call the Unemployment?"

"Far be it for me to tell you what to do, sir. We got to run now. But be sure to give us a call and let us know what the bureaucrats who hand out our money have to say for themselves on this one." *Click.* "This is Tom Rollins here for 'Brickbats and Bouquets'. Speak now or forever hold your — "

I get hit with an anxiety attack whenever I think of those two. Right now I'm having a humdinger, a real Ed special. I'm sweating, my breathing is rapid and shallow, my heart is bumping my breastbone. I heave the covers off in one convulsive movement.

Calm down, Ed. Calm down. I roll on my back, stare down the

expanses of my ample, pale body. Eyes trained between the little hillocks that are my breasts, I survey a white swell of belly; a little coppice of hairs rises in the vicinity of my navel. In the beyond, hidden below all this, lie legs and feet and orangish, ridged toenails.

God, The Beast is slowly, day by day, week by week, driving me crazy. He has sat in judgment on me and pronounced me guilty. There is no appeal from his terrible court. Just ask me how that loser, K, felt in *The Trial*.

Victoria used to tell me it was a symptom of my immaturity that I can't let things like this go. The inability to make distinctions of value, she called it. But it isn't that. Very well, I know there are greater injustices being borne than the ones I bear, there is injustice in the very air we breathe. Infants are scalded by hapless and drunken mothers, concert pianists contract multiple sclerosis, Martin Luther King is assassinated, and Idi Amin is granted political asylum. In the scheme of things what has happened to me is nothing, less than nothing. I know that. For God's sake, nobody even knows who McMurtry and The Beast are talking about, and if they did, no one would care except my father. He would be ashamed.

Pop sends me snapshots from Brownsville and on the back of them he writes things such as, "Old Ralphy Madigan took this one. He admires your mother's legs," or, "Photo courtesy of Shirley Phillipotts", as if I knew these people. They are his world now, these new friends from Minnesota, Montana, North Dakota, Michigan, and Saskatchewan whose life journey has been a pilgrimage to a shrine distant from the snows.

In these photographs he and my mother sit under a striped canvas awning tacked to their junky trailer and held up by spindly aluminum poles spiked in the dusty earth. I barely recognize them. In the freer air of the great Republic to the south, mother has dyed her hair chocolate and taken to wearing red rubber sandals and one-piece swimming suits. Pop is a stranger in a Detroit Tigers baseball cap, Bermuda shorts, and mirror sunglasses. I never saw him in shorts before in my life. Never.

I could have believed he was born in his khaki work pants. I could have believed his first words were: "It isn't right. Fair's fair." For it's from Pop that I absorbed my bittersweet understanding of injustice. We're very much alike, although he can't recognize it.

You see, Pop was a small-potatoes building contractor and big-league idealist. He never understood business. What drove him to despair was that he couldn't land the larger jobs. "I was low tender," he'd say to my mother, "what the Christ is going on there?"

Whenever I look at the Polaroids he mails me I wonder if, behind the mirror sunglasses and the white smile in the dark face, he isn't still asking that bewildered question: "I was low bidder all those years, wasn't I? What in Christ was going on? How come I never got it?"

Not that he didn't inquire. My father doesn't have much formal education but he used to write eloquently stilted letters to boards and committees requesting explanations. Of course, he never got satisfaction and their evasions only made him melancholy. "I was low," he'd mutter. "I'm always low. I pare my costs to the bone. No fat. There's practically nothing left for me. Don't they trust me?" he'd ask, turning to my mother.

And then he'd write another letter asking, Didn't they trust him to do quality work? Because he could *guarantee* quality work.

They almost never deigned to answer the second time. Pop was such an innocent.

No, nobody knows who The Beast is talking about, so who cares?

I know. I care. I have phoned the open-line show to explain to him that I receive neither unemployment insurance nor welfare, but live on the capital I raised from cashing in my life insurance policy. What an act of blind faith that is, my throwing myself on The Beast's mercy in hope of redress. I barely begin to make my case when the line goes dead, and then in the background The Beast speaks from my radio. "Well, ladies and gentlemen, it's him again. This high wind we're having today must be shaking the nuts out of the trees."

I have written him letters begging him not to encourage McMurtry in his persecution of me. I flatter The Beast and remind him that with great power comes great responsibility. It does no good.

I have never set eyes on The Beast, but in my fantasies I see him seated behind a microphone in a deserted radio station. He is forty-five years old or thereabouts. His rich brown hair has been permed into a profusion of pubic-looking curls. His shirt, undone to the third button, exposes a baby-pink, hairless bosom, on which rosy expanse dangles one of the last great bronze medallions to grace a chest west of Warsaw.

From his voice alone I have extrapolated this, I have invented his biography. I can see him. I *know* The Beast. He is the kind of man who cups and conspicuously hitches his genitals before taking a seat. He went to a radio arts academy in Oklahoma. He orders his wife to lose weight. He has turned his son into a bed-wetter and his daughter into a drum majorette. I would be willing to wager dollars to doughnuts that this monster of iniquity has decreed one night a week Family Night and on that hallowed eve his children, denied television, are compelled to talk to him.

My fantasies lean toward strangulation. I have broken into The Beast's studio. He is alone.

He springs to his feet, upsetting his chair in terror. It makes an ominous sound toppling over in the studio. "You!" he exclaims.

"Yes," I intone solemnly, calmly advancing. "It is Ed. It is he whom you have wronged."

"No! No!"

We grapple. My righteous thumbs embed themselves in his Adam's apple.

"Aarrgh! Aarrgh!" cries The Beast, tearing at my swelling forearms with his fingernails. *Homo horribilis* is being strangled on air, live. Ten thousand watts of power are pumping out his death agony across the province, into thousands of households.

And then the bloody phone rings. Rings and rings and rings. Just when I had the son of a bitch where I wanted him.

TWO

A phone call, a surprising, startling phone call, loosened my death grip on The Beast's throat. It was my wife. A curious development, because not only have Victoria and I not met face to face for over a year, but she has resolutely refused to speak to me during our separation except through her lawyer, her mouthpiece, Benny Ferguson. Our last conversation occurred on the summer evening that I inveigled a tenant in her apartment building into unlocking the lobby door to me. He fell for a convincing dumb-show search of pockets for keys I didn't have.

Mine was not a successful re-wooing. I succeeded in insinuating myself into her suite by some childish yet compelling tactics, but one thing led to another, the result being that I locked myself in her bathroom and refused to come out.

The day I barricaded myself in her bathroom is the day from which I date our present impasse. Our happiness together I date from that day in June of 1973 when I arrived at the door of Victoria's flat bearing three madras plaid shirts on hangers and a pair of blue jeans with the cuffs tied shut and the legs stuffed with underwear and socks. Although we had been seeing each other for over six months, Victoria clung tenaciously to her privacy and independence; she never permitted me to stay with her for longer than a single night, and she made it clear that she did not want a roommate, male or female. She was determined to be free, an attitude I found unacceptable. So that day in June I explained to Victoria that my roomie Benny had received a shitload of dope

14

from a guy in Vancouver and was intending to deal it out of our apartment. I told her I was terrified of being busted while he conducted business, and asked if I could temporarily move in until trafficking was suspended. My lie got me in the door. Later, Victoria had trouble persuading me I should leave. Throughout the summer I continued to widen the breach in her defences and to infiltrate the citadel, bit by bit smuggling in my worldly possessions, quietly establishing squatter's rights. Despite herself Victoria got used to me, even though she kept up a kind of weak resistance until September, when university classes resumed and distracted her. Victoria was a conscientious student.

I have wonderful memories of that July and August. I remember her as already a remarkable woman at twenty-two, full of courage, passionate, opinionated beyond the appeal of reason. When we drank beer and argued, her face would flush so red with conviction that I was sure I could feel it radiate heat across the width of the table. Perhaps she did not believe in the things she defended as much as she believed in herself and in her inability to ever be wrong. That may account for why she struggled to save me for so long.

The only thing she seemed to have a doubt about was her nose. It was large, had a high bridge and flaring nostrils, and saved her face from being merely beautiful. That summer she wore her hair in a shag cut, probably because the crinkled hair and big nose taken together made her look exotic, vaguely Assyrian. The rest of Victoria was an approximation of middle-class ideals of perfection: a translucently fine complexion; strong, even teeth; a slim, leggy, full-breasted body that always smelled faintly and pleasantly of soap, toothpaste, and baby powder.

To sum up, she was everything I wasn't: assured, idealistic, ungrubby. She had had success stamped early in her heart as I had had failure stamped early in mine. She had been vice-president of her high school's student government, a member of the honor roll, editor of the yearbook, popular. I also learned, in time, that when Victoria was seventeen, a high school senior dating a university man named Max, she had been deftly deflowered and had awakened to the knowledge that she enjoyed sex a good deal.

In contrast, I was a long-term social pariah who had never had a date in high school until my graduation, when my mother scared up a girl for me through her vast network of friends and relatives, a girl horrible and desperate enough to grace my arm while I waddled through the grand march of graduates. In anticipation of my first real encounter with the fair sex, I spent a lot of time studying "The Playboy Adviser", French-kissing my left biceps, and practising unhooking a bra of my mother's I had stolen out of the laundry hamper.

It was this high level of sexual expertise (barely supplemented by three wild, roguish years of university life) that I brought to bear on my seduction of Victoria. Add to this the fact that I was corpulent and considered by some to be verging on sociopathic and one is confronted by one of those baffling conundrums of the heart: What was Victoria doing with me? I had no answer then, but later, after I had been introduced to her family, I thought I could see why she was drawn to me. Maybe it was because I was as different from her father as a man could be, and that what Victoria at first valued in me was eccentricity, unpredictability, and an emotional range that she equated with depth of feeling rather than a lack of restraint. Certainly the first time I wept in front of her she was stunned.

Oh yes, that was a fine summer. Victoria was working as a secretary, earning money against her return to university in the fall, and I was preparing for grad studies by teaching myself the French I hadn't troubled to learn in high school. When I wasn't conjugating verbs, I was refurbishing Victoria's tiny apartment on the third storey of a rickety old revenue house. One day she would return from work to find the kitchen painted canary yellow, another to discover the bedroom was painted blue and there were carnations in a bowl on the dresser. I was happy. I stripped the old, yellowing wax off the living-room floor and polished and repolished the linoleum until the reflection of my face beamed back at me. I washed windows and revarnished window frames and baseboards until the place was redolent with vinegar and varnish.

By five-thirty when Victoria arrived home from work, the flat, which was directly under the roof, would be sizzling hot, but I would serve her chilled lemonade and one of my famed cold collations: devilled eggs, salami, French bread, pickles, bean salad, Jell-O chocolate pudding. After eating and changing, we would walk downtown to escape the oppressive heat. Sometimes we sat through the same movie twice for the pleasure of the air-conditioning, sometimes we met friends to drink beer and talk politics, talk books, talk films, talk the meaning of life, talk anything. We were testing our wings; none of us talked for truth but for victory. I talked for her. I performed, I ranted, I gesticulated, I demonstrated, I impugned, I drunkenly soared in a flight of rhetoric. I had somebody. I talked for Victoria.

It was always late before we started for home, strolling along in the lush, warm darkness. On a week night the streets would be deserted except for the occasional carload of drunks tooling around in a Camaro, Firebird, Cobra, or Mustang. Victoria, braless in a T-shirt and jaunty in safari shorts, often attracted attention and remarks.

One night in August one of these muscle cars crawled over to the curb, engine rumbling throatily, and a number of beery Visigoths hung out the windows to give vent to their admiration. I, with a long and woe-filled experience of being subjected to the unwelcome attentions of extra-chromosome types, turned catatonic with terror. Victoria did not. When I counselled silence and circumspection I was not heeded.

"Ignore him, Victoria. Do not even look at him."

"*Hey, baby!*"

"Forgive them, Victoria, for they know not what they do," I said, picking up the pace.

Loud, suggestive sucking noises.

"Hey, baby, lose Jumbo and come for a ride!"

"What a treat. A ride in the fartmobile. Just what every girl wants," Victoria said. She has a talent for invective if roused.

"Oh Jesus. Don't get them mad, Victoria."

"Hey, I got something to show you, baby. Wanna see a one-eyed pant snake?"

"Go have a wet dream, greaseball."

"For God's sake, Victoria," I said between clenched teeth, "do you know what you're talking to? This is the kind of person who collects Nazi regalia, for chrissakes."

"It's made to measure, baby, I guarantee. Check out the fit."

"Fit it in your hand, algae. From the looks of your complexion that's where it usually goes."

Quite naturally he turned his attention to me, favoring weaker prey. "Hey, Fatso, what you got to say for yourself? You as mouthy as the broad?"

I didn't answer.

"Hey, I'm talking to you, Georgie Jell-O!"

Victoria said, "Leave him alone, creep."

"So you talk for both of you, eh? So what's Tubby got I don't got?"

"*Me*, for one thing."

How my heart leapt, even in that moment of imminent peril. *Me! Me! Me!*

"Some prize," he said.

"Get lost, pustule."

"*Fuck you, bitch!*"

The driver revved the engine, popped the clutch. Tires squealed and smoked. When the tail lights had swept around a corner, I said, "They don't know how lucky they are. I was on the point of freaking out. It could have been a mean scene for them."

"Come on, Ed," said Victoria, "let's get going before they decide to come back. Let's go home."

Off we went, hand in hand, my legs and heart pumping in time to the refrain ringing in my head. *Me! Me! Me!*

It was several months after this declaration that the seed of the idea of going to Greece was planted. Victoria had assembled our portable desk (a door laid across two sawhorses) in front of the living-room window to reap the benefit of the October light. I lay on the sofa attempting to persuade her to join me there. At the time I was mournfully singing "I'm Mr. Lonely" at the top of my lungs.

"Ed, shut up. I'm trying to concentrate." She was laughing, though.

"Bobby Vinton appeals with his plaintive mating call. Dare you resist his blandishments?"

"I'm trying to finish a paper."

"What paper can possibly be more important than the duty to reach out and touch another human being in his hour of need?"

"A paper on Greek mythology due tomorrow."

"A paper on Greek mythology could only be enriched by a fuller understanding of the Dionysian revel. Let us disport ourselves with Attic enthusiasm."

"Ed, give me a break."

"Okay, okay. Offer yourself to me body and soul and I promise to type the paper for you tonight. Greek's honor."

"I thought you're supposed to read a book for Schwingler's seminar."

"When the Greek's blood is heated with the madness of Dionysian revel," I declared, smiting my breast, "he thinks not of the paltry pedagogue Schwingler!"

"You aren't going to give up until you get your way, are you?"

"That is an approximation of the truth, yes."

"You just better type this paper then. I mean it," she warned me, before entering freely into the spirit of the thing.

By December the "Greek afternoon" or the "Greek evening" had become a household phrase. By degrees we developed a festival of wine, song, and feasting to dispel the cold and darkness which crept into the soul during a Canadian winter. Whenever I saw Victoria's spirits flag I would begin secretly to gather the ingredients necessary for a "Greek evening". From the delicatessen across town I would buy spinach pies and Greek pastries. A store of metaxa and retsina would be laid in, albums of Greek folk music would be obtained from the public library, and a roast of lamb hidden in the freezer of the tenant who lived below us. Then one day when Victoria stumbled in out of a January blizzard, bundled, scarved, mittened, snow flakes frozen in her eyelashes, she would be welcomed by the scent of roasting meat, music on the stereo, me proffering a glass of retsina, and the cry: "Everybodies get heppy! We got a Greek night!"

So it would go. We had some good times. We ate and roared toasts and splashed metaxa down our throats as the stereo blasted out the sound track of *Zorba the Greek*.

I would propose: "Death to the Colonels!"

"Long live Melina Mercouri!" Victoria would rejoin.

"More sex, please! I am Greek!" I would yell.

In one of these moments of craziness I offered, "Next year in Crete!" and Victoria took me up on it. It was an idea easy to fasten on to in the black months of January and February. She began by collecting travel brochures and books. From that she progressed to explaining to me that cheap living in Greece would allow me to write. Writing was a thing I sometimes talked about doing, not very seriously of course, but in the way young men who study literature often do. I said her idea made sense. The next thing I knew, Victoria had taken a part-time job as a checkout clerk at Safeway and was making me set aside something each month from the salary I received as a teaching assistant at the university. This money was to finance a stay in Greece.

Nothing brought us closer than our talk of Greece, than the minutiae of budgeting and planning, than the book of traveller's Greek we traded phrases back and forth from. I felt free to feed the fire because I believed that a hard-headed, practical girl such as Victoria would draw back at some point. After all, what the hell did the two of us want in Greece?

Finally, in the slush of March, we came to a decision that if we were going to live in conservative, reactionary Greece our stay would be made pleasanter and smoother if we were married. Not only that, if we had a wedding we could sell the wedding gifts to raise money to finance the trip.

It was agreed we would marry in June and then work until some time in November. The day the first snow flew we would begin preparations for our final departure. The symbolism of that appealed to Victoria. I never looked beyond June and the wedding.

But that is all in the past, and now, riding a city transit bus that shakes along snowy streets, I must consider more pressing things such as Victoria's phone call and, with it, her perplexing invitation to lunch. She wasn't unfriendly, merely curt and formal, exactly what one might expect given the circumstances. But why have I been summoned to a meeting? It can only be trouble of some kind. Perhaps the question of custody of Balzac. I can't understand why she has chosen to stand firm on that issue. Not that I mind. If he is the last feeble link between us as man and wife, so be it. Victoria, after all, is the one who wishes our marriage ended as quickly, cleanly, and finally as possible. I, on the other hand, have not been prepared to relinquish my spouse with any semblance of dignity and good order.

This, I know, given the standards of the present age, is viewed as a grievous fault of character. I have seen a number of men of my age and acquaintance bow out nobly and back into the wings to allow the understudy to assume the role of male lead. However, Ed is jealous, Ed is possessive, Ed is selfish. I understand that contemporary couples ought to dissolve *relationships* harmoniously, with all the alacrity of a single-cell amoeba dividing itself in the interests of new life. Some generous souls speak well of the perfidious wife-snatcher in public and meet him for the occasional drink after work. Not this cookie. My petty antics are legendary in the circle of Victoria's friends. They have enjoyed the spectacle of me in hot pursuit of the woman I love, travelling after her just as fast as my hands and knees will carry me.

The bus groans and shudders along icy, rutted streets. The city is in the second week of a severe cold snap. For twelve consecutive days the temperature has dropped below $-35°C$. Brisk, penetrating breezes drive needles of cold through pant legs, lodge aches in septums, gums, and teeth, burn faces with dazzling pain. Pedestrians weep and snuffle and wince from building to building.

Scratching a patch of clear glass out of the frost on my window I stare out at the frozen world while the bus grinds over the bridge. I can see the river's crust of ice and snow, which has heaved and buckled where the current runs strongest in mid-channel. A ribbon of water twists amid this shattered ice, steaming like a flow of ashy lava. On the river bank the tawny spire of St. John's Cathedral raises a cross against a white sky.

I'm apprehensive about seeing Victoria again. For years I cam-
ouflaged love with acrimony, seeing our marriage as a series of
bargains that had to be negotiated from a position of strength. I
thought that to admit how much I needed Victoria was bad
strategy. Of the two of us there was no doubt I was the weaker —
and for that reason the least able to yield. At one time Victoria
loved me. But she never needed me. I understood that from the
beginning and hated what I understood. Now we have little but
what I made us heir to: the dreary formulae of recrimination,
elaborated by a genuine wish on her part to break free from me
and my lover's heart.

The bus drops me in front of the public library. From there it is
a short, numbing walk to the Café Nice, where I have been
ordered to report for lunch. Once inside the Café I shed my parka
and lurk behind a large fern in the vestibule, scouting the premises.
Good intelligence is an important function of all successful counter-
insurgency operations. Know your enemy and the disposition of
her forces.

I gingerly part the fronds and swing my eyes over the lunch-
hour throng. At this time of day the diners are a rather conventional crew, younger professionals and businessmen and business-
women, a spattering of well-dressed and well-heeled ladies savoring their second martini before tucking into the tourtière. In the
evening the Café is given over to the city's cognoscenti and artsy-
fartsy set. Just the kind of place that attracts Victoria and her pals
the way jam attracts wasps.

As the name Café Nice suggests, the restaurateur is a Gallomaniac
with a particular passion for Provence, although anything French
passes muster. There are travel posters displaying delectable French
views, there are French cinema advertisements, there are notices
of art exhibitions in Paris, and there are reproductions of impres-
sionist masterpieces hung on the walls.

But the Riviera ambience is predominant. The tables have fake
marble tops in which are stuck red-and-white sun parasols. The
Mediterranean theme is embellished by a large wooden trough
abutting a window overlooking the street. In this the proprietor

of the Café Nice has dumped several yards of fine white sand, upon which are strewn gaily colored beach balls suggestive of wave-lapped and sun-kissed shores.

It is by this window that Victoria sits smoking a cigarette and watching condensation dribble down the windowpane. She hasn't changed much. Her hair is longer than when I saw her last and lies in a fat, loosely plaited braid across her collarbone. She is wearing crisp, starchy-looking blue jeans and one of those tweed jackets I always disliked because they emphasize her shoulders and de-emphasize her breasts. This is her tough, no-nonsense ensemble, so I can expect a serious conversation. That bodes ill for me. However, on the other hand I'm glad to see she doesn't look particularly ornery, merely abstracted and perhaps a little tired.

The question now is how to cover gracefully the intervening distance under the scrutiny of a baleful, wifely eye. I shift from foot to foot and wring damp hands. I'm pretty sure I'm here to be called up on the carpet; demands are going to be made and the law is going to be laid down. All this is made worse because Victoria turned thirty-three in December.

I have a theory about the early thirties. Of course, Victoria says I have a theory about most things. The early thirties are a danger-ous time because people get unpredictable. Roughly the age Jesus downed tools and walked out of the carpentry shop.

I turn over in my mind what she might want. Maybe the car. She paid for it and I haven't had it repaired since the "accident". Rust is already spotting the door panel that that old fart McMurtry scraped. Victoria will give me hell for that. She always hated my careless attitude towards property. Whenever I was given a lec-ture for neglecting or abusing something, the price tag took centre stage in the harangue. When I forgot to clean my electric razor for three months and the heads seized while she was doing her legs, Victoria demanded to know, while frenziedly scrubbing its innards with a toothbrush: "Ed, is this any way to treat a seventy-two-dollar razor?"

Better lose the car than Balzac. Our last confrontation was over the set of the *Comédie humaine* she bought at a garage sale shortly before we split up. When Victoria left she demanded the books. I pointed out to her when I refused to surrender them that she had obviously bought them for me. As support for this reasonable contention, I cited my upcoming birthday and the fact Victoria can't read French. *Voilà!*

She's not getting Balzac. For one thing, I'm not even through a third of the musty, foxed volumes of the *Scènes de la vie privée*. Ah yes, old Honoré surely knew the human heart. He'd held his ear to that intricate mechanism and heard the little cogs of malice, duplicity, greed, and lust creaking away, making their sinful music. So far the book about the marriage settlement is my favorite. Oh God, please don't let her start in about the Balzac again.

Peering through the lacy maze of crinkled greenery I feel my apprehension at meeting Victoria growing. It has been a long time and I'm not sure I can trust myself to act decently. After I locked myself in Victoria's bathroom last summer I promised myself she wouldn't catch me grovelling again. But I have never been particularly good at holding to resolutions or improving my rather lamentable character. Not like my father. Pop, there was a man for resolutions, a Bismarckian gentleman of blood and iron. He used to tape *Reader's Digest*'s "Increase Your Word Power" above the bathroom mirror so he could study it while shaving. "If you use a word three times," he used to say, "you make it yours for life."

It doesn't seem that much else is for life, but Pop was going to get whatever could be had for the duration. Increasing his word power added color and force to his letters to the boards and committees which had slighted him, but that wasn't his motive for studying. He believed in being "well-rounded". It's one of his great sorrows that I'm not.

Now or never, Ed. Death before dishonor. I hitch my shoulders back and strike boldly out into a field of carpet-daisies. As it turns out, Victoria is so lost in her thoughts she does not take her eyes from the rivulets streaking the window until she hears me struggling with the wicker chair. She glances up sharply, startled. Her face looks small and dark in the shade of the parasol; winter has chapped her lips and scored little lines in the pale, bitten flesh. She smiles at me in a wary but unhostile manner. This half-welcome surprises me.

"Ed," she says, extending her hand.

I can't take it because in my nervousness I've sat down too abruptly. Now I'm fumbling with a squeaking wicker chair that refuses to be shifted to the table without a struggle. While I wrestle with the arms, bounce my bottom and heel the carpet, it keeps snagging the nap and tipping precipitously forward. A typical Ed entrance. I realize I'm mumbling to myself.

"You look very well," Victoria says. Lady Gracious.

"I don't. I've put weight on again. Goddamn it." I lurch forward in stages to the edge of the table, accompanied by high-pitched squeals from the flimsy chair.

"You know why that is." Victoria can't help herself. I'm supposed to confess gluttony. She actually appears to be glad to see me fallen off the weight-watcher's wagon and prime stock for the fat farm. I stare back, grim and tight-lipped.

"It's not as if you're ignorant about what you should eat. It's just that you won't eat anything that's good for you." This is a familiar refrain from our days of marital bliss.

"Yeah, yeah. Fruits, vegetables, cereals. White meats. Fish. Nuts. Complex carbohydrates," I mutter, reviewing lessons learned.

"How's your blood pressure? Are you going for your regular blood-pressure checks?"

"Jesus Christ, is this why I was called in? For the annual company physical?"

"A simple inquiry after your health."

"No. A simple inquiry after my health would be: 'How you doing, Ed?' And then I could chirp back: 'Fine. And yourself?' "

"You may not realize it, but not even I want to see you dead. You ought to take care of yourself better," she says.

The waitress arrives at our table. I can't believe it. The girl is got up in the uniform of a French sailor, right down to the pompom on her hat. My mind runs to the Battle of Trafalgar and Lord One-Eye Nelson. "England expects that every man will do his duty." Sometimes I catch myself saying what I only meant to think.

"Pardon?" says the girl.

"Sorry. Don't mind me. Too much sun." I reach up and tickle the tassels on our parasol. The girl passes out the menus and gives me a sceptical look. I ought to pull myself together.

Victoria studies the menu. She is used to me and isn't easily ruffled.

"What are you having, Ed?"

"I thought a complex carbohydrate would be nice."

"Sir?"

"Ignore him," says Victoria, not even troubling to look up. "Two spinach salads with house dressing, two mushroom omelettes, and a half-litre of dry white wine, please."

"Make that a litre," I say.

"Ma'am?"

"A litre then."

The waitress gathers up the menus and bustles off to the kitchen.

Victoria busies herself lighting a cigarette. "You made her uncomfortable. That wasn't necessary. Behave yourself."

Victoria, as usual, is right. "I didn't make her uncomfortable. *You* made her uncomfortable. They expect the man to order."

"Save your breath. I'm not getting drawn into one of those interminable and invariably childish arguments that you concoct to cover your tracks."

I'd forgotten how wise in the ways of Ed she is. "Well," I say, trying to look injured, "don't accuse me of things I didn't do."

"Same old Ed." Victoria sighs, breathes smoke. "I guess you can't expect a leopard to change its spots."

"Or a skunk to change its stripes."

"Don't put words in my mouth, Ed. Believe it or not, I didn't come here to pick scabs on old wounds. Let's try and keep it pleasant. I haven't much fight in me at the moment." The skin around her eyes looks smudged, grey. When she smiles, her lips part with visible effort; there is strain in the corners of her mouth, her fingers pick nervously at a loose thread in the weave of the tablecloth.

"I don't know why I'm here. I didn't ask to be dragged away from my warm radiator all the way to the Côte d'Azur. Just remember that."

"You're always so goddamn indirect, aren't you? You don't like the restaurant? Is that it, Ed? Could it be that you find it pretentious? Too affected for an honest soul like you? Well, you aren't particularly honest — just rude. I'm buying this lunch, so we'll eat where *I* want to eat. And if you've got something to say to me, say it. Don't start sniping."

"Sniping at a tank. A poor little peeshooter taking pot shots at Panzer Wictoria. Would I dare?"

"I wonder what a psychoanalyst would make of that? Talk about a peeshooter and a tank," says Victoria. She's very good. In six years of marriage I seldom did better than a draw. Victoria comes from a long line of Scottish Presbyterian fanatics. The kind who hid in caves and ate heather or whatever, rather than admit God wasn't their first cousin.

"Don't pull that Psychology 101 crap on me, honey. Don't forget I'm the expert on those guys."

"You'll never forgive me for talking you into seeking help, will you?" says Victoria. By help she means a certain Dr. Brandt I saw weekly just when my imagination began to fail. I had trouble adjusting to the new perspective.

The spinach and the wine arrive. Victoria and I munch in silence. Chewing winter spinach, I discover, produces an odd sensation. Maybe it's thinking of all that dough Brandt ate up, but I'm beginning to imagine I'm chewing dirty, tattered, gritty dollar bills. Money must taste like this, bitter. I think of creased and folded bills, think of the greasy wallets they have ridden in, the lint-laden pockets they have lain in, the sweaty décolletages they've been crammed down. That's it, that's enough. I push the bowl away.

Victoria breaks the silence. "I dropped by the china department in Eaton's last week to see if you were free for coffee."

Although I'm curious as to why Victoria has suddenly taken to seeking my company, I make no comment. The pause grows to an uncomfortable length while she waits for me to respond. Finally she says, "The woman there said you quit months ago."

True. Two months ago to be specific. The money I realized from cashing in my life insurance policy will soon be gone. . . . I don't like this talk about work. It makes me nervous. It makes me think of my shrinking bank balance.

"Can we drop this subject?"

"Don't be so touchy. I'm just curious to know how you're managing."

"You asked me to lunch after all these months of separation to ask me how I'm managing? Get serious. What do you want, Victoria?"

"I didn't say that's why I asked you to lunch. But now that the subject has come up — how are you managing? Are you getting unemployment insurance?"

"No!" I protest, much more loudly than I intended. "No goddamn unemployment insurance!" McMurtry, I realize, has made me sore on that subject.

"Keep it down, Ed. People are looking."

So they are. I lower my voice, crane my neck around the parasol pole, and hiss, "Not unemployment insurance. *Life* insurance. I cashed in my policy. So I could live on my capital like a nineteenth-century Russian landowner. I'm an incorrigible romantic."

Victoria lays her fork down. "What life insurance?" she demands. "I didn't know you had any life insurance."

Neither did I until three months ago. That's when my steady ways in the Eaton's china department finally convinced Pop his son had stabilized and was showing signs of maturity. As a sign of confidence in me, he handed over to me a life insurance policy he had been paying premiums on since the day after I was born.

Nothing reveals my father's mind as clearly as that. It ought to be graven on his tombstone: *Loving husband, father, and policy-holder.* The man insured everything, a symptom of a profoundly superstitious mind. As long as he was laying out hard-earned money for coverage, nothing would happen. Why? Because it was just his luck to pay for protection he didn't need. He used to gripe, "Twenty years now I've paid insurance premiums and has anything happened? Have I got a penny back from those leeches? No way. Isn't that typical?'' The implication being that if he stopped paying, something dreadful would happen.

All that was near and dear to him was insured: house, car, business, Mom. Insured to the maximum, to the hilt. We were insurance-poor. The bigger the premium, the more potent the spell. When I was eight he showed me where he kept the key to the safety deposit box and explained that if he and Mom were to ''pass on unexpectedly, God forbid,'' I was to give the key to my Uncle Bert. ''You've got nothing to worry about,'' Pop said. ''There's a hundred thousand on your mom alone.''

Of course, I did worry. *I worried he'd forget to pay the goddamn premiums and bring disaster to us all.* I'd caught superstition from him the way I might have caught the flu. My mother always said: ''Eddie's got a case of Daddy's nerves.'' Any wonder?

I can't imagine what I'd have felt if I'd known he had a policy on me. I get a mite antsy even now when I recall I've cashed it. For the first time in over thirty years I'm not covered.

Our waitress delivers the omelettes. ''I didn't know I had life insurance until last year,'' I inform Victoria under the smooth bare arm settling the plates on the table. ''It was a policy Pop took out on me when I was a kid.''

Victoria is incredulous. She has never completely adjusted herself to my father's weird and wondrous *Weltanschauung*. ''Earl took a policy out on you? Whatever for?''

''To help defray the cost of a university education.'' That was the ostensible reason; however, I'm sure it was bought as a prophylactic against those polio epidemics so frequent in the early fifties. Pop's white magic. ''The idea was to cash it when I was eighteen. But when the time rolled around he didn't need the bucks, so he just held on to it. The policy was a present, a reward for exemplary service in the crockery wars.''

''And you bailed out. Earl ought to have known better than to put temptation your way.''

''Go on, stick together. Pop and you always conspired against me. I remember you two huddled in a corner at Thanksgiving

four years ago, whispering. You were going to commit me to law
school that time. Wasn't that the plan? You can confess now, I've
been jettisoned.''

"Thirty-two years old," Victoria says, shaking her head.
"Thirty-two years old.''

"Not until April. Don't age me any more than you already
have.''

"Ed, when is all this going to stop? What are you going to do
with your life?''

It's a question I've been pondering myself for some time now.
So the answer comes easily and promptly. "Simplify it.''

"Simplify it. God, I don't believe it. What is that supposed to
mean?''

I've got a quick answer for that one too. "Nothing much is
wrong with me except my age. Being thirty is what's the matter." I
recite Frost. " 'Two roads diverged in a yellow wood / And sorry
I could not travel both / And be one traveler, long I stood.' " A
woman at a neighboring table smiles indulgently, mistaking me
for a lover declaiming verse to his beloved. I am merely making a
tactical point.

"Oh, Christ.''

"Well, have you taken a good long look at any of our friends
lately? That's what they're all doing.''

"No they're not.''

"They are.''

"Here we go," Victoria says. "It was always your worst
habit, reading into others' actions your own motives. Nobody is
doing any such thing.''

"They all are, and Frost was talking *particularly*," I ballast the
word with leaden emphasis, "about people like you and me, or
Benny, or Sadler." A strange image is forming in my mind. I can
see Frost, or rather McMurtry masquerading as Frost, in a plaid,
billed cap with huge ear lugs. I blink hard and he dissolves.

"You're a loon," Victoria says.

"I'm not. Think about it. We've lived just long enough to
make out the paths in all those trees. Big-decision time. No more
fooling around. Don't you feel that? I certainly do.''

"This is interesting coming from you," says Victoria, looking edgy as she stubs out her cigarette; "you never showed any signs that you saw anything passing you by."

"There they are, two roads — " I lift a forefinger, "one choice. We can choose to simplify our lives, or we can choose to complicate them."

"And you have chosen to simplify yours," says Victoria with an acidic smile.

"In a way," I say. My theory and its ramifications are subtler than this. I ransack my mind for illustrations. "Perhaps it would be closer to the truth to say that the inclination for one path or the other is in us all. Our tendencies just become more evident as time runs out on us. And, of course, each individual's path can take a wide and interesting number of variations from the two basic forms. Take what Sadler did. He chose what I'd call religious simplicity. Not uncommon."

"Sadler is crazy. You can't make an argument on the basis of what a crazy person does."

"He was always crazy. It's just that now his craziness expresses itself in a way unacceptable in your circles. Back when we were going to university and Sadler was a big-time campus radical urging Luddite atrocities on the computer centre, none of your friends thought he was particularly nuts — which he evidently was. But now it's a different story because he's chosen an unpopular lunacy. Some television preacher offers him salvation one morning and Sadler falls on his knees on the living-room carpet. Suddenly everyone claims Sadler is nuts. Looks like the same Sadler to me."

"You make it sound like it was a revelation or something. He didn't just fall on his knees. You always exaggerate for effect. Marsha said he was depressed for weeks. All he did was watch early-morning TV. That Christian talk-show host got him at his lowest ebb. The conversion business was a direct result of mental illness. Sadler is nuts."

"Not any more than he ever was."

Victoria does not buy my argument. She has the atheist's illiberalism. She begins to argue anecdotally. "Try and tell that story to Marsha. Did you hear why she finally left him?" I barely have time to nod. "Because he had an operation to have his vasectomy reversed after he joined that church of screwballs. Can you believe it? They're Protestants but they're against birth control."

"Not exactly," I qualify, "they're not against birth control. They're in favor of abstinence. You see, there is a distinction —"

Victoria interrupts. "Marsha gave him fair warning. She told him if he went ahead with it she was leaving. Although what the point of the reversal was I don't know — it hardly ever works anyway. But you tell me that isn't nuts — reversing a vasectomy."

"Any man who had a spark of sanity would undergo any number of vasectomy reversals to induce Marsha to leave him. But that isn't the point. The point is Sadler's fundamental nature. What you fail to understand is that he's the ultimate simplifier. The very antithesis of your bet-hedging, quibbling complicator. Sadler wants Truth with a capital T. He always did. And when he signed on with the Independent Pre-Millennial Church of God's First Chosen, or whatever they call themselves, he didn't go making his membership contingent on a bunch of mental reservations. No sir. He understood that being one of God's First Chosen isn't easy. He swallowed it whole. I kind of admire that."

"God, this is typical. It's so like you to defend him out of perversity because any other reasonable and sane human being wouldn't."

I'm offended. Victoria doesn't understand scientific objectivity. "I'm not defending him. And I'm not saying he isn't nuts. I'm explaining him to you. When Sadler reached his early thirties he became what he was always deep in his heart, a wild-eyed prophet. We're all becoming what we really are. Time and circumstances are like sunlight and earth and water to all of us little acorns yearning to be oaks."

"Ed, you're still the only man I've ever met who makes me want to literally scream. Fifteen minutes with you and I can feel the pressure building here." Victoria touches the region of her diaphragm. "And the horrible thing is I know you won't be stopped, can't be stopped, until everything you want to say gets said."

"Don't be melodramatic, Victoria."

She rests her head in her hands, a model of weary resignation. "Finish your speech," she says.

"It isn't a speech."

"Goddamn it, just get it over with!"

"You have to help."

"Don't needle me, Ed."

"I need a push. I forget where I was."

"Where you were," she says, "was on the topic of acorns and oaks."

"Aristotle," I say, "sort of."

"Let's not review the intervening two thousand years between Aristotle and Ed," Victoria says. "I'm on my lunch hour."

"Ha ha."

"Ha ha yourself."

"What I was trying to say, Victoria," I resume, "is that we're all approaching the time of life when the oak-tree potential in the acorn becomes manifest. In Sadler's case we end up with John the Baptist. Haven't you noticed that everybody we know is coming out of the closet, so to speak?"

"Example," says Victoria, listlessly, right on cue. Her cooperation indicates she is eager to get this over with.

"Example — well, Benny's a good example of Sadler's opposite. He's a complicator."

"And just what's the difference between Benny and Sadler?" Victoria is showing signs of impatience. "Aside from the fact one is nuts and the other isn't?"

"Easy. The simplifiers want less, the complicators want more."

This only increases Victoria's annoyance. "Less what? More what?" She angrily lights a cigarette.

"*Everything.*" I ought to stop myself but can't. I've been musing on life lately and have the intrepid explorer's eagerness to pass on his discoveries. "Let me explain. A complicator finds safety in numbers, people, things. It doesn't matter. He takes pleasure in possessions. Here's what I mean. Suppose a guy wakes up one morning and realizes he can't stand his wife. If by nature he's a true simplifier he'll just up and walk out on her. If he's a true complicator he finds himself a girlfriend.''

"And this is how you've been spending your time, dreaming up crap like this?''

"Listen to me and you'll see. It isn't crap. Think of Benny's house. Have you ever really looked at it? Magazines everywhere. For chrissakes there's a *World Almanac* in the bathroom on the toilet tank. He *reads* the *World Almanac*. Benny believes in being 'informed'. He believes that facts are truth. He displays all the characteristic features of the complicator.'' I'm on a roll now. "Let me enumerate.'' I hold up one hand and begin counting off fingers. "First we have Benny's fascination with facts, with information. Typical of the legal profession — of which he imagines himself a leading light — a shabby coven of complicators and obfuscators without parallel. Second, unlike the simplifier, Benny places his faith in the flesh. Look at his sexual habits. Women, women, women. Only one of whom, let me remind you, is he married to. The thing is, Benny believes in data and sensation. He believes that his perplexity is a result of not having enough information, and his lust the result of too few women. Hence his belief in one more feature-length article in *Time* or one more bimbo.''

Victoria is growing angrier. There are ruddy spots of color on her cheeks and this prompts me to hurry to finish. "Sadler on the other hand, rumor has it, is chaste and ascetic. He has no interest in facts. All he wants is contained in the covers of The Book. The last five hundred years of discoveries in astronomy, biology, physics, chemistry, and psychology weigh less than nothing on his metaphysical scales. I'm trying to achieve such purity of viewpoint myself. Of course, I'm travelling in a slightly different direction, but I can't deny he's been an inspiration to me. Mind over matter.''

"I can imagine the direction you're travelling,'' says Victoria. She seems to be growing more and more agitated. She is glancing nervously at her watch and twisting the expansion bracelet.

"That's the wonderful thing about one's thirties,'' I comment. "Almost anything can surface. Old radical friends — and you and I can think of a number — emigrate to the suburbs, build two-car attached garages, take their daughters for lessons in bourgeois dance, and coach competitive sport. On the other hand we find the individual who decides he doesn't care what Granny or Aunt Edna thinks. He says to himself, 'There it is. I'm queer, queer as the day is long. I'm going to prance and wear satin pants until I'm eighty. I don't *care*.' Admirable.''

"You always put things in the nicest ways, Ed. You're so understanding of others.''

"Oh-oh. Here we go with 'If you show me your sensitivity I'll show you mine.' Knock it off, Victoria.''

"In my experience you have little to show. I wouldn't hold my breath at the unveiling.''

"Say what's on your mind, Victoria.''

"How can I with you saying what's on yours?''

"I suppose your outrage is occasioned by unkind references to your old buddies? Well then, let me say something nice about same. I am pleased by the sudden crop of babies. Of course, as I've said before, time is marching on. The spectre of infertility looms. The dirty deed must be quickly done, but I concede that the result, the product, is nice.''

"Shut up, you boor.'' Victoria is furious.

It is clear we are going to fight, so I decide to get my licks in quickly. This is advisable with Victoria, since in seconds you may be pummelled senseless and incapable of retaliation. A charge of calculated disloyalty is often wounding. "On the other hand, we do see marriages dissolving, don't we? Quite a substantial number. Perhaps once again a case of biology being a hard taskmaster. It's a tough decision deciding whether to stick with what you've got or look for something better, isn't it, Victoria? If you want better, dump the spouse now while you've still got a few good miles in you. What you've got to market — as a man or a woman, no sexism, please — is fading fast. The bloom will soon be off the rose. The semi-soft hard-on, bum droop, and saggy tits are just around the corner. *Tempus fugit*.''

The muscles of Victoria's face and throat go rigid, as if she has been slapped. Fasces of tendons spring along her throat.

"You son of a bitch.'' These words are uttered from a depth of sadness and bitterness I hadn't imagined. Something is very wrong. There is a bright gathering of tears in her eyes. I quickly glance away, partly from shame, partly because if I don't Victoria will break down. Strange. In seven years of marriage she cried only twice in my presence. But, Christ, when it came. Always against her will, torn out of her. It was worse that way: snot bubbles, face twisted and red, stray hairs plastered in the spit at the corner of her mouth. Just wouldn't stop. Choking and stuttering on the effort of trying to quit.

People are passing on the sidewalk beneath us. The exhaust of cars waiting at the intersection for the light to turn green runs in billows against the side of the Café Nice, then spins up to writhe briefly on the warm window glass. The muffled pedestrians, some in stiff nylon snowmobile or ski suits, shuffle through these white clouds like space voyagers on a planet of visible, deadly gases.

"I ought to have my head examined," Victoria is saying, "coming to you at a time like this. How did you know exactly what to say to stop me dead in my tracks? What is this sixth sense of yours, Ed?"

I keep my eyes off her face. The white wine in my glass is gold. "Pardon?" This is a polite, surprised, and diffident request for an explanation. I cannot follow this sudden turn to our conversation.

"I don't know what got into me," she says. I hear her voice growing reedier by the second. "Perhaps I felt you owed me some advice after all these years I carried you draped over my shoulders; maybe I thought that if nothing else after nine years of living together you would know me better than anybody else."

I feel the old familiar neurotic stab of apprehension. I lift my eyes to her face. "For God's sake, Victoria, what the hell is the matter?"

"It never fails," she says, blundering along, "that anything I have to say gets turned back on me by you, so that I look foolish and pathetic. You never cared if you looked either, but I have my pride. I won't feel that way."

"Victoria, what is it? Please."

She knows she will cry now; it can't be avoided. She begins to gather her things from the table. Head down, she says: "I didn't think it possible but you didn't even ask me how I was. How many months? Not even that."

"For Christ's sake, how are you? How are you, Victoria?"

Her face is dark and bitter with choler. "Guess. Take a hard look and guess, asshole." Then before I can react, can hoist my bulk out of the unsteady chair, she walks swiftly towards the exit.

By the time the bill has been calculated and I have paid, Victoria has disappeared. The exhaust pipes of idling cars churn out banks of dense white smoke, the packed snow squeaks under the boots of passersby, the entire street rests stiff, dumb, obscure. My heart pounds and pounds.

THREE

Victoria's disappearance outside the Café Nice seems ominous, a forbidding sign. It is nearly midnight and I still haven't managed to reach her. Her old phone number is no longer in service and information has no new listing for her. This leads me to believe that Marsha Sadler was speaking the truth when she phoned me a month ago to drop a ponderous hint that Victoria had given up her apartment and moved in with her new boyfriend, co-vivant, or whatever such people are presently called.

Although Marsha frequently sees Victoria because they are members of a foreign film society, when she phoned I was inclined to discount the credibility of her information. As a source, Marsha Sadler is not particularly trustworthy. Bill Sadler's flight from her sinewy arms to the comforting embrace of the Independent Pre-Millennial Church of God's First Chosen appears to have unhinged the woman. She now resents anyone who is married, happily or otherwise. With dogged determination Marsha seeks the hairline fractures that can be found in any marriage, and into such cracks she scrabbles her witchy fingernails and, tugging with spiteful vigor, does her best to make them gape as wide as the jaws of hell.

The peculiar thing is that when we meet she carries on as if a strong bond of sympathy exists between us because we have this in common: *we were deserted by our mates*. During our chance encounters Marsha grips my arm with her painted talons and confides that, although Victoria is her friend, she relates to my "life situation".

Marsha resembles a veteran airline stewardess. She displays the hard-bitten confidence, professional grooming, caramel tan, and jingling jewellery of such gals. Of course she isn't a stewardess. The caramel tan and the jewellery are courtesy of her father, who sends her to Arizona every January to lollygag in the sun. He owns a condominium in Phoenix. The hard-bitten confidence is innate.

The only woman whom I fear more than Victoria is Hideous Marsha; yet Hideous is my last hope of reliable information. Since six o'clock I've been making phone calls to anyone who might know where Victoria is living. At the moment the total stands at eight. No one would tell me anything of any significance; almost to a woman they feigned ignorance. No, they didn't have Victoria's phone number. Had I thought to call information? Really? No listing? Living with another man? They hadn't heard.

They were all lying through their teeth because of things I'd done to Victoria's paramours in the past. Not that I ever did anything truly evil. Just light harassment. Telephone impersonations of collection agencies, that sort of thing. Although I did put one gentleman caller's phone number and vital statistics in the personal column of a homophile tabloid.

The only scrap of information I managed to turn up was a Christian name: Anthony. I got this out of Miriam, an older woman with whom Victoria works. She is neither as wily nor as militant as some of the others I phoned; nevertheless, she knew she'd done a bad thing letting it slip. Nothing more was forthcoming. Anthony. It isn't much more than a toehold but I'll see what I can parlay the name into with Hideous Marsha.

It just isn't working. Galloping pell-mell from room to room of my apartment hasn't eased my apprehension. Elbows crooked and carried high like a racewalker's, forearms sawing back and forth at my waist, I wriggle down the hallway, veer around the planter spilling plastic ivy, streak across the kitchen, and churn back upstream toward the bedroom like a 240-pound spawning salmon. I've lost count how many times I've thundered round the circuit, breaking stride only for pit stops to void my bladder in nervous, parsimonious spurts and dribbles, or to change the album on the stereo. Right now Credence Clearwater Revival is belting out "Proud Mary".

Trust Hideous. Trust Hideous Marsha Goddamn Sadler to make a bad day worse. The phone must have rung a dozen times before she deigned to answer it in that cool, distant way she has.

"Hello, Marsha Sadler speaking. I hope you know what time it is."

"Marsha, it's Ed."

There was a slight hesitation while she decided whether to be civil. The possible interest of the call apparently outweighed the inconvenience of the hour. "Ed! How are you? So good to hear your voice again. It's been ages, hasn't it? But then I spent the Christmas holidays in Phoenix. You should see me. I've got the most glorious all-over suntan." Said with a giggle. "But you'll have to hurry, it's fading fast. Drop by and have a drink some evening."

As conversations go with Marsha, this one began sanely and sensibly enough. There is in Marsha Sadler a bedrock of self-importance and self-interest that makes her reasonably predictable. However, having said that, I have to qualify it by adding that Marsha wishes to be appreciated as a "serious person capable of growth". Her growing pains are often a trial to those around her. This year she is adding inches to her stature by attending a graduate class in English literature.

In the past her interest was confined largely to pop psychological treatises available in paperback at the corner drugstore. They pointed out to her many a straight and narrow path down which she sauntered only to discover they opened into Californian box canyons. None of these books altered Marsha's personality, but they lent her darker machinations and meddlings in other people's business the appearance of sincerity and genuine concern.

"What a life you lead, Marsha," I said jocularly, "grilling your lovely limbs in Arizona."

"Ed, you make me sound decadent," declared Marsha, full of hope. One of her fondest desires is to be thought just that. She revels in sexual innuendo the way a cat rolls in catnip. "Surely you wouldn't deny me the *natural* pleasures of life."

Taking a firm grip on my gorge, I replied, "Or even the unnatural, Marsha."

She tittered. I tittered.

"Ed, you're incorrigible!"

"Marsha, you're insatiable!"

Another round of adult chortles. I was beginning to sweat with shame. God only knew how long this would have to go on.

"Ed, I'd forgotten how quick you are."

"Sadly, that's what all the girls say!"

A squeal of delight. That's it; I don't have much self-respect left to squander. I decided to change the subject, so I cleared my throat. "But, seriously, Marsha, how was Arizona?"

The adverb was a signal to Marsha. It gave her the opportunity to prove she's not just a bundle of sexual tensions. "Ed, it's always an experience. You wouldn't believe the light."

"The light?"

"The light," she repeated. "The desert light. I don't know. It's kind of spiritual. Anyway, it was great. Then I went on to Palm Springs for a week before coming back."

"That's wonderful," I said, imagining hecatombs of depleted tennis pros littering the sandy wastes, marking Marsha's passage.

"It is wonderful, isn't it? It's like I always say — you know what I always say about marriage and Arizona, don't you?"

"No. Regrettably, I don't."

"I always say there's no way I would have married Bill in Arizona. The light there is too revealing, too pitiless. Anyway, shit smells in the sun. He'd have stunk to high heaven."

I attempted to head off trouble. Hideous Marsha was getting ready to start in on Bill. I wasn't going to be sidetracked. "Speaking of light," I broke in hastily, "I wonder if you could shed a little of it on a matter for me, Marsha? I've just about succeeded in demolishing my apartment looking for Anthony's phone number. Victoria gave it to me and I put it away some place and now I'm damned if I can find it."

Marsha didn't appreciate being interrupted. "Anthony?"

I took a deep breath. It's all a venture, isn't it? "Yes. You know Anthony. *Victoria's* Anthony."

Her reply confirmed I was correct in my supposition of a connection. At least she didn't contradict my wife's claim to him. "Victoria gave *you* Anthony's phone number?" she said, making clear she viewed this contention with scepticism.

"Uh-huh."

She paused. "If you've lost his phone number, why don't you look it up in the phone book?"

This was hardly the time for Marsha to suddenly turn vicious and logical. "Because I thought it was unlisted," I said, not particularly convincingly. "That's why I thought Victoria *gave* it to me — because it was unlisted."

"No," said Marsha in a guarded voice, "he's in the phone book."

On reflection I realize I ought to have given her plenty of time to rubber-hose poor Bill in that startling, revealing Arizona light while I looked on and applauded. Then she would have been more kindly disposed to me.

"Ah," I said, casting around in my mind, wondering what to do next. A long, painful wait for her to volunteer information wasn't a success. "This is really embarrassing," I confessed at last, "but I can't recall Anthony's last name. It's slipped clean out of my mind. Imagine forgetting the name of your wife's lover," I said with a bark of wry laughter. "There must be something psychologically revealing about that." I was offering bait which the old Marsha, the student of the human mind and human interactions, would have risen to, mouth gaping.

"Yep," she said.

There I was with a phone humming in my ear. Yep, that was it. In my confusion I faltered, lost my grip, and made another appeal to last season's Marsha. That is, to warm, wise Counsellor Marsha. I worked tremolo into my voice. "It's so hard," I said. "I'm finding the adjustment so damn hard."

This ploy was not much more successful. "We all carry scars, Ed. You've got to learn to live with rejection like everybody else," she said.

What was I to do? My situation was that of a desperately unfunny comedian performing his stale patter before a bored, even hostile audience. But if it's your only routine you have to carry on despite a cool reception. Carry on with rills of nervous perspiration trickling down my sides and the idiocy of what I was saying clamoring louder and louder in my ears. I nattered on breathlessly. I said that just by listening Marsha was helping me get in touch with my feelings. I said feelings were important, it was important to say how you felt. I paused. Marsha said she *supposed* that was true. I said I felt worried, really worried. Why? she asked with a touch of interest. And having got that far, I gabbled the story of all that had transpired in the Café Nice from the time the first bread stick was crunched until Victoria had fled, weeping. "So you see, Marsha," I concluded, "Victoria did want to talk to me. Something's the matter. I'm really worried. Please give me her number."

"Let me think," replied Marsha. "What we've got to do in this situation isn't entirely clear."

"We?" I didn't relish her use of the plural pronoun.

"I think it would be best if I get hold of Victoria tomorrow — arrange a lunch or something. Leave it to me. I'll find out what's going on. Then you can drop by here tomorrow night and I'll fill you in. In the meantime just relax, get a good night's sleep, and don't worry. Marsha'll take care of everything."

This took me so aback I lost my hold on my tongue. "I don't want a go-between, Marsha. I want a number."

"Trust me, Ed. There's no way Victoria will want to talk to you right now, not after what happened. You must admit you were a bit insensitive."

"I don't have to admit anything."

"It seems obvious you were. Otherwise, why did she run away?"

"Nothing under heaven and earth is obvious. That's my goddamn point. I want the situation cleared up and I find you running interference. Butt out, Marsha."

"Ed, learn to rely on others. There are none of us so strong that we don't need help at some point in our lives. It isn't wrong to lean on somebody else."

"Come on, Marsha, cut the crap. Give me the fucking phone number."

"Not until I've talked to Victoria. I've got to trust my own judgment. I don't think this is the proper time for you two to talk — not when you're both so upset."

"Who's fucking upset?"

"You obviously are, Ed. And stop using that word. There's no doubt you're upset. In the last few minutes — when we started discussing Victoria you'll note — your voice has gone all high and funny and squeaky."

My ears started to ring. The old blood-pressure thing. "What is it? Do you want me to crawl? Is that it? Beg? Well, I am. I'm begging." I actually dropped on my knees beside the phone stand. "You can't see me, Marsha, but I'm in your favorite position — male submissive. I'm on my knees. Picture it, Marsha."

"Ed, get hold of yourself."

"Not low enough? Lower? You got it!" I flopped on my belly and the smell of dirty feet rose out of the carpet and assailed my nostrils. "This is Ed reporting. I'm on my belly. I'm grovelling, Marsha. I'm prostrate." *Why do I do these things?* "Merciful Marsha, I implore you, give me my wife's phone number!"

Marsha neglected to respond. I lay on the floor, panting. How soon our passions are spent. The phone droned in my ear. Finally Marsha spoke with her customary icy authority, customary when addressing me. "Ed, are you still there?"

"Yes."

"Are you really on the floor?"

"Yes."

"Then get up."

I did.

"Are you sure you're quite finished?"

"Yes."

"All right. I'll see you tomorrow. About nine-thirty."

"I'm warning you," I said half-heartedly, knowing I was beat, "if you don't give me Victoria's number I'll keep phoning all night."

"Then I'll just have to leave my receiver off the hook, won't I? Goodnight, Ed." Click.

She did it, too. Left it off the hook, that is. I'm such a stupid jerk. Never warn anybody. Just do it.

So now I'm pacing, which is what I always do to keep hysteria at bay. If Victoria hadn't behaved so completely out of character, I wouldn't be this strung-out. And because I can't be with her, can't reach her, my apprehension is augmented. I expect the worst.

The engaging Dr. Brandt, the psychiatrist I visited when Victoria and I were newly married, barely had me inside his office door when he decided to roll up his clinical sleeves and go to work on this neurosis of mine. This didn't please me because at the time what I saw as my problem was a temporary loss of imagination. That is, I was panicky because I could not construct a scenario of success in my future. I didn't regard the apprehension I experienced when I was away from Victoria as a particularly thorny difficulty. At that point I had resolved I wouldn't let her out of my sight aside from the eight hours a day we spent apart at work. That solved my problem.

Dr. Brandt, however, chose to label my attitude towards Victoria as unhealthy and described it as "infantile separation anxiety". According to him, whenever circumstances prevent me from being with Victoria, my perception of the world reverts to that of a child. My emotional ties to Victoria, Brandt said, are not the mature ones of a husband to a wife, but those of a child to his mother. Therefore, when I am prevented from being with Victoria, I experience the separation anxiety of a young child, an anxiety compounded by an adult's ability to imagine dreadful contingencies: rape, murder, automobile accidents, etc. Furthermore, he went on to say that in his clinical experience he has seldom encountered a "socially functioning individual" who perceived his environment to be as threatening and consistently hostile as I apparently did. If my world-view was not significantly modified by therapy

I could expect to experience a breakdown in the future. At best I was sure to suffer some severe dysfunction. He thought I already displayed symptoms of burgeoning agoraphobia.

Yet I believe that after only seven sessions with Dr. Brandt I was coming close to convincing him my portrait of the world was more accurate than his own. But perhaps I flatter myself. Still, he asked me to find another therapist. Instead, I went home and announced to Victoria that Dr. Brandt had pronounced me cured. Victoria never did tell me what he said when she phoned him, seeking corroboration of the miracle.

On reflection, what I find interesting is that Dr. Brandt, a man of science, steadfastly refused to test my claims about the world against the evidence. It's not that I deny the practicality of his approach. If a patient expresses displeasure about how the world is constituted, one had better change the patient, since one cannot change the world. The only other possible alternative is for the patient to re-invent the world, and that is a capability given to only a very few.

For the time being I struggle with my dreadful intuitions. When my phone rings at two o'clock in the morning I never assume it is a drunk with a wrong number. No, it is always news of a death in the family. "Eddie, Daddy's gone. A coronary."

Two rings and I scatter the blankets, heave my bulk upward, and pound out to the phone, where, throat parched with horror, I plaintively croak into the mouthpiece: "Yes! Yes! For God's sake, tell me!" Only to be reviled by a drunken gourmand demanding egg rolls and chow mein, or a lonely Lothario with coarse, mumbled offers to sniff my panties.

And now I whirl from room to room, fearful for Victoria. Cancer?

I've been afraid of Victoria getting cancer for years now, even though I know that to harbor such fears is to submit to superstition. The old woman, Victoria's great-aunt, is responsible for lodging that black apprehension in my mind. It was she who raised the subject at the tea party held in the week before Victoria's and my wedding took place.

Victoria was in the habit of describing her family as utterly boring and conventional. Her mother, she said, had constructed an entire ethical system around the notion of "niceness", and living with her father, she said, was like living with a clock. However, neither of her parents struck me as being either boring or conventional; I always had the feeling that both of them had loose boards in their attics.

For example, I found her mother's idea of hosting a tea party to allow the groom to meet the female relatives and friends a little odd. It wasn't arranged with an eye to making me uncomfortable, but that was the result. There I was, the only male in the company of twenty-three women sipping tea and eating sandwiches the size of postage stamps. No, I tell a lie. I wasn't the only man there; my father-in-law Jack was in attendance also. He had come home early from the office to lend me "moral support". Evidently Jack's desertion of his post was unusual enough to make news in family circles, because whenever another lady arrived at the tea party, Victoria's mother would tell her, with an air of sharing a great confidence, "Jack took the day off to lend Ed moral support."

Then Jack would say, "Half a day, Frances."

He was an engineer of some description. His father had been an engineer and he had two brothers who were engineers. He looked like a man raised on girders and graph paper, as if exactitude were bred into his bones. Looking at him put me in mind of a mathematical equation; I got the feeling one could no more argue with him than one could argue with numbers. Throughout the tea party he sat in a distant corner of the room and watched me. Whenever I looked in his direction he averted his eyes and gazed off through the glass patio doors.

Meanwhile Victoria and I made polite conversation with the ladies.

"I understand you and Victoria met at the university, Ed?"

"Yes."

"Let me guess. Was it at a Mixer Dance? I bet it was. That's where I met my husband, Harold. You'll meet him at the wedding."

Etc., etc.

This sort of chatter I could handle with aplomb. In fact, I was on the point of congratulating myself on my poise when one old girl suddenly addressed me very loudly, in the manner of the profoundly deaf. "Young man," she said, "has my grandniece had the decency to inform you of the family curse?"

With that the room went absolutely still and all eyes settled on the great-aunt. She was a queer-looking old duck, bright blue eyes staring out of a face that had been battered white with a powder puff. I smiled weakly at her while I tried to balance a teacup on my knee and prayed silently for succor.

"You should be warned of what you're getting into," she continued shrilly. "There's cancer in our family. All kinds of it!"

"Now, Auntie," said Victoria's mother, "there's cancer in all families."

"Not like ours," the old girl said, wavering between pride and anger, "*we're full of it!*"

Jack got conspicuously to his feet. "Come along, Ed," he said, "and have a look at my shooting range in the basement."

As I followed him out of the living room I heard the great-aunt say, with immense self-satisfaction, "Somebody had to let that boy know. It's only fair. And another thing, now that he's been told, he can't come back at the family and say he wasn't warned."

Of course, Jack never made any mention of what had gone on upstairs. That was how he dealt with things or people that failed to please him: he refused to recognize their existence. In the not-too-distant future Jack would make me disappear also, but for the moment he was still sizing me up, forming his opinion of me, and so I was being taken to the firing range.

I had heard a bit about Jack's marksmanship from Victoria. When I had asked her what her father liked to do, she had said, "Cut the lawn and shoot air pistols in the basement."

The shooting range wasn't as elaborate as I had envisioned it, just a white line painted on the basement floor where one took up one's position to fire. Ten yards distant from the line a wire was hung with bull's-eye targets; behind the targets a canvas tarp absorbed the impact of the pellets with a resounding *thwack!*

Before we commenced gun play, Jack said we had to put on

safety glasses to prevent taking a pellet in the eye. How such a thing could occur, unless we let off a salvo at each other, I couldn't see, but I didn't ask questions. Once we were suitably goggled, Jack showed me how to load the pistol and demonstrated the two-handed grip and the wide, straddle-legged stance I was to assume when "discharging my weapon". Finally I was allowed to approach the line. When I had taken up the prescribed stance and sighted down the barrel of my piece, Jack said, "Ten rounds rapid fire. Commence firing."

In my nervousness and haste I squeezed off eleven shots instead of ten and hit the target only twice. Jack didn't use the word cheating, but he carefully explained to me that a score was computed on the basis of *exactly* ten shots. Then he stepped up to the line and showed me how it was done. After peppering his target he solemnly totted up his score and recorded it on a large chart taped to the wall. From what I could see, his records went back to the early sixties.

That's the way we continued, alternating turns and merrily firing off our air pistols in total silence except for Jack's terse command: "Commence firing!", an order he addressed not only to me but also to himself whenever he toed the line and levelled his pistol. This fun had continued for about a half an hour when he remarked, "We're running low on ammo, Ed. I think I'll pop off to the store and lay in a few more rounds. Won't be a sec."

He left so abruptly I didn't know what to do with myself while I waited. One thing was certain, I didn't want to go back upstairs and subject myself to the tea party. Out of boredom I started fooling around with the air pistol. I twirled it on my index finger. I stuck it in my pants and practised my draw. I attempted the border roll of the shootist of the wild west. I shot at the target over my shoulder, behind my back, between my legs. I tossed the gun from my right hand to my left hand and snapped off a shot. That's how I took the light out over the laundry tubs.

It was while hiding the broken glass in the drain in the basement floor that I heard voices. Because of the arrangement of heating vents and ducts in the house, it was possible, from that particular spot, to hear clearly everything that was being said upstairs.

I heard someone ask, "And where will you and Ed make your home, dear?"

Victoria startled me by saying, "We intend to go to Greece."

I wasn't the only one startled. Victoria's mother squealed, "*Greece?*"

"Yes, Greece," said Victoria firmly.

"Isn't that interesting — Greece," said someone. "And what will your husband do there?"

"He's going to write."

I was beginning to feel very uncomfortable listening to what was going on upstairs. I didn't like it one bit.

"Write what?" demanded Victoria's mother. "Will he write for magazines?"

"No. He won't write for magazines."

"How do you mean to say he'll write? Do you mean to say he'll write like Hemingway, or someone like that?"

"Yes."

"Well," said someone else, "he must be a very interesting and clever young man to be able to do that."

"Yes," said Victoria, "he is. That's why I'm marrying him."

No one can imagine how dreadful I felt hearing all that. I had never taken the business of going to Greece really seriously; I thought common sense would finish that idea off when the time was ripe. Until that moment, talk of Greece had been private talk, having no connection with reality. Now Victoria had made a public announcement committing us to something I didn't want to do. Suddenly I knew I didn't want anything to do with Greece. I now saw it in an entirely different light; the land of wine and song had become a harsh court of bright light in which I was to be measured and surely found wanting. I couldn't write. If required to attempt it I would fail; I would reveal myself as neither clever nor interesting. It was an old story preparing to repeat itself; I was going to disappoint as I had disappointed all my life. If that pop pistol in my hand had been the real item, who knows what Jack might have found on his basement floor when he returned with more ammo? I felt pretty low at that moment and afraid of losing Victoria if my true self were to be exposed.

My spirits, however, recovered over the next two days, although they took a dip during the actual wedding ceremony. It was the oddest thing. When the minister asked if I would keep my wife in ''sickness and in health'', the image of the great-aunt with the white face and the terrible blue eyes sprang to mind, and I was gripped again with such a fear of losing Victoria that I could hardly answer. Later, jokes were made about the pallor of the groom.

It's that old bitch who got me worrying about cancer, and cancer is what I'm thinking about remembering Victoria in the Café Nice. But I'm going to stop all that right now, this very minute, and make an end of it.

Credence Clearwater has sung itself out. The black disc spins mute. I hear the wind rising and stop in my tracks with a groan. Peeling off my damp shirt and then letting it drop to the carpet I limp to the window and thrust my bare chest out to the cold pane of glass to cool myself.

One of those unpredictable February blizzards has poured out of the night with a muffled roar. The two tall evergreens which front the building and give it its name, The Twin Spruce Apartments, lash their tops in a wind which the street lights reveal is streaked with a thin, flying snow. It spatters grittily against the window in fierce gusts, fine and hard as salt.

I'm shivering. I decide I would be better off getting some sleep. In the bedroom I strip and crawl between the sheets, feeling lonely and hollow. I have never cared for these moments of darkness before sleep comes during which the mind is helpless. As a child I would watch the shirt hung on the chair back slowly fill with the horrible, solid flesh of an escaped madman; the criminally insane stalked the night.

I had to light torches against the mind's blackness. My choice was *Huck Finn*. The book was a favorite of mine. Huck was, like me, superstitious. He lived in a world in which danger could be deflected by signs and ceremonies. Like Huck's Pap I put a cross of tacks in the heel of my shoe. I also hung a lucky penny on a string around my neck, which left perfect green circles under my sweaty armpits when I slept.

I talked to myself then, I talk to myself now.

The bed I lie on is a raft, a raft riding the silt-laden, chocolate currents of the Mississippi. The darkness which surrounds me is the southern night, warm and still, enriched by the heavy, fertile smells of growth and decay. Far away on the river bank to starboard a dog barks sharply, once. The sound is strange, distant yet distinct across the water. A brief light shows itself high on the bluffs, a kerosene star shining behind oilskin in a cabin window. Water rips languidly round a snag unseen in the blackness, the raft spins a quarter-turn when the current coils momentarily like a snake.

There are two people on this raft, the boy Huck and the man Jim. I play both parts, modulating voice and accent as required. Ed is bound for the Gulf and for the moment I know no impulses but the river's. Borne on its broad, strong back through a night of huge, flaring stars an arm's length above me, and soothed by the faint music of the river's surge, I feel a great peace. For several minutes I lie silent, lulled by the gentle tugging of the current. I clear my throat and speak softly into the night. "A body gits to feelin' mighty low, 'n po', 'n lonesome come night on dis ribber, doan he, Mars Huck? A body gits to feelin' der hain't no pusson in de worl' tall dat cares nuff'n fur 'n ole nigger like Jim."

"Drat you, Jim! I was most asleep! How you carry on!" Huck cries. Victoria used to reply in a similar vein but in a more modern idiom when I carried on like this.

"Dat sho is a turrible lonesome feelin' when you onliest fren' doan wants to keep you comp'ny on no raf'. Sho nuff is, Huck honey. Hain't ole Jim bin good to you, chile?"

"Ain't you *s'posed* to be good to me? Why d'you think I brung you along, if it warn't to be good to me?"

"Dat's de troof, Huck. Dat's a fac'."

The raft glides around a bend in the Mississippi and a riverboat comes into view, sparks tossed into a sky of pitch by the handful, deck lights blazing like the eyes of angels.

"Lookee thar, Jim! What you speckilate that is a-makin' fur us? Sidewheeler or sternwheeler?"

"Doan ax Jim. Doan ax an ole burrhaid nigra, chile, to speckilate on dat."

"Sternwheeler!" cries Huck, triumphant.

"I calc'late dat's de *Natchez* boun' fur St. Joe."

"Could be," allows Huck, topped, crestfallen.

"Dem sparks a flyin' out ub de smoke stack am a wonder, hain't dey, Huck?"

" 'Deed they are." A long silence follows. The great floating hotel of gaiety and pleasure blazes a stately progress down the river, a snatch of music wafts to our bobbing raft, tiny handsome men and stunning women lean against the railings of the upper deck and gaze into the sombre evening, their faces white. Then the sternwheeler churns out of sight and the great train of light spreading from its stern flickers, disappears.

"Goodnight, Jim," says Huck at last.

"Goodnight, Huck honey."

A little conversation before sleep is a comforting thing. And that's not a bad sight to hold in the mind, those sparks streaming upward from a riverboat chimney into the dense, blue-black canopy of an Arkansas night. As Huck notes at one point in the relating of his *Adventures*, "There warn't no home like a raft, after all. Other places do seem so cramped and smothery, but a raft don't."

No, a raft don't. And experience has taught me it rides the dark a good deal easier and lighter when it carries two.

FOUR

It would be hard to imagine a worse day. To begin with, the weather is foul. Snow fell until nine o'clock this morning with a stupefying persistence, strangling side streets and burying sidewalks in the old white and crisp and even. I predict at least a two-heart-attack afternoon when the shovels come out. Minimum. Jesus, it's even several degrees colder than it was yesterday, despite the fact a storm usually brings milder temperatures. But when the snow ceased falling, the mercury started. Even now, at noon, the sun hasn't managed to burn a patch of blue out of the zinc sky. It stares down, a blurred eye of milky, diffused light.

I have a headache. It isn't enough that yesterday's rendezvous with Victoria has driven me bonkers with worry and that I have to wait nine more hours before I get any news about her from Marsha. No, that isn't enough. Today has to be Every Bloody Second Fucking Tuesday.

This morning when I woke I remembered the eight manuscripts I have to read and the class I have to conduct later this evening. If today weren't Tuesday I could be out tracking down Victoria. As it is, I'll have to dismiss my eager scriveners early to get to Hideous Marsha's apartment by nine-thirty. I'll tell them my agent is in town. They'll understand.

No, maybe I better not mention an agent. It's bad enough facing them as it is; I don't need another lie on my conscience. How did I let myself in for this? I could say I believed I'd be found out and sent packing, which is certainly true. I did believe that. I

thought I might carry on the hoax for a while, scrape through
two months at most. An easy five hundred bucks. How was I to
know I'd be shepherding such a batch of innocents? Fat ladies in
scruffy shoes with the backs trodden flat, one of them covered in
suspicious-looking bruises; a thin girl who sometimes soundlessly
weeps at the back of the room for what reason I don't know; Dr.
Vlady Mandelstam, the Russian-Jewish émigré who has hopes of
repeating Nabokov's *succès d'estime* in a second language. Dr.
Vlady, who haltingly communicated to me in nearly unintelligible
English his love for Jack London and the language of "nobble
Shaksper". And Rubacek, who believes every mendacious word I
feed him, takes notes while I speak, and doggedly pursues my
friendship.

Every Bloody Second Fucking Tuesday I ask myself why I did
this terrible thing. The answer is that I needed the money. But
that is the excuse of a criminal. I'm not just taking money under
false pretences. No, I am sinning against the dreams of other men
and women.

Yet my claim to be a successful writer was only meant to
encourage them and I modelled my impersonation on their dreams of
success, not my own. After all, at one time I wanted a different
kind of literary fame than the sale of a package of six scripts to
Magnum P.I. That lie was uttered to breathe hope into the bruised
lady, the thin girl. In private I confided to the aesthete, Dr. Vlady,
that I only did script-writing to buy time for serious intellectual
work, for an "art novel".

Exactly what Rubacek wants to hear I haven't figured out yet.

The trouble I find myself in puts Eaton's china department in a
new and slightly more favorable light. Of course, if I hadn't quit
I'd have been fired, wouldn't I? So what's the point of regrets?
Perhaps, however, I might have hung on by my fingernails for a
few more months if Pop hadn't dropped that insurance policy in
my lap. I saw it as a chance to pursue the simple life. The Chinese
sage said it all: "Beware of your desires, for ye shall certainly
attain them."

The fact remains, I was never meant to sell china. Only truly saintly men are cut out for that; the sort of men who trudge the roads to Benares, or reside on icy hilltops speculating on infinity. It takes more faith than I can summon.

The china company representatives, men invariably short, bald, and moist of palm, had this faith. How I wished I could, like them, color my voice with awe when I said the words "diplomat line" or "basic foundation for the royal service". They possessed an unvarying confidence and belief in china. I didn't have it. I didn't believe in china.

Mr. Brown did. I will not mention his firm, ancient and respected as it is. For Mr. Brown, porcelain was the last, thin, fragile line between civilization and savagery.

"Remember Melmac?" he'd say. He had a bee in his bonnet about Melmac. "Used to come in soap," he'd say contemptuously. "Gone the way of the buffalo. But we're still here. Two hundred and forty-seven years of gracious dining and British craftsmanship. Tell your customers that, Ed."

I didn't want to tell my customers anything. I didn't want to talk to my customers. I was getting so bad in the last months of my employment that if I was the only unoccupied clerk on the floor and a customer made for me, I broke for the washroom.

Customers, I learned, come in all temperaments, shapes, and sizes. All of them horrible. The middle-aged were intent on value, Mother Courage types who could gallop a wagon through the midst of the Thirty Years War without turning a hair. The elderly fell into two categories. The sweet and doddering were worst. I have spent hours smiling and snapping pencil stubs in my trouser pockets while they meandered slowly down memory lane with me in tow. But only a cad and a swine would vent his frustration on them. No relief to be had. The prescription was to suffer and grin as if one were in one's right mind.

The hard-eyed biddies swathed in muskrat and possessed of all their faculties were a different story; these I considered fair game, like McMurtry. Many of them were regular and valued customers of the department, old battleships whom I christened in my mind with the venerable names of fighting ships of the line: H.M.S.

Courageous, H.M.S. *Royal Oak*, and H.M.S. *Victory* were among the tougher. When I saw these old broads swing their barnacle-encrusted hulls hard about to unleash a broadside of vituperation at Ed's waterline, I felt the obsequious smile I'd learned to fasten on my mug unravel. I heard myself giving sharp answers in a phony English accent I unaccountably adopted on such occasions.

"Madam, I shall repeat what I told you scant days ago. We do not have a gravy boat in the particular pattern you require. That pattern, I should hazard to say, was discontinued approximately the time General Gordon was slain at Khartoum. Surely you recall that tragedy? It was in all the papers, I believe. No? Strange. In any case, as I have already intimated to you several times, we don't have it in stock. We never, ever, ever shall have it in stock. I suggest you consult a reputable antique dealer, *madam*."

There were complaints laid against the "the rude, fat Englishman". Understand, I'm not complaining but explaining. With every day that passed, my position at Eaton's grew more insecure. I had two warnings from my superior before the cavalry arrived in the guise of an insurance policy and I was rescued from the certain ignominy of dismissal with cause.

This unhappy train of events has led me here, to Tuesday, once again unprepared to orchestrate another Community Outreach Creative Writing Encounter. I hate reading those manuscripts, postpone it as long as possible. It is like holding up a mirror to my face and gazing at the distortions of the imagination. For you see, my Huck Finn bedtime episode of last night is not in the least unusual. As long as I can remember, I have been carelessly casting myself uninvited into novels where no self-respecting novelist would have me. This literary gate-crashing of mine must be a sign of a wretched thirsting after immortality.

When I was a child my preference for *Classics Illustrated* comic books made me a subject of derision for contemporaries whose tastes ran to *Wonder Woman, Superman*, and even *Little Lulu*. I did not bear up well to mockery, never have. For a time I shamelessly accepted the critical orthodoxy and made voluble professions of admiration for the antics of Sluggo and Dennis the Menace. I was motivated by a desire to be liked, an impulse that invariably leads me into no good. But one day I broke, as I always do, under the strain of deception, and during the interminable recounting of a Sgt. Rock anecdote by adenoidal Julius Kreuger, who kept interrupting his thin tale to say: "Wait, wait, I forgot before he done what I just told you — you'll like this, this is something, really — *before* he chucks this grenade — " I heard myself shrieking that Sgt. Rock was a slobbering moron and likely a slobbering moron sissy besides, and that Cyrano de Bergerac could whip his ass any day of the week!

Julius demurred and after he had sat on my face for twenty minutes I allowed that I might be in error. Never cross the Establishment.

Being a ten-year-old middlebrow had its perils, yet the happiest memories of my childhood are of bread and jam and a new *Classics Illustrated* balanced on my pudgy, dimpled knees. It was all shot and powder for the imagination — *The Red Badge of Courage, The Ox-Bow Incident, The Count of Monte Cristo, The Man in the Iron Mask, Ivanhoe, King Solomon's Mines* — and once primed and charged I went off in surprising ways. I was known to emerge (say after the fourth close reading of *The Last of the Mohicans*) into the sunshine of my backyard transformed from portly little Ed into the fearsome Chingachgook. There I stalked the hereditary hunting grounds in a breechclout cobbled up from bathing trunks and facecloths, my face and naked chest emblazoned with zigzags and wriggles of Mom's lipstick. From the back of my head the pheasant feather I had expropriated from her Sunday hat rose like an exclamation mark, held quivering in place by a rubber band that slowly squeezed off the blood supply to my scalp.

As Chingachgook capered recklessly about the suburban grass, whooping, howling, and dispatching shaven-skulled Mingos to the Happy Hunting Grounds with his tomahawk, neighbor ladies watched slack-jawed with amazement and thanked God for what they had been spared. In the aftermath of such performances my father would order my mother to prevent these public costume dramas. Angry voices would rise to my upstairs room.

"I can't watch him all the time."

"For chrissakes you're his mother! If you don't watch him, who will?"

"It's a stage."

"All right. It's a goddamn stage, and I give him thirty seconds to get over it. Thirty seconds. You know what Prokopchuk asks me the other day? When am I taking him to Hollywood? Then he winks. I got to put up with that kind of crap?"

"Well, that means a lot coming from Bill Prokopchuk, doesn't it? His boy is seven years old and can't ride a bike yet."

"Jesus, what do I care? You think I care? He isn't my kid. We're talking about *my* kid. Do something with the one I got, for chrissakes." At the very least Pop wanted me kept inside the house and out of sight. If I could not be made to forgo the pleasure of impersonating Fagin, Natty Bumppo, or the Melancholy Dane, he argued I ought not to inflict my performance on innocent bystanders.

I was an embarrassment to him. I knew it even then. It would not be hard to portray him as an insensitive villain, but it would be neither fair nor true. Pop may have worried that I made him look ridiculous and absurd, but he also worried about me. He wished to spare me pain. He wanted to encourage me to be "well-rounded".

This was part of his own larger struggle to fit in, something he never quite managed to do. Not that he didn't work hard at it. Every Saturday afternoon in the dog days of summer found him in front of the TV set watching the Game of the Week. He would stare at the screen intently, the picture of a man concentrating all his resources of will. Sometimes his lips moved breathlessly, repeating what the color commentator had just said, committing his words to memory. He looked like a man preparing himself for a Monday morning quiz on the weekend's action — which was how he looked at it. Pop didn't really like baseball, but he believed that for business reasons it was necessary to *talk* baseball. Still, he was hopeless. Stan Musial, he claimed, was his idol; but do you think he could remember Stan the Man's number?

I, on the other hand, adored baseball — on TV, that is. But Pop insisted on me actually playing the game. He undertook heroic measures in an attempt to fashion me into a passable athlete. The same pig-headed, hopeful persistence that kept him writing letter after letter of inquiry to boards and committees also kept him pegging baseballs to a sullen, flinching fat boy.

For forty-five minutes every night after he came home from work we played catch, or I took batting practice. The shadows lay purple in the rich green summer grass and the smoke of barbecuing meat rose blue beyond our hedges while I, sweaty and resentful, hacked away with my pint-sized bat.

"Keep your eye on the ball."

"I am!"

"Ed, you're not."

"I am, too!"

"Don't cry, Eddy."

"*I'm not. It's dirt in my eye!*"

"It'll come, son. Don't get frustrated. Just listen to Pop."

I see him standing in Sad Sack khaki pants and work boots, the sun in his eyes. Nat King Cole was singing on a radio in the next yard. He was wrong. It didn't come.

Most times he was practically out on his feet, so tired he wavered a little stooping to pick the ball from the grass. There was always sweat on his face and hair falling in his eyes. Before we were done, his lips had tightened into a bloodless cut in his face. He had back trouble, something to do with a disc. It wasn't hard to see from whom I inherited my panther-like grace and stunning hand-eye co-ordination. The old man threw off his front foot like a girl, with a girl's buggy-whip arm motion. Did he think he was fooling me with his stories?

"We'll make you into a top-notch first baseman yet," he'd call to me across the lawn. "I played first base. You don't need a lot of speed at first base."

In my humiliation and rage I wanted to yell back at him: With who? Who'd you play first base with? The Hooterville Handicaps, you spastic you?

I didn't yell at him, though. That came later when I was sixteen and in high school. Pop had given up on baseball by then in favor of me putting the shot. As implausible, as insane as it sounds, my father actually *bought* me a shot as a present.

"All right," I said, hefting it from hand to hand, "where's the cannon?" I thought it was a joke.

"You, Ed," said Pop, "are the cannon."

It took some time for me to comprehend that he actually wanted me to throw that thing in an upcoming high school track-and-field meet. I refused.

"It makes sense," he argued, "you've got the size."

"No."

"Ed, you've got to put your mind to doing things you find hard. It builds character and prepares you for life."

"No."

"Look here. Look at this book. I bought you a book. It shows you how. It's all laid out with photographs."

"No!"

"Why?"

"I don't want to."

"Ed, that's no answer. You've got to take part in school activities."

"Why do I have to take part in school activities?"

"To make you well-rounded. And it's a preparation for the world of business. You lay the foundations for success now, Ed."

He had pushed me near tears. "Then maybe you're the one ought to heave the old shot around! If it's so good for christly business! *Because you're such a terrific goddamn success story, right!*"

It was only then he finally realized I knew. I've never forgotten the look that passed over his face.

A week later, driven by guilt, I began to practise putting the shot in the backyard, following the principles outlined in the manual Pop had bought. The lawn was soon pocked with tiny craters. I was asking forgiveness, but he did not encourage my perseverance as he earlier would have. He refused to acknowledge, even in an off-hand dinner-table remark, that I was conforming to his wishes. Once I caught a glimpse of him watching me from his bedroom window behind a discreetly parted curtain. After two weeks my mother said to me, "Your father says there are holes all over the back lawn. He wants to know if you know anything about it."

I moved my practices down the block to the park.

When I was younger, the purpose of sport had not been to build character but to seduce me from my fantasies. It was no more successful then than it was to be later. The final straw for Pop was coming home and finding me wandering around the property got up as Vercingetorix, the unfortunate warrior chieftain who raised all the tribes of Gaul in rebellion against their Roman occupiers. The sight of his son shuffling around with his wife's Persian lamb jacket buttoned at his throat like a cloak, a two-foot-long moustache of yellow wool yarn Scotch-taped under his nose, and a collander stuck on his head, was just too much for the poor man. He confiscated my comics and announced they'd stay locked up until I was old enough that they wouldn't have that kind of effect on me.

He'd missed the point. If what I read didn't have exactly that kind of effect on me, what was the point in reading it? I never outgrew my reliance on fantasy. My personal aesthetic is a simple, sensual one. I wish to taste the faint tang of urine in the kidneys with Mr. Bloom, and to savor the tea-soaked *petite madeleine* which evoked a delicious shudder of memory in M. Proust. I wish to escape my blunted senses, my time. For me there is one pertinent question: Am I, having read this or that book, inclined to clap the metaphorical collander on the old noggin?

Pop was not then and never has been interested in such questions. That summer he was exercised by a more practical matter: how was his son's time to be occupied? His answer was lessons, and a stretch of hard time in Little League baseball with my skinny contemporaries. Hardy little ruffians who joyously chanted, "Ed, Ed, the donkey's dead! Died with a potato on his head!" as I writhed in the dust after being beaned with a hard, rising fastball. Summer stretched before me as an arid waste of boredom, relieved only by the discomfort of bruises, blisters, and taunts.

Until I realized that while my father could place my tattered treasures under lock he couldn't shut down the public library. That was where the originals were kept. My summer suddenly became cool, lazy, and inviting. While my parents thought I was sensibly occupied with a variety of lessons (tennis and swimming) and frequent Little League baseball practices, I was sequestered among the library bookshelves gorging myself on contraband chocolate bars and salted peanuts as I splintered lances with Ivanhoe, pursued the renegade Simon Girty, cackled a capella with Mr. Hyde, and hauled iron with Shane. I missed the colorful illustrations of the comics and found the language of many of the books puzzling, but reading was pure heaven when I thought of the alternative — bruised shins and scraped elbows. It was also that memorable summer I made the acquaintance of Huck and Tom and Jim, and fell utterly in love with the ravishing Miss Becky Thatcher.

The other consequence of this abandoned summer of forbidden pleasures was a weight gain of seven pounds that left my mother perplexed and worried. ("I can't understand it, Doctor. He's been so active this summer, yet he keeps gaining weight. Could it be his glands?") The long-term consequence has been a pathetic reverence before the altar of literature.

It was this reverence, coupled with penury, which hastened my present problems. After the first rosy flush of liberation from Eaton's, the cold dawn of calculation shed its grey light on the obvious: the tidy sum my life insurance policy had yielded could not possibly last me the year's sabbatical that I felt entitled to after my stint of grinding labor. This realization led to a mild depression that lifted only when I got the phone call from the University Extension Officer offering me — no, to speak accurately, *pleading* with me to accept — the job as instructor of the Community Outreach Creative Writing Encounter. Literature, I told myself then, does not spurn her unworthy suitors who stand season after season through hail and sleet and snow, singing beneath her bright window.

Still, it was only through a number of mishaps and misunderstandings that the offer ever came to be made to me. The first and decisive one being a coronary thrombosis which hospitalized the instructor hired to conduct the Community Outreach Creative Writing Encounter, or COCWE, as those of us in adult continuing education like to think of it. Under such unforeseen and pressing circumstances, any warm body that was reasonably punctual and could plausibly imitate semi-literacy would do.

Initially, however, I was very suspicious of the offer. I naturally presumed that the whole thing was a tasteless joke cooked up by a cadre of Victoria's vindictive little chums. Such offers are made to people like me only in jest. But the longer I played along with the woman on the other end of the line, the clearer things became, and the greater my horror grew with the realization that she was serious. Apparently I had met her at one of those benefits for Central American freedom fighters at which Victoria used to demand my attendance. Not only had she remembered my name, she had also remembered my spurious and likely drunken claim to be a man of letters.

It was a claim I was driven to make in those long-ago days when my wife supported me in indolent ease. Pasha Ed was how my jealous male acquaintances used to refer to me. Others were less kind. My embarrassment at being unemployed prompted the idea of passing myself off as a writer. Also, by then I knew the idea of going to Greece was beyond reviving. Posing as a writer wouldn't encourage Victoria to make me prove I was one.

At the time the whole world seemed intensely interested in what I was up to. Election enumerators quizzed me on my occupation; sales clerks inquired after my place of business when I tried to write a cheque for a purchase. People I was introduced to at parties turned vocational counsellor when they learned I was unemployed. My doctor, while thumping my sternum, absentmindedly asked me how I like my job. *What do you do?* I seemed to get that question every time I turned around. The truth was I didn't *do* anything.

But, I asked myself, if you *could* do something what would you do? Unhesitatingly I answered, *write.*

There it was. The esteem in which I had always held authors

and the pleasure their books had given me only confirmed my decision. To make such a claim, in France, say, would have been base, despicable. Masquerading there as an *écrivain* entails little risk or hardship for an impostor. France names streets and avenues after its authors. It is a country where the public raised a furor over Rodin's statue of Balzac, incensed that the great man had not been done justice in bronze. In Canada, however, writing, like soldiering, is an occupation for those young men for whom all hope has been abandoned.

So I decided to impersonate a writer. An act of defiance like my stubbornly persisting in launching the shot in the teeth of the laws of gravity and my own nature during those sweltering afternoons in a deserted suburban park. For anyone who cared to listen I was a writer. When asked where I published my short stories (I was, I said, a short-story writer at work on a novel), I told them *The Paris Review*. The name didn't mean anything to Victoria's friends but it made me feel I'd arrived. My policy, if asked how to find one of my stories, was to cite a reference at least two years back. And seem vague. "I think," I'd say, "it was Vol. 9, No. 7. Or was it Vol. 7, No. 9? Anyway, if you do a little digging it won't be hard to find. It's called 'Les Arbres de Stockholm'." There was no risk. Nobody could care less. Nobody ever bothers.

But obviously I had made some impression on that woman, at least to the extent that in a moment of crisis she found herself offering me two hundred and fifty dollars a month to take a group of tyro scribblers under my wing Every Second Bloody Fucking Tuesday. Two hundred and fifty dollars a month is what I pay in rent for this miserable hole I am squatting in.

A restless conscience almost led me to confess my charlatanry, and I almost refused the job. I almost said: "Look, lady, I am not now and never have been a writer. I am sorry for the inconvenience the delusions I was suffering under at that time of my life have caused you now. I am very sorry."

But wait a minute, Ed, clamored the voice of reason. How can you say you're not a writer? When Victoria abandoned ship, didn't you produce a 75,000-word western about Sam Waters,

buffalo hunter, Indian fighter, and quick-fisted marshal? Of course
you did. And he who writes a novel, is he not a novelist? Just so.
And should the sweat and labor and grief and tears of a novelist go
unrewarded? *Not if there's any justice in this world they shouldn't.* For
the moment this ingenious line of argument sufficed. I accepted
the position as leader of the Community Outreach Creative Writing Encounter.

Of course, when examined, my attempts to justify accepting
the job didn't hold water. The 75,000 words I had scrawled
didn't amount to a book. There was more justice in describing my
process of creation as a case of automatic handwriting than its
product as a novel. What I wrote in that desperate time after
Victoria had announced she had had enough of me was patterned
on the childhood fantasies that had sustained me through the
misery and indignity of being fat, awkward, and a mouth-breather.
Translated by imagination into Chingachgook, or D'Artagnan,
or Vercingetorix, or Huck, I had been able to forget the taunts
and heavy-minded impertinences of the neighbourhood morons
who followed me gleefully while I waddled along crimson-faced
with self-loathing and murderous anger.

So leathery Sam Waters, with his laconic speech, his deliberating,
cold eyes, his stunning, lightning-quick fists, was the sort of
fantastically potent icon that cuckold Ed's vulgar, wounded ego
would create. A tough *hombre* who could gentle a mustang or a
cantina spitfire; a grave, slouching, *lean* figure to be found propped
against doorposts and fence-rails, Stetson tipped over his eyes as he
coolly waited for the drover to walk out of the orange ball of sun
burning at the end of an empty street. A man whose courage was
so serene and incorruptible that the calculation of odds never
entered into his decisions to uphold and protect the good, the
true, the beautiful. The Sam Waters I had struck from the base
metals of my mind would have bellied up to the bar with Socrates
and asked for a shot of that there hemlock too, pardner.

Despite my fervid admiration for this cowpoke there was something about Sam that troubled me, like a face one knows but
cannot place. He came to the page too easily, fully formed. Sitting

there in my dingy apartment, the bass of a neighbor's stereo thudding distantly like a voodoo drum, the first paragraph of *Cool, Clear Waters* had come to me all in a rush.

> Sam Waters had been a plainsman, a buffalo hunter, a wind-drinker, a free man, before he became the sheriff of Constitution. And because of the long vistas he had looked steadily into and the clean rain he had tasted, he didn't care much for towns. Sam Waters was too big a man to feel easy in towns. They made him feel pinched and cramped and restless. And the worst thing about them was that their smells made it difficult for him to breathe, and no town smelled worse than Constitution, because Constitution stank with the worst smell of all — hypocrisy.

I will not comment on the deficiencies of this passage. I will only say I wrote these words with a sense of exhilarating release, as if an aching tooth had been torn from a tender, swollen gum. But even then I felt a prickly uneasiness linger. I could not shake the feeling that I knew this man. I believed we shared a history.

My attachment to Sam, however, could not compensate for the ludicrousness of my calling myself a writer. Of course, I skated over all such thin spots with extreme care during my chat with the extension officer. When I said my book hadn't had a wide readership I wasn't being modest. I was leading her to infer that a small but nevertheless select audience had savored my prose with much appreciative smacking of lips.

The truth was, the book had never been published, hadn't even been submitted to a publishing house. As far as I knew, its readership consisted of myself, and possibly, just possibly, Victoria. For on completing my sagebrush *magnum opus*, I had mailed my absent wife a photostat copy of the manuscript, a palpable refutation of her charge that I was incapable of completing anything I began. But I doubt Victoria read it. She was full of hard feelings at the time.

Which puts me in mind of the eight unread student manuscripts stowed under my bed. There will be no more flinching

from duty, Ed. I patter off on bare feet to my bedroom, drop on
all fours, and peer under the bed. My breathing becomes stertorous
and sets long, serpentine boas of slut's wool to eddying along the
floor. I ought to vacuum.

There they are: the inevitable television scripts for *Three's
Company, Dallas, Dynasty,* or *Taxi*; a short story or two; and the
latest instalment of Dr. Mandelstam's bewildering novel about a
dog who acquires, through surgery, the disgusting habits of *homo
sapiens.* Dr. Vlady volunteered to me the provenance of this work.
"You knowit Mikhail Bulgakov boog?" he demanded. "Wall,
this boog is ironic rewerse!" To which I nodded sagely, even
though I had not the slightest understanding of what he was
talking about.

Only Stanley Rubacek never hands in material, secure in the
knowledge of his own genius. And mine possibly, too. He tells
me there is nothing doing until we reach an agreement. So I have
no idea of what he is writing. Not that I care.

Every Bloody Second Fucking Tuesday finds Stanley barricaded
behind his stack of smudged and bleary foolscap. It is my custom,
when desperation overtakes me and I am at a loss what to do next,
to call upon a member of COCWE to read from his manuscript.
Discussion then follows. Stanley has always politely but firmly
refused to read. He fears plagiarism.

Stanley spends his time in class brooding over his pile of
manuscript, bulging shoulders hunched protectively, forearm shield-
ing its southern approaches from prying eyes. Occasionally he
plies a vigorous pencil when visited by the divine afflatus. Rubacek
writing sounds like someone wire-brushing old paint off house
siding. It has entered my mind that he may be dangerous.

A kind of general dread coalesces into a heavy lump in the pit of
my stomach whenever I think of Every Bloody Second Fucking
Tuesday. In my mind's eye I can see the long corridor which leads
me to room 31, and the reflected light lying in waxy puddles
down its length of polished tile. If I walk this corridor with
energy and business-like purpose my heels ring out like a doomed
man's. Also my students hear me coming. So Every Second Tues-

day I walk soft-footed the first five yards, creep-slide the next ten, and steal on tiptoe the final five. Then I hover indecisively outside the door of the classroom, trying to compose myself and rehearsing my opening remarks, while one distracted ear fills with the hum of voices filtering through the door of room 31.

Opening remarks are crucial. I always mean to begin critically, yet end encouragingly. That, I believe, is the formula. Still, it never fails that the moment I enter that room, whatever I meant to say flies clear out of my head. All I can think of is confession. Public confession. I feel an overwhelming need to make a clean breast of it and lift from my stooping shoulders their trust, their admiration, their dreams. I want to tell them I never sold scripts to *Magnum P.I.* or "took a meeting with Tom Selleck in a cabana at a Hollywood poolside". And, I want to say, neither will any of you.

But that would be terrible all the way round. So I have stood for long minutes before their uplifted faces trying to recover those lost words, turning over manuscripts, fumbling aimlessly in my briefcase, buying time as I ransack a vacant mind.

Confess, I think.

My long silences always produce terrifying doubts in their minds. They take them as a sign of displeasure at their efforts. The room fills with the nervous musk of schoolrooms and courtrooms, of places where people are called upon to defend themselves before the powerful and capricious. The pale girl at the back of the room, incapable of blanching whiter, seems to yellow. The overhead lights glitter in Dr. Mandelstam's wire-framed spectacles and his gold tooth glimmers wanly in a fixed and artificial smile. The fat ladies stare at their broken, scuffed shoes or examine, against columnar thighs, fingers that look like Vienna sausages.

You have to say something, I remind myself, growing more and more anxious.

Only Stanley Rubacek sits massively self-confident behind his life's work, scratching his scalp through thinning hair, showing as he does a floral tattoo on the back of his left hand. He can't be more than five years older than I, but there are deep lines cut in his cheeks and he has lost his teeth; I sometimes catch his upper plate slipping. His gaze is always direct. *Come on, let's strike a deal*, his expression seems to say to me.

I cannot find a path between confession, the truth, and lies. And so I hear myself saying, "These are wonderful. A source of inspiration I will carry with me to my own typewriter. Well done, one and all."

Suddenly, Dr. Mandelstam's gold tooth blazes forth like the sun, nearly blinding me.

FIVE

ideous Marsha's father has
installed her in one of those trendy condominiums which in the
past few years have risen near the river. They replaced the old
three-storey houses which decayed in lock-step with the elderly
widows who lacked the means to maintain them. At first these
houses were chopped into tiny suites, warrens for university students and welfare recipients, but the widows finally died and
their heirs loosed the developers' bulldozers for the coup de grâce.
With the houses went the elms and mountain ashes which mingled their leaves in high Gothic vaults that turned the narrow
streets of July into long naves of shadow streaked by sunlight rich
and yellow-white as cream. Victoria and I inhabited one of those
dying houses when we were first married. On summer evenings
we strolled those streets while unseen sparrows chorused above in
the breeze-swung branches. I miss those quiet, green stretches.

It was during our walks down our lovely street that I attempted
to stonewall the trip to Greece. The argument ran on for weeks.

"Ed, what do you mean we don't have enough money? We
have the cash we got as wedding presents, and we have the money
we've saved. It's enough."

"I don't want to get halfway into my book and have to come
back. I want to see it right through to the end, without interruptions."

"You will, Ed. Just relax."

"Next year. We'll go next fall."

"We'll go this fall."

71

"Half of that money is mine, Victoria. I have some say."

"Nowhere near half of the money is yours. I'm the one who punched the keys at the checkout all last winter, remember?"

"Why can't you be reasonable about this? What's the rush?"

"I want to *live*, Ed!" She said that so vehemently and with such a rush of color to her face that I almost surrendered before her desire for experience, for life. But I succeeded in steadying myself. I was not going to risk everything. I had no intention of jeopardizing what I had: Victoria, the trees lining the street, the elegant old houses that wrenched my heart. In the end I wore her down. We would work another year; the extra money would allow us to live like kings in Greece. I think she believed we were still going even three years later. It was only when she suggested we have a baby that I knew she had given up on the idea of Greece.

It is a different street now. The condos which supplanted the trees and houses come in two styles. They are what I like to call Babylonian ziggurat, an industrial hymn to concrete, and the more homely Zuni-pueblo preferred by the under-forties. The pueblo is, of course, where Marsha is to be found. Sitting in my car looking at those huge, jumbled cubes and their glowing windows I feel more keenly the cold and my exhaustion. The Encounter went badly tonight. Or to put it another way, it went so splendidly that I am wrung by remorse.

At six o'clock tonight, an hour before the curtain went up on COCWE, I suddenly recalled with panic that two weeks ago I had promised the class, at their insistence, to read to them this Tuesday from my work in progress. Since no such work exists, this was a foolish promise. Earlier I had got around their questions as to why they couldn't find my first novel in libraries or bookstores by bemoaning my publisher's small press run and explaining that the company had quickly let the book lapse out of print. But I had also spoken casually about a work in progress. This was my undoing. As the weeks passed, the class importuned me to treat them to a selection. Of course, I could have dodged the issue somehow. Upon reflecting, however, I have surmised I may have unconsciously made that promise to entrap myself, to furnish myself with the opportunity for an oblique confession. My commitment to read would force me to write something, and reading what I wrote would reveal me for the fraud I am. I would be eased.

That was only the first step. The second followed inevitably from my nature. I forced this onrushing unpleasantness out of my mind, delayed, dawdled, forgot. So tonight I had nothing to read, nothing except *Cool, Clear Waters*. But when the crisis was upon me I knew I couldn't read that. Sam Waters was too private, too cherished, a figure to run the risk of having him exposed to sniggers.

There was nothing else to do but cheat. I hammered out at my typewriter a passage from a book I though it unlikely anyone in the class had read, an historical novel by Alfred Duggan. Tonight, when I was done reading and I glanced up at those exalted faces, I knew, with a rending sensation, that they had loved it. All but Stanley, that is. The fat ladies expressed awe at my erudition (destrier, hauberk, etc.), while Dr. Vlady judged my battle scene surpassed only by Stendhal's account of Waterloo in *The Charterhouse of Parma*. I was a hit with nary a tip of the old topper to Mr. Duggan.

So here I am, out of the frying pan and into the freezer. Cold and difficulties. The story of my winter. Racing and roaring the engine, I can raise no more than a ghostly, tepid breath from the heater. The side window is slowly frosting over; white fog creeps inward from the perimeter of the glass, congealing in a scum of ice. I fear that if I don't move soon I'll be frozen in place like a ship stalled in arctic seas. There is no sense in putting it off any longer. Up there where the windows burn, the Witch of Endor waits.

Marsha swings her door open to me, smiles. "Hello, Ed," she says, popping up on tiptoe to swipe a welcoming kiss on the corner of my mouth. This kiss of peace exchanged and no mention made of last evening's contretemps, Marsha offers to take my coat. While she stows it in a closet I saunter into the living room.

It is evident that Marsha lives better now than she did when she was Bill's wife. He, like many liberal-arts types, ended up a teacher, and a teacher's salary puts no one in a riverside condo. Marsha's present living quarters are her father's doing. The old gentleman is big in fast-food franchises and down on Bill, so when Marsha gave Bill the heave ho there was no heart gladder in the land than Daddy's, and evidence of his gladness is everywhere to be seen. I sink ankle deep in pile. Far off, in the distance, several folding Chinese screens stand in splendid isolation. There is an ornate divan upon which I imagine Marsha reclines in the character of odalisque when entertaining gentlemen callers. There are small tables scattered with expensive-looking knick-knacks and numerous low-slung chairs. I make a mental note not to sit in one. A husky fellow such as I mightn't be able to hoist himself out of one of these; the laws of physics militate against it. No, it appears my bottom is best suited to a basket chair hanging from the ceiling on a massive chain, a chair that could pass for a cage for a giant condor or for a prisoner of the Mongol hordes. I am regarding it with a calculating eye when Marsha comes up behind me. "Would you like a drink, Ed?"

"Please."

There is a liquor cabinet hidden behind one of the Chinese screens. "This is right—Scotch—isn't it?" she asks, handing me the tumbler.

"Yes, you got it right." I salute her with lifted glass. "How did you remember?"

"It would be hard to forget. You stood out like a sore thumb at those parties in our university days. Everybody else doing dope and you wandering around, toting a twenty-six of Islay Mist."

"An affectation on my part." Which is not true. I never went for that heightened-awareness crap. I was looking for anesthesia.

Marsha makes for the divan. She is wearing a white caftan with billowing sleeves. It sets off her Arizona tan very forcefully. Marsha is one of those women for whom age and a little more flesh have done wonders. In her early twenties she looked winsome and scrawny, but now she comes equipped with standard features: breasts, a noticeable surge of buttock under the caftan. She wears her hair short; studs wink in the lobes of neat, well-formed ears. Her face is long, thin-lipped, large-toothed.

Marsha settles herself on the divan, crosses her legs and arranges her arms in a flurry of skirts and sleeves while I hop onto my perch. The basket makes a half-revolution to the left; the links in the chain tighten with a groan, spin me slowly back again. The process repeats itself. I stab at the floor with the toe of my shoe to counteract this lazy to-ing and fro-ing. The chair is hung too high. Not only am I looking down on Marsha and her divan, I have to strain to touch the floor with both feet.

"And it turns out that you were right," says Marsha, resuming talk of who ingested what. "The way the story went then, booze was bad and grass harmless. Now they tell us the evil weed damages your genes, gives you lung cancer. You can't win. I don't know. I still smoke on special occasions. It's relaxing. A joint now and then, what's it hurt?"

I nod agreement. Marsha seems in a good mood and I don't want to spoil it; also, I'm busy trying to read her demeanor. She can't hide that she has something to tell, and that what she has to tell pleases her. It may be bad news for me, but I know now that Victoria hasn't got cancer. Nobody, but nobody, with news like that to deliver has a half-smile playing on their lips. What a relief. Although I knew it was foolish, that fear lay at the back of my mind all yesterday and today. The Big C.

For the first time in twenty-four hours I unwind a little. If I don't press Marsha too hard, too soon, like I did last night, it will all come out. So I follow in the train of her last observation and cheerfully natter away. "Well, Marsha, nothing is completely harmless any more, is it? Take milk. My grade four teacher, Mrs. Appleyard, drilled it into our little noggins that milk was 'the perfect food'. Mom used to warn me if I didn't drink the vile stuff rickets would make little Eddy's legs look like a hula hoop. Now they say moo juice clogs the arteries. What the hell?" I conclude. "We weren't meant to live forever. I eat *everything*. Why worry?"

This last bit of philosophizing is a mistake. Marsha, true child of her generation, believes something ought to be done about death. If it can't be abolished, arrangements should be made to have it indefinitely postponed. "Still," Marsha says, "diet is very important. And exercise. Exercise is wonderful." As she says this I'm sure she casts an appraising eye at my girth.

"Yes, a number of people have told me the same thing. I jogged for a while, but I tended to overheat and caught a lot of colds. I found it wasn't healthy."

"I'm training now," says Marsha. "I go to a spa."

"Mmm." I sip my drink and try not to appear encouraging.

"I weight-train. Are you surprised?"

I gather I'm supposed to be, so I dutifully declare my wonder.

"A lot of men don't approve. They think it's unfeminine. What do you think, Ed?"

I hate this kind of setup. It's heresy-hunting pure and simple.

"Anything that stops short of a hernia and a truss is well within the boundaries of femininity in my books," I say. "But speaking personally, I wouldn't want to see any wife of mine in a truss."

"Oh-oh," says Marsha, "guess who's feeling threatened."

"Not me."

"All men find the idea of strength in a woman — strength of any kind — enormously threatening. Bill certainly did. What are all you men afraid of?"

I swallow the last of my Scotch. There are some people I should never argue with, and Marsha is one of them. Things always get out of hand. I don't answer because I don't want to antagonize her before I get news of Victoria.

Taking my silence as a sign she has scored a hit, a very palpable hit, Marsha decides to be magnanimous in victory. She returns to body-building, which appears to be her favorite mania at present. Like any recent convert she feels the need to testify and proselytize.

"Weight-training has made me feel at home in my body," she volunteers.

"Mmm."

"A person feels better, has more energy, moves more gracefully. Weight-training means nobody has to feel ashamed of their body any more. If they want to, they can improve it."

"What's that crack supposed to mean?"

"I'm not criticizing, Ed."

"Look, Marsha, let me tell you something. I've been taking cheap shots ever since I was seven years old about the earthly tenement in which my soul is so conspicuously lodged. I'm sick and tired of it. Lay off."

To emphasize my point I slop out of my chair; my feet strike the floor with a resounding thump.

"Where are you going?" says Marsha, alarmed at the idea of escaping prey. "You're not leaving."

"*Fat chance*. No, Porky Pockets just wants another drink. Watch him waddle his way to the bar, thighs rubbing together. Oink, oink, oink."

"You can pour me one too. I'm getting tense. You're making me very tense. You always do."

I pour the drinks and carry them back to Marsha. "Don't be angry, Ed," she says. "We're old friends." She pats the divan. "Sit down."

"I don't think it'll bear the load," I say, choosing to lower myself on to the carpet.

"It's times like this you remind me of Bill."

"I happen to like Bill, so I'll take that as a compliment, and not in the spirit you intended."

Marsha draws up a leg and locks her fingers around the knee. From under the hem of the caftan emerges a long, thin, white foot with painted nails. It rests at the edge of the divan at my eye level.

"That's generous of you," she says, "because Bill doesn't like you. He hates your guts. Or maybe I ought to put that in the past tense. Now that he's full of Christian love, maybe he *used* to hate your guts."

I don't know why I am always surprised to learn that people don't like me, because quite a number don't. Even as a little kid I rubbed people the wrong way, and I've come to the conclusion it was not so much what I did, but my manner of doing it. Style always counts for more than substance. But I had never suspected I'd had that kind of effect on Bill.

"Oh? And what did I ever do to Bill?" Oddly enough I really

want to find out why Bill should hate me. I don't like to be hated.

Marsha smiles in the unpleasant way she has when her bitterness with life rises into her face and she must try and disguise it. I think I understand something about her no one else does. Marsha still loves Bill. None of their friends can see this because they don't realize it is possible to love a lunatic. Her smile never wavers as she says, "For a fairly sharp character you miss a lot, don't you, Ed? It wasn't what you did to Bill, dear, it was what you did to Victoria. That was it."

I try to hide my confusion by raising my glass to drink. I compose my mouth along its rim. "And what concern was it of Bill's what I did or didn't do to Victoria?"

Marsha's toes curl under with pleasure. "Come, Ed, I can hardly believe you didn't see it. Bill had a thing for Victoria. Maybe not a grand passion, but not just a bolt in the pants either. A lot of men seem to want to think women are naturally better than they are, and that was part of it with Bill. He tended to romanticize her, see her as a long-suffering, noble soul. I couldn't fit the bill, of course. But he could make himself see Victoria as a victim, rather like the wife of that disgusting bureaucrat in *Crime and Punishment*. I can't recall his name at the moment. Can you believe it? I just read the book a month ago and now I can't remember the goddamn name. Isn't that crazy?"

"Marmeladov," I say, "his name is Marmeladov."

Marsha looks sceptical, considers, and then replies: "Why, you're right. It *is* Marmeladov."

"Of course I'm right."

"Poor Ed. Right about everything that doesn't really matter and wrong about everything that does."

Marsha is doing quite a job on me. I have to admire how she works — indirect, sly, a measure of truth in everything she says. I was never a good husband. Not even a passable one. There is nothing to refute. All I can do is lamely say, "I didn't know Victoria and I attracted that kind of attention. I didn't know we were items of conversation."

"Come, Ed, don't be modest. The two of you always had a

loyal and interested following. Like Liz Taylor and Dick Burton. Perhaps I shouldn't say it, but there was very nearly a pool drawn up on how long your marriage would last. And any number of people took delight in watching *your* career. There's a certain amount of pleasure that comes from seeing somebody who is obviously intelligent fail. It's reassuring. It emphasizes the importance of character over brains. And Victoria — well, you know, in the beginning she talked too much about what you were going to do. People resent that. Victoria was very naive when she was young — life with you improved her in that respect.

"Still, maybe that's why she attracts men the way she does. She's loyal. Like old Shep. And given the right qualities in a man — a certain phony intellectualism, let's say — she's even admiring. She can't help but be, and not even her best friend would make extravagant claims about her mental equipment. She's easily impressed.

"And finally there's no discrediting the fact that it was common knowledge she was unhappy with you, and that she had an occasional romantic fling. That made her a centre of attraction for some. Not that I'm saying she was up there on the block for the asking. I'm not saying that. Victoria picked and chose, showed discrimination. More than one of your acquaintances thought he might get lucky. Hope springs eternal in the human heart. I know it did in Bill's." Marsha, finished, drinks her Scotch in her cool way. I want to grasp one of those large, bony toes and twist it, twist some fear and pain into that self-satisfied face.

I turn on my back so she is not looking directly into my face when I ask the question. There are speckles in the stippled ceiling plaster. "And poor Bill, were his prayers ever answered?"

I think she giggles. "Does it really matter at this late date?"

The terrible thing is that it does. Even at this late date. "I suppose not. Does it matter to you?"

"What? That my little Billy screwed Ed's Victoria? Not in the least." She sounds no more convincing than I. After a moment's hesitation she says, "I'm more concerned with what he's up to now."

What Bill is up to may prove interesting. In any case, a change
of subject would be welcome. I roll back on my side. "Do tell," I
say. "Bill hasn't gone out and lost his heart to one of those
pink-pant-suited sisters of the First Chosen now that he's been
refitted for action and is fertile again, has he?"

"Hardly. As far as Bill's concerned there can never be another
woman in his life but me." Marsha's voice is tinged with irony.
"It's all because we had that goddamn church wedding."

I recollect Bill and Marsha's wedding with much fondness.
Initially Bill had insisted they be married in a civil ceremony at the
courthouse, but Marsha's Daddy wouldn't hear of it. Only a few
guests were allowed in judge's chambers and Daddy, for business
reasons, felt it incumbent upon him to invite practically everybody listed in *Henderson's Directory*. Bill, of course, stood firm on
his principles. He was having no truck with organized religion in
any of its ghastly manifestations. His obdurate behavior made
Daddy desperate. Marsha's Pop offered to write a thousand-dollar
cheque and donate it to the Waffle branch of the NDP if Bill
would get his hair cut and be married in the United Church.
Daddy would hand over the loot at the reception if Bill behaved
himself as agreed. So, in the interests of social justice Sadler
compromised himself. However, Daddy never produced the cheque,
because, he said, a contract made under duress wasn't a contract in
anybody's books.

Now it seems that Bill's political expediency is having unforeseen consequences.

"Because we were married in a church," Marsha is saying,
"Bill claims we are married in the eyes of God, which means
married *forever*. He says that if I divorce him it doesn't change a
thing. We're still married. He quoted something from the Bible.
You know that bit about whatever God has joined, no man can
put asunder? Talking to him is an experience, really. He says as
soon as I'm saved we can resume our life as man and wife. I swear,
Ed, he's completely out of his mind."

I'm enjoying this. "You ought to be patient with him. After
all, he's an idealist, always was." I would like to add that he's also

a simplifier, but that involves an explanation of my theory and there isn't time.

"He's an asshole, always was. And now he's taken to phoning our old friends and urging them to repent their sins. Which he lists at some length, I might add. You can't believe the embarrassment it's causing me. I still see a lot of these people. He doesn't."

I wonder why Bill has not troubled to contact me. Does he hate me so passionately that he desires to withhold from me the opportunity to repent and save my soul? "Who's he called?" I demand.

"A lot of people."

"Like who?"

Marsha hesitates. "Well, Benny for one. Benny says if he doesn't stop he's going to get a court order to stop him."

Benny. There's a black soul in need of saving. We were roommates at university but ever since he agreed to represent Victoria in her divorce action he's been no friend of mine. "Wonderful! Wonderful news!" I cry. "Let me guess which of the seven deadly sins Bill accused friend Benny of. Lust. That has got to easily have been number one on the list. How often he regales his smutty little chums with tales of his carnal exploits in the firm's secretarial pool. And then covetousness. The man salivates at the thought of the bench. Imagine Benny sitting Solomon-like robed in the weeds of the Queen's justice. And envy. He's an envious son of a bitch, Benny is." Even while I enumerate Benny's wickednesses, which leap so readily to mind, I am thinking of the others who must figure prominently on Bill's top ten of those to phone when he wants a break from the singing of hallelujahs or the mortification of the flesh. I wonder if he's called Victoria, who is, after all, an adulteress. "And anger," I add. "The sin of anger. Benny has a terrible temper. You wouldn't believe how he used to carry on and scream at me—scream, mind you—when we roomed together."

"Wouldn't I?" Her eyebrows arch like a cat's back.

"Good old Marsha," I say, without a trace of fondness.

"Good old Ed." Her voice too is expressionless. An uncomfortable silence succeeds. It seems we can no longer carry on the charade of old pals jawing over old times. The evening has arrived at the point when business ought to be talked. I clear my throat, begin. "I take it you've seen her. What's the problem?"

Marsha regards me with a calculating air. Inexplicably she says, "I got a wedding invitation today. My youngest brother is getting married."

What the hell is this? I smile and nod.

"God, you can't imagine what a wedding in my family is like," Marsha continues. "The men are creatures from the Stone Age; you wouldn't believe what their attitudes to women are. If I go stag, the way I did to my cousin Cecilia's wedding, all my uncles, God, all my *great-uncles*, will be dancing with me out of pity and telling me I'm prettier than the bride. And Daddy will invite one of his franchise managers who happens to be under forty-five, divorced or a bachelor, and manoeuvre the poor schmuck into a chair beside me at the banquet. Do you know what these guys like to talk about? How many ten-gallon pails of lard they go through a week at their outlet. It's supposed to impress you. It's a gauge of sales. Ed, you can't imagine what it's like to be a single woman, worse, a *deserted* woman, in the midst of those Neanderthals. It's humiliating. But how do you not go to your own little brother's wedding? It's just not possible." Marsha is finished. Her eyes narrow, she waits.

So there it is. Marsha isn't giving anything away without exacting a price. I take a deep breath. "I hope you don't find me forward," I say, "but I'd be charmed to escort you to your brother's wedding, Marsha."

"All right, Ed. Do you own a decent suit?"

"Of course I own a suit."

"I said a *decent* suit. I know you, Ed. Don't you dare show up wearing a Nehru jacket or some other god-awful thing. If you don't have a decent suit I'll buy you one. I'm not substituting one embarrassment for another."

I bristle. "Piss off, Marsha."

"Okay, okay. But don't forget to have it dry-cleaned. And keep February 26 open. Unless," she qualifies, "you know —

maybe I'll have a friend by then. I'll call."

Marsha is a classy broad. "Fine," I say. "Great. Now, what about Victoria?"

Victoria, I learn from Marsha, has fallen in love again. It is an indication of her perennially blooming optimism that she keeps surrendering her heart in this careless and carefree way. This time it has been given to the man whom until now I knew only as Anthony. I learn that he is young and, according to Marsha, the consummate renaissance man. Anthony Peters is a sometime contributor to art magazines, a sometime poet, a sometime film reviewer, and an academic who is presently engaged in writing *Fantasies and Fasces: A Study of the Ideology of Popular Fiction in the Modern Age*.

It was Hideous Marsha who introduced Victoria and Peters at a Film Society rerun of *The Two Husbands of Dona Flor*.

To hear Hideous tell it, the chemistry was so perfect that they practically fell panting into each other's arms while the film was still flip-flopping on the take-up reel. Since that fateful, steamy night they have been a number. However, it is only recently that Victoria let her apartment go and moved in with Professor Peters. It seems that Anthony requires stability, that it was too trying, their disorderly domestic life, socks at Victoria's, *Oxford Dictionary* at Anthony's. His work was suffering. This would never do, because *Fantasies and Fasces* is going to catapult him out of this provincial backwater and back home to Ontario. He's even thinking of the possibility of graduating out of Canada, going Ivy League maybe.

Marsha gives this brass idol one more vigorous rub so that he gleams even more painfully in my dazzled eyes.

Not only has she taken pains to hint that Peters is some kind of sensualist par excellence, she also wants it clearly understood that he is absolutely *brilliant*.

"He's remarkable," says Marsha. "Everybody is agreed: *Fantasies and Fasces* is going to be a seminal work."

"Who's everybody?"

Marsha gives me a drop-dead look.

"Could everybody be the author of *Fantasies and Fasces*?"

"We're displaying hostility. Don't let envy overcome, Ed."

"Okay, if everything is so wonderful with this paragon, why's my wife come bawling to me after a year of silence?"

"Because she wants to have her cake and eat it too. And because they've had a lovers' quarrel." Marsha pauses significantly. She wants to be asked.

"All right, what about?"

Her smile is luminous. "She didn't want to talk about it at all, but finally it came out. Victoria's pregnant."

"Pregnant?" I almost laugh in her face. Victoria doesn't get pregnant. I should know, we tried for years. The least of her problems is a tipped womb.

"It's just about the worst possible time for Anthony. He's just getting established, he needs quiet for his work. It's not that he's unsympathetic to her feelings, but he thinks that it would be better if they waited two or three years. His book would be finished then." I hear Victoria's reasoning in Marsha's explanation, her attempt to put the best possible face on the one she loves. She did that for me, too.

It strikes me that what Marsha is saying is true. "Jesus Christ, pregnant," I say. "That was it. Pregnant."

Victoria always wanted a child. At first she argued it would hold us together, and then the notion of a child was sufficient in itself. Pop thought a baby would be good for us too. On my twenty-fifth birthday he collected me after work and took me out for a drink. We went to a cocktail lounge for happy hour. He ordered a grasshopper. Pop never went to cocktail lounges and seldom drank, so he didn't know a grasshopper was a lady's drink.

"They've got beer," I pointed out to him.

"I thought I'd experiment," he said. "It's very refreshing."

I was never much at ease with Pop, but that has to be the worst happy hour I've ever logged. He talked about the joys of family life. He told me that I couldn't begin to imagine what my arrival had meant to my mother and him. "You changed my life, son.

When I saw you for the first time I made up my mind to put forth 110 per cent effort in everything I undertook. At last I had somebody to work for," he confided.

"Didn't you have yourself to work for before me?"

"Believe me, Ed. At a certain stage in a fellow's life he wants to start building for his posterity."

It was like Pop to express our relationship in such grandiose terms. Momentarily he saw himself in the role of patriarch, Ben Cartwright perhaps, explaining to a quizzical Hoss the larger meaning of the Ponderosa. Pop had loved *Bonanza*; for him, Sunday nights were sacred. What he could bequeath to posterity. Jesus.

I feel terrible. A dull ache is settling in over my kidneys. Sometimes when I am very nervous, very tense, I get muscle spasms in my lower back.

I hear Marsha saying, "Of course, Victoria has this now-or-never feeling. I don't think she's being entirely reasonable. Sure she's thirty-three, but they'd still have time. Why she wants to have a baby anyway is beyond me. I can't see it myself."

"How was she, Marsha?"

"Not bad. Not good. She'll be all right. Tomorrow she's going to take some time off work, move into a motel and take a few days to think things over. Though what she's got to think over I can't imagine. You ask me, she's only got one choice."

"What motel?"

"Who knows?" Marsha leans toward me. "Take my advice, Ed. This is private. Keep your nose out."

My back is tightening. If I don't get off the floor soon I mightn't be able to. I lurch to my feet, in stages, like a camel rising under a load.

"What's the matter?" says Marsha, alarmed. There must be something showing in my face.

"Where's your bathroom?"

She points. "Down the hall. First door on the left. Are you ill?"

Without answering I hobble off, bent-backed. The bathroom

gleams with tile, frosted glass, a huge mirror with bulbs all around its perimeter. I see myself reproduced in these surfaces, a ghostly Ed in frosted glass, a misshapen Ed in the tile, a pale Ed staring back at me out of the mirror over the sink.

It's the only room in most apartments with a lock.

SIX

fter spending twenty-five minutes mastering my feelings in Marsha's bathroom while listening to her threaten to call the police, the fire department, or both, to get me out, I returned home to sleep the sleep of the dead. This was possible because before dropping off I decided what course of action to pursue. I'm going to find her. Victoria wanted to talk to me.

So, beginning at nine o'clock this morning I phoned all the motels and hotels listed in the Yellow Pages. First of all I inquired after her under her married name, then her maiden name. Finally, I requested Victoria Peters. Most of the desk clerks hung up before I got a chance to ask whether they had a guest registered under the name of Victoria Laine. Cleo is her favorite singer. A shot in the dark.

So there I sat, a little depressed. I was slipping the telephone book into a desk drawer when I saw the stationery, stationery I had stolen from Benny Ferguson's office months ago. Stationery emblazoned with the letterhead of the legal firm he works for. I decided I ought to cheer myself up.

Life plays one the strangest tricks. Because we had been room-mates at university for three years, I had assumed Benny and I were some kind of friends, but Benny must have nurtured a grudge against me I'd never detected. Why else would he agree to represent Victoria in the divorce action? In a little less than a year his unarticulated grievance has swollen to bilious hatred. Can't he understand I have to defend myself with whatever poor tools come to hand? The stationery is one of these tools.

I fed it into my typewriter and began a letter to The Beast.
Killing two birds with one stone.

> Dear Mr. Rollins:
>   I am writing to you to demand, on behalf of my
> clients, the Jewish Anti-Defamation League and the
> Society of Free and Accepted Masons, a retraction of
> statements uttered by you on your radio program "A
> Piece of Your Mind" on January 2, 1982.

Legal stationery is so useful. A letterhead liberally peppered
with B.A.s, LL.D.s, and Q.C.s is a welcome addition to anyone's
arsenal.

The Beast's guest that day had been the noted sexologist and
world-renowned authority on sexual dysfunction, Dr. Norman
Gullickson, of New York, New York. His first questioner was,
quite predictably, McMurtry. The old gentleman desired to know
a sure-fire way to spot homosexuals.

As soon as I heard what he wanted, I knew what was behind
it. A week before, McMurtry had stumbled on me in our apartment building's laundry room drying a load of women's slips.
McMurtry's lizardy old eyes slitted with disgust as he watched a
gay gale of flimsy garments, a fuchsia, cerise, green, temptress
black, and virginal white maelstrom, swirling behind the glass of
the dryer. He knew I lived without benefit of female company.
What conclusion would he draw?

The slips were artifacts of the late regime, left behind in an
unrifled drawer when Victoria had departed in haste. For the
longest time I had held them against her return, but it was, at last,
plain to me that this was a vain hope. I had decided to launder
them and donate them to the Salvation Army Thrift Store.
McMurtry had discovered me going about my depraved business.

A week later he was to beg guidance through the modern
sexual labyrinth from the world-renowned and noted sexologist
Dr. Gullickson.

"Tom? Is that sex expert there?"

"Yes I am," said Dr. Gullickson. He had the breezy, professional manner of a person frequently interviewed, of a man at ease on the airwaves. If I remember correctly he has his own radio program in New York on which he dispenses advice to the sexually unfortunate.

"What I want to know is," said McMurtry, "is there any way you can tell them hummasexuals from us normals?"

"I'm not sure what he means," said Dr. Gullickson to Tom.

"He's an old gentleman. A regular," apologized The Beast, one pro to another.

"*What?*" complained McMurtry. "*I didn't get that!*"

"How do you mean?" shouted Rollins. "How do you mean, sir?"

"Well, we got one in the building where I live, and for the longest time I never thought, you know? And then I find out he wears women's underclothes."

"Ah," said the Dr. "A transvestite. He must be talking about a transvestite. They're not the same thing at all — a transvestite and a homosexual." He turned his attention to McMurtry, raising his voice to a piercing pitch. "Do you mean a transvestite, sir?"

"I don't care what you call them. We had a word for them in my day. What I want to know is how you spot them. I mean if they aren't dressed up."

"I think, sir," said Dr. Gullickson, "you're operating under a misconception. The traditional stereotypes of homosexuals that have plagued Western societies just don't bear up under examination."

McMurtry wasn't listening. "Like, do they have a sign they give each other?"

"A sign?"

"Yeah, a sign. Maybe like the sign the Jews give one another. Or the Masons. With them it's the ring. It's how all these people stick together without us knowing it."

"Let's just stop this thing right here," broke in The Beast. "I think I ought to make a comment on what we've just heard here, friends. Now I know for some of us, old opinions and old prejudices die hard. But I say — *let 'em die!* I also want to make it clear

I've got many good friends and even acquaintances who adhere to
the Hebrew faith, and I want to protest on behalf of them, on
behalf of the entire Jewish community, what has just been inferred
here today. Without thinking twice why I'd go anywhere, any
place, any time to testify to what the fine Jewish people of Canada
have contributed to this country.

"Likewise, everyone out there knows the good work the Shriners
do for children's hospitals, and many of us have enjoyed their
world-famous circuses." The Beast paused to marshal his professional outrage. "The name of my show is 'A Piece of Your
Mind'. Well, we've had a piece of yours, mister, and let me say
this: *It stunk!*"

> It has come to the attention of my clients that on the
> above-mentioned program certain statements deleteri-
> ous to their interests were made. The Jewish Anti-
> Defamation League finds particularly offensive your
> claim to have many Jewish friends. It demands a public
> retraction of this claim and a public apology to Jews
> everywhere.
>
> Similarly, the Masons are disturbed by your thought-
> less endorsation of their fraternal organization, fearing
> it may seriously hamper recruitment of new members.
> They too demand a retraction of statements made by
> you on January 2.
>
> If such action is not forthcoming within a week, my
> clients may be forced to seek other avenues of redress.
>
> Respectfully yours,
> Benjamin R. Ferguson
> Barrister and Solicitor

Writing that made me feel cheerier. There is no better antidote
for the terrible feeling of powerlessness which clutches modern
man by the throat than a vigorous exercise of the imagination. It
is the allurements of the imagination which has allowed all those
ragtag guerrilla movements of the last three decades to succeed,

that and the will to endure for the sake of the future. It is only the lack of the latter that has prevented me from accomplishing great things in my own right.

I think Benny knows that it is me that has been using his stationery. That's why he doesn't bother me any more, no new steps have been taken to effect the divorce, and I've heard not a word about the set of Balzac for months. Perhaps, though, Ferguson is merely taking a long breather before once again entering the fray, head bloodied but unbowed. However, I like to believe the silence about the twenty-six volumes may be because Victoria has reconsidered her position. Time heals all wounds and she, after all, has no real, intrinsic interest in them.

It was during an argument over *l'oeuvre complet* at a property settlement meeting that I filched the ten sheets of legal stationery off the stack on Benny's desk while he was ferociously rummaging in a drawer looking for cigarettes. Sucking on a butt was one of the ways he used to overcome the strong feeling our discussions about *l'oeuvre complet* aroused in him.

I miss our little get-togethers, the cut, parry, and thrust of negotiations. Whenever time hangs heavy on my hands I wish I could stroll down to Benny's office and reawaken the slumbering monster. Our debate never really ended and it is hard now to remember when it began. All I know is that it lasted long enough that Benny and I came to refer to *l'oeuvre complet* simply as Balzac, as if it were a person.

Of course, it was beyond the powers of Benny's feeble, essentially forensic imagination to understand what the custody battle for the set of Balzac was all about. Victoria had bought and paid for them it was true, but it was equally true her intention was to make a present of them to me. In the end the books came to symbolize love, the giving of it and the withholding of it. That was why Victoria was determined to have them returned, and why I refused to surrender them.

Long and wearing negotiations were undertaken to settle this question. Benny represented Victoria and I acted in my own interest. That I dared to do so enraged Benny, who thought it

beneath his dignity to bandy words with a layman. On many
occasions he made it clear that he felt I ought to seek legal counsel.

Fat chance. I had no intention of giving up my advantage, that
advantage being a thorough understanding of the workings of
Benny's mind. In the three years we had roomed together at
university I had never once been bested by Benny in one of our
frequent disputes. This was because I had studied his psychology
and learned that Benny has no bottom, no staying power. He
falters in the last furlong. The secret to grinding him to dust is to
make Benny feel that there will never be any end to the business at
hand. (In my mind I refer to this as the Viet Cong approach.)
One must invest every argument with a spacious sense of infinity.
Instead of the light at the end of the tunnel growing stronger and
brighter, it must seem to recede, grow dimmer, flicker, tremble
on the brink of failing entirely.

I thought that this approach produced splendid results in our
meetings vis-à-vis the set of Balzac. It took him three conferences
to get me even to admit the books were in my possession. After
that we went on to the question of ownership. Two more meetings and I agreed Victoria had paid for the books, but only after
Benny flourished a cancelled cheque under my nose.

Made overconfident by this minor victory in what I regarded as
a kind of Hundred Years War, Benny strutted over the vanquished,
berating me, demanding I sign the property division he had drawn
up, an agreement which returned *l'oeuvre complet* to Victoria.
Whereupon I flounced indignantly out of his office, warning him
never to use that tone with me again. It took him a week of
coaxing to lure me back. At that point I was satisfied that things
were going well; Benny was clearly displaying signs of great
mental strain whenever in my vicinity. They were the same symptoms I had showed when employed in Eaton's china department:
haggardness, testiness, elaborate and false politeness.

We began where we had broken off a week before.

"All right, Ed," he said, showing me a clammy slice of teeth
and gums that he tried to pass off as a smile, "let's review the
situation. You agree Victoria paid for the books?"

"Certainly." I said this with great conviction, to raise his hopes.

Benny took a tape recorder out of his desk and set it on his blotter. "Would you mind if I taped this conversation? For the sake of accuracy?"

"Not at all."

"Would you mind stating that when the recorder is on? That you agree to be recorded?"

"Not at all."

No one could accuse Benny of subtlety. When he had depressed the record button I put on my best Russian accent and said: "I confess to counter-revolutionary sabotage at the Krupskaya Tractor Works. Also to having uncomradely thoughts about Comrade Stalin. I throw myself on the mercy of Soviet justice."

"Fucking asshole."

I pointed out to Benny that the machine was still running. He shut it off.

"You always were a fucking asshole," said Benny. "You always will be."

"Benny, Benny, don't you remember how you used to preach the perfectibility of man?"

"What?"

Of course he didn't, because that was the past. Benny lives only in the present. There he sat, slumped behind his desk, barely recognizable to me. How many years ago was it that he had urged freedom on me, on everyone? What a noble savage he was, in revolt against the suburban decorum in which he had been raised. Benny was a Rousseauian primitive who hardly ate his meals out of an open fridge, who satisfied his poignantly urgent sexual drives with clamorous gusto, poor Ed often stumbling upon copulations that seemed to occur in every room of our rented flat except the one traditionally reserved for recreations of that sort.

He called himself a radical but he was one only in the sense that he had bewitched a small following with his graphic, hopeful vision of the demise of bourgeoisiedom. His frizzy-haired disciples were enchanted by his scenarios of the coming desolation: the rusting barbecues; untended, rank suburban lawns; the casual couplings amid the ruins. Out of all this he promised that a new clear-eyed, hairy race would arise, free of the hateful legacies of civilized memory, suckled on mother's milk, strengthened by goat's cheese.

Carried away by his own prophecies, in 1972 he led a small band out of the city to form the ill-starred Darien Commune. (It was I who helped him pick the name. "Or like stout Cortez, when with eagle eyes/ He stared at the Pacific — and all his men/ Look'd at each other with a wild surmise — / Silent, upon a peak in Darien.")

But the goats went unmilked, firewood unchopped, vegetables unharvested. Eight months later Benny was in law school on a generous stipend granted by the father of a communard he had impregnated and then married on the strength of great expectations. The girl had been fleeing her past. Her father was a lawyer, a constituency vice-president of the Liberal Party, an avid five-handicap golfer, and a notorious trifler with women. Ferguson led the girl firmly back to the bad old life, albeit in easy stages, where she discovered somewhat to her chagrin that she was perfectly happy.

Benny's transmogrification was so gradual as to be almost imperceptible. He explained to his friends that he was entering the system to gnaw it from within, vowing that he was going to become a legal-aid lawyer, the comforter of widows and the fearsome scourge of slum landlords.

I knew instinctively he was a lost man.

And there he sat before me, what I took to be the end result of ten years of compromises, a gentleman who plays squash at The Courtyard, whose ranting fervor has cooled to mere *brio*, a sensitive type who writes a cheque in support of the symphony because it's the thing to do. Although he never goes.

Unlike me, Benny has never really been out of step in his life, will always be the very picture of fashion. Man of the moment then, man of the moment now. While I, no matter how hard I try, will be caught with my hair long when it ought to be short, my trouser bottoms cuffed when they ought not to be cuffed. I will never speak the current lingo like a native.

On impulse I asked, "Do you like your life, Benny?"

"What the fuck's that supposed to mean?"

"I'm serious, Benny. Do you like your life?" I *was* serious. I wanted to know. I have a strong interest in discovering and questioning happy people. The most surprising types are.

"Sign the goddamn paper, Ed, and let's go home." He tossed the document across the desk. I looked at it lying there, one of its crisp pages turned back on itself, and I felt one of those inexplicable moments of sadness that fly across the consciousness the way a handful of cloud flies across a blue summer sky, driven by winds high above us.

With perfect sincerity I said, "Jesus, whatever happened to us, Benny? Look at the two of us, for chrissakes."

Benny couldn't even guess what I was talking about. "Look, Ed, I've been patient with you for old times' sake. You were always a fucking goof. When I was twenty-one I thought it was funny. Shit, I thought everything was a joke. But I don't think it's funny now and I think you're pathetic. I'm not the same guy I was. You can't treat me like you used to. You've got no right to laugh at me or belittle my work. *I* made something of myself — which is more than you can claim. And another thing. I can't afford to piss around with you any more, being polite. I've got a backlog of cases and my father-in-law is crawling up my back to get this cleared away. I haven't got time to talk about life with you and its meaning and the rest of that crap. Pardon me, but I've got other things to do besides entertain you."

"Whatever gave you the idea you were entertaining?"

"Sign the fucking paper."

I tried to explain why I wouldn't. "I can't sign that, Benny. It's not really the books that matter. I want Victoria to admit to me that she wanted to please me, that she was thinking kindly of me right up until the last minute. I want her to admit that she thought enough of me to buy me a goddamn two-hundred-dollar birthday present. Bought it only one week before she walked out on me. That means something to me, Benjamin."

"Maybe it's time you learned that nobody is interested in your little fucking private fantasies and what they mean, or don't mean, to you. There is one set of rules for everybody. I'm interested in seeing my client's property is returned. That's all. Legally those books are hers.''

''But morally mine.''

''Can't you get it through your head?'' he asked. ''We're talking legally. We're not talking morally.''

''I'd like to hear you make that statement before a jury, twelve good men and true. Justice will out.''

Benny's face darkened, his hand leapt to his tie knot. It made an expensive sound when he loosened it. ''Okay,'' he said, ''gloves off. You can drag your feet and whine and *kvetch* all you want. But I'm tightening the screws. I'll have Balzac seized by court order. If it takes a year, if it takes two years, I'll have Balzac returned to Victoria.''

''She cares nothing for Balzac!'' I shouted. ''I, on the other hand, *love* Balzac!''

''No matter how long it takes, you slimy motherfucker, we'll get him back.''

''Now we get to the crux of the matter,'' I declared, leaning across the table, rubbing my thumb and fingers together in the time-honored manner. ''Moolah. The big shekels. I'm sure you'd be only too glad to drag this sordid business out. But we'll see how Victoria feels about being impoverished so that you can persecute an innocent man at her expense. Because this is personal with you, isn't it? You always resented me, didn't you?''

''No, I resented your fucking supercilious attitude, that's what I resented!'' cried Benny flushing, rising from his chair, looming above me, confronting my eyes with a vast expanse of blue pinstripe. ''Who the hell were you to judge us?''

It is a common misconception that those who don't get involved with others' causes must inevitably be either judging or disapproving. That has seldom been the case with me.

''Benny, if you only knew how I wished I could have believed,'' I said in a subdued voice. It is the truth.

''Believe this, Ed. If you think you'll wear Victoria down with legal costs you have another think coming. No fucking way. Because from this moment on she's going to be treated as a hardship case, charged with office expenses only. I'm not taking a fee. My time's gratis. We'll see who breaks who, you fat tub of shit!''

That last remark of Benny's was very foolish. Didn't he know me well enough to realize that rude references to my physique would turn my mind to vengeance? It was shortly after this pungent remark that I skimmed the legal stationery off the top of his desk while he banged drawers in a furious search for a pack of cigarettes. I hid the paper inside my jacket.

We continued our exchange until Benny lost patience and ordered me out of his office. I refused to go and asked him whether he'd care to attempt to remove me. Benny is a physical as well as a moral coward, so he called security, who dispatched a much-decayed specimen of the corps of commissionaires. Because of my respect for his age and his service to king and country I allowed myself to be taken by the elbow and directed through the offices of Fitch, Carstairs, Levine, and Lemieux, all the while chanting at the top of my lungs, ''Free Balzac! Free Balzac!'' It is a sign of the present age that no one joined in, even when he got me out on the sidewalk and a sizeable crowd had gathered to watch me chant ''Free Balzac!'' and make encouraging motions with my arms, urging them to participate in my demonstration against establishment justice.

Fourteen years ago someone would have.

SEVEN

A few minutes ago I mailed my letter to The Beast, and that made me feel like a take-charge kind of guy, decisive. I no longer have any doubts that I'll find Victoria. The important thing, I tell myself, is to have a plan, to organize.

Organization, I must admit, isn't one of my strong points. Nevertheless, fired with zeal, I take a map of the city and divide it into quadrants with ruler and red pen. These quadrants I number 1, 2, 3, 4, ranking them according to what I calculate would be the likelihood of Victoria's choosing a motel or hotel within their boundaries. Pausing to admire the map I feel a stirring of confidence; this disciplined, logical approach to the solution of a marital conundrum is entirely un-Ed-like. It is a new, somewhat invigorating experience. I gnaw my pen and consider. On the whole this is proving to be a success. I forge ahead.

Next, I mark the approximate location of all hotels and motels on my map with tiny pencilled o's, using the addresses given in the Yellow Pages as references. This afternoon I'll drive to these places and scout their parking lots for Victoria's battered blue Volkswagen. If I fail to find it, the corresponding zero on the map will be inked red, thereby eliminating it. It's strange how closely linked fastidiousness is to a sense of control, even power. This exercise is making me feel better, without a doubt.

The careful plotting of hotels and motels takes me until one o'clock. It's amazing how many of them there are to be found in even a moderately sized city of 150,000. When I'm finished I beam down at my neat and tidy handiwork.

There is, however, no time to rest on one's laurels, because the car has to be loaded with supplies for an extended patrol of wintry streets. God only knows how long it will take to unearth Victoria. I set to packing a cardboard box. Items: a thermos of black coffee laced with brown sugar and dark rum, to keep the cold from creeping into my bones; a carton of Player's Plain; a family-size bag of Dad's Chocolate-Coated Oatmeal Cookies. And last of all, a two-quart red rubber hot-water bottle into which I'll void my bladder if I become car-bound on an extended stake-out. (I remember this as an article employed by a hard-bitten gumshoe in a detective novel.) Thus equipped, and nothing left to chance, I climb into my little yellow Fiat and drive off in search of my wayward wife.

Eighth Street runs through the heart of Quadrant 1. It is one of the city's chief arteries of entry and exit and therefore is bordered with fast-food franchises, service stations, shopping malls, family restaurants, chain stores, and plenty of motels. Prime hunting ground.

Moving in a westward, spasmodic flow of traffic that lurches through intersections and bucks along in the ruts worn in the road ice, I cast cautious glances to my right, eyes peeled for motels. It is mid-afternoon, the lowering sun strains behind a fine, crystalline snow which fuzzes the outlines of the signs that picket the roadside. Some of these signs wink and blink with violet or orange neon; others solemnly revolve in the grease-stiffening cold. The majority, however, are megaliths that loom against an ashen sky, pharaonic testaments to hamburger empires. The golden arches of the House of McDonald are prominent, as is the boast "4.6 billion burgers sold". (A tyrant's brag, "My name is Ozymandias, King of Kings: / Look on my works, ye Mighty, and despair!") The Family Size Bucket of the colonel from Kentucky squats impaled on a sixty-foot concrete pole, sullenly vying for attention with the intaglio of A & W, a mahogany-and-orange blandishment against a pale winter sky. Nearby the huge sombrero and yucca cactus of a burrito palace are rimed with gritty snow and old ice.

It is in the face of all this visual chaos, so opposed to order and simplicity, that I suddenly, perhaps a little guiltily, recall my vow to simplify my life. When I made that promise I had in mind the image of the ancient Greek subsisting on a fragment of pungent cheese, coarse bread, a handful of sun-warmed olives, a little watered wine; a man who discussed the Good, the True, the Beautiful with grave delight, and piped clear music in a sylvan glade. But I feel the absence of hills clothed in myrtle and thyme; of the Great Mother, Homer's wine-dark sea. Good resolutions, it seems, require good scenery.

Here amid the Ponderosas, Bonanzas, Gulf Services, Consumers Distributings, Speedy Mufflers, Firestones, Smitty's Pancakes, Dog 'n Suds, Canadian Tires, Essos, Burger Kings, and Sambos, I spot the Sleepy Hollow Motel nestled in an urban thicket of sign poles. I touch the brakes, wrench the wheels out of the tire tracks that ladder the pavement, and with the sound of a car horn blasting outrage behind me slither into Sleepy Hollow's driveway.

Parking lot succeeds parking lot and that of The Palisades offers nothing more than did those of the Sleepy Hollow, Slumber Land, The Rest Eezy, or The Motorola, all of which I have subjected to a thorough inspection undertaken on foot.

Bundled against the cold, my parka hood tightened until the drawstring is lost in my jowls and my chubby features are scrunched, I gloomily tramp about in search of Victoria's crumpled and dented car. Since four o'clock the wind has been rising and now it is unbearable, running over exposed flesh like a flame and licking tears into my eyes. Fingers and toes have turned brittle in mitts and snow boots, and my lips feel like leather. Having completed my circuit of the premises of The Palisades, I crawl with a grateful whimper into the comparatively milder climate of my car, light a cigarette, munch a cookie and drink a lot of rum and coffee.

I'm going to be arrested. It would be just my luck. I see myself, a suspicious figure lumbering through the six-o'clock darkness of a winter's evening. Ed tripping over shards of caked snow broken up and scraped into ridges by a snow-removing machine. Ed skirting the long, harsh patterns of light thrown by the windows of occupied rooms, weaving between parked cars, hugging the barracks-like building, daring to hope that a peep through parted curtains might reveal my lovely Victoria, and having my feverish hopes chilled as snow spills over the eaves and cascades into my eyes, icing my hot, expectant face.

And then, from behind, the strong hand gripping my collar.

I sip from my thermos, stamp my feet on the floorboards. Perhaps it is too late to continue my search. In the night, at a distance, the cars look the same, all wear skullcaps of fresh snow.

The L-shaped courtyard of the motel carves the stinging wind into eddies. Waste paper suddenly darts out of the darkness of the parking lot to rise into the bright, streaming snow lit by the one remaining functional floodlight set on the fake log ramparts that give The Palisades its name. There they fly erratically like hunting bats; or flap languorous wings like rays moving in a strange, sunlit sea, before swooning and tumbling back into blackness.

I am not at all surprised that Victoria has chosen to hole up in a motel while she tries to reach a decision as to what to do about this unexpected pregnancy. She has always shown a preference for rented rooms as the setting for the momentous decisions of her life; crappy little rooms where nothing familiar, nothing invested with awkward memories, can influence her. It was in just such a room (framed reproductions of a Portuguese fishing port, television chained to its stand, worn and snagged carpet) that a number of years ago she decided we should have a child. That was in Toronto in an "economy hotel" where I had been reluctantly taken to relieve a lingering depression.

What was the cause of my melancholy? I cannot say exactly. Some of it was that I did not like my job. I was a lowly library assistant, which meant I shelved books for eight hours a day. More of it was that I had the feeling Victoria was drifting away from me. I had always assumed that she saw the world much as I did, but an offhand remark of hers one day contradicted this notion. We were talking about the past and she said, "You know it's strange, but hearing other people talk, I'm always surprised by how little of the past I remember. I seem to live pretty much in the present."

I didn't believe her; I told her she remembered as well as anyone. It was just that she remembered different things. I would prove it to her. "Tell me something about the first year of our married life," I said.

She mentioned a few things, but seemed vague.

I urged her to be more specific.

"I remember you organized the big laundry party and all of our friends took their dirty clothes to the laundromat and drank wine out of a wineskin until the manager threw us out because you kept yelling that there ought to be a prize given to the owner of the biggest pair of boxer shorts."

"That was the second year of our marriage."

"Was it? Maybe it was. So what?"

I began to question her more closely. "Name two movies we saw the summer I moved in with you."

"Ed, give me a break. Who remembers the movies they saw any given summer?"

"I do. We went practically every night for the air-conditioning. Two movies. Come on, name them."

"I can't. End of discussion, okay?"

"Two measly movies, Victoria. Out of dozens."

"This is ridiculous, Ed."

It seemed that what she claimed was true. She did not remember the way I did, did not have the same feelings of loyalty to our shared past. I was frightened that she thought so little of the past, because if the past cannot be called in to redress the provisional present, to speak as an advocate to the heart and plead the claims of steadfastness, how could I expect to hold her? To me it seemed that whatever I offered in the fleeting present wasn't enough; I needed, too, the weight of the past. I began to try to help her recall. This led to fights.

"When did I grow a moustache?"

"You started in on that yesterday and I told you then to shut up. I don't care when you grew a moustache."

"I'll give you a hint."

"I don't want a hint."

"I grew a moustache to look older. Why did I want to look older?"

"Ed, please."

"You remember, Victoria."

"Honest to God, Ed, one more word and I walk out of the apartment, I swear."

"Think!"

She walked out. "Because I was going to be a teaching assistant!" I yelled after her. "I wanted to look older than my students, remember?"

I slowly came apart that summer and autumn.

Pop thought he knew what was the matter with me. He said to Victoria: "It's that job he has. A monkey could do his job. It gets to Ed. His mind needs stretching. He needs a challenge."

He didn't want to believe what had happened to me. Years afterward, in the middle of a fight about my father, Victoria said that he had only come to visit me in the hospital once and all the time we sat in the visitors' lounge he complained that the place smelled. She said he kept telling me it was no place to think things through. I had to think things through, he said he understood that, but I ought to do it someplace peaceful, like a cottage on a lake. He'd rent me one if I wanted.

Victoria said she even caught him asking me if I were being held against my will. He turned to her and said, "It's been known to happen, a person kept in a place like this against his will." He didn't come back to see me, nor did he allow my mother to visit me.

Of course, I don't remember any of that. It was all reported to me by Victoria. A session of shock therapy obliterated whole reaches of my memory, electricity making a simple erasure of hours, days, I suspect even weeks. Yet certain stretches of memory are entire, wholly intact, perhaps their clarity even heightened by the absence of context. For example, I remember distinctly the library, the river bank, the sleepless nights, and *Dr. Friggenstein's Finishing School for Wayward Misses*. Shock therapy didn't wipe any of that away.

God, how could I forget the library? The job stacking books at the University Library was the only one I could find after graduating, or at least the only one I could bring myself to take. I thought a library would be a nice place for me to work because I liked books. In any case, Victoria said the job was only temporary, just a few months of employment before we left for Greece.

I ended up working there for three years, pinned by inertia. Victoria's job mobility was not hampered in any such way. When she realized Greece was retreating into the future, she quit her menial job and got hired as a social worker at a salary approximately double mine.

I carried on well enough to get by for two and a half years. After that I began to dread going into the ranges; I sometimes panicked at the idea I might not find my way out from among the books. I hated the hot, oppressive silence of the narrow aisles between the shelves, the walls of books that my shoulders brushed as I shuffled along pushing a loaded truck. The radiators ticked emphatically, someone coughed harshly and persistently, a pair of shoes creaked, alerting me that my floor supervisor, Mrs. Muchison, was stealthily observing my work habits. The book in my hands sounded like a small fire crackling when I ruffled its sere pages with my thumb.

I wandered for hours in this maze, fingers fumbling with cracked book spines, shifting misplaced volumes, mumbling PR6045. A91B8; PR6045.A91Z498, head aching, watching my fingers burnished a sickly yellow by the fluorescent lights as they clawed and scrabbled, smarting with paper cuts, in among the books.

As my condition worsened, I began frequently to lose my way in this labyrinth. Heart thundering, I heard my shoes clattering with panic in the stifling aisles as I sweated and groped, searching for the proper range on the wrong floor of six. I was reprimanded for slowness, sloppiness, inattention to detail. I was trying, but the canyons of books lengthened, the library's walls grew taller and steeper, the light feebler. Call numbers and letters dwindled, faded. I put a magnifying glass in my pocket.

At night I couldn't sleep. I ran the tub full of cold water and sat chilled and numb for hours on end. I smoked and paced in my bathrobe through the silent hours of early morning, windows thrown open to admit the shushing, wet sound of tires on hot pavement, walked and smoked until my legs tightened and I collapsed on to the sofa and sank into the dreamless sleep that I was granted between 5 and 7 a.m., only to awake to return, mouth parched, to the weight of all those books pressing in on me.

Victoria, concerned, urged me to find a hobby. I bought an old Audubon Society bird guide in a second-hand bookstore, a fat, compact book badly damaged by frequent drenchings on field trips. The pages were crinkled, the covers warped, and the colored plates of the birds marred. The cardinal's scarlet had bled in the rain and stained many of the dowdy birds — sparrows, thrushes, and wrens — pink. I couldn't have cared less. The book was just a prop, a justification for my haunting the river bank.

On the east side of the river the carefully groomed park has not yet swallowed up the entire distance between the two bridges. A part of the river bank, more rugged and cut by ravines, is still covered in original growth. The native bush turns this stretch of land still and thick with green light, and through the poplar and willow a narrow path beaten by joggers threads its way.

In that disturbed time I often found myself walking that path on a summer's evening. I would walk quickly along until a bend hid me from the sight of anyone who might be following and then I would plunge off into the woods that crawled up the bluff overlooking the river. Several yards into the tangle of brush and deadfalls the land began to rise abruptly and the undergrowth thinned. Breathing heavily I scrambled up, feet slipping in leaf mould, face switched by willows, hands ripped by wild-rose thorns.

As I climbed I would cast about me for some small clearing where I could crouch unseen; one unlittered with broken wine

bottles, charred wiener sticks, blackened logs, withered and be-
draggled condoms; one high enough up on the river bank that I
could watch, through the slim trunks of the poplars, the river
running in the setting sun with the placid dignity of molten
bronze. Overhead the light glittered wistfully in the leaves shivering above me, birds I did not trouble to identify in my Audubon
guide darted among the trees, and I could hear small animals
thrashing in fallen leaves.

When I found a spot, I would sink down sweating on the damp
compost which carpeted the ground, hug my knees, and stare. On
the trail below me joggers pounded heavily on, their breath harsh
and sibilant in the quiet. One evening a teenage couple stole
upwards hand in hand towards me, whispering and twisting
among the trees to a place no more than twenty feet from where I
was hidden. There they proceeded to couple urgently and furtively,
their white bodies shimmering in the broken light.

How did I feel hunkering there in the thicket? I recall wishing
never to leave its green solace, wishing never to be found. Every
evening that passed I sat a little longer chained in its peace, watched
the light die a little more, felt the chill of coming autumn stipple
my skin and creep deeper into my flesh.

Sometimes I thought of Huck Finn on Jackson's Island, the
part of the novel in which his friends search the river for Huck's
dead body and he, hidden in the bushes, watches Judge Thatcher
and Becky and Tom and Joe Harper and Aunt Polly crowd the rail
of the ferryboat to peer down into the muddy waters for his
corpse, the cannon booming loud enough to raise the dead. And
all the while Huck crouches mere yards off their gunwales on the
island, screened from their sight, and behind him, miles further
back in a wilderness of trees, the black man Jim crouches too, an
unknown continent, waiting to be claimed by Huck.

During my last visit to the river bank I could not bring myself
to leave. The cool grey of twilight became a prison, the shadows
bars. Night fell. The yellow windows of the hotels and office
towers on the opposite bank shone on the moving waters of the
black river, the glow of the city rose into the sky and washed out

the stars that swung low on the horizon. I sat on. Cold crept out
of the ground and into my flanks, a breeze combed the crowns of
the poplars and rattled their leaves.

Much later I heard my name called. It came to me from a
distance, very faint. At intervals of some minutes it grew clearer,
closer. At last I saw a flashlight tossing in the night like a light on
a boat.

"Ed!" she called. "Ed!"

I wanted to let her pass without a sign, to stay hidden. I wanted
to hear her voice fade as Huck had heard the booming cannon
fade. I wanted to be left alone, to pity myself.

And then I thought of the desolateness of this urban wood and
was afraid for her. I shambled down the slope crying her name,
thinking of rapists.

Victoria led me home. One of my hands was closed on hers, the
other dangled the bird book, my attempt at achieving balance.

Toronto, where I found myself two weeks later, was enduring a
September of wind and flying grit that made my eyes run with
cold and ground dirt between my teeth. I was there because
Victoria had decided on the culture cure to heal a broken spirit. I
was to be regularly dosed with art galleries, museums, bookstores,
the theatre, the symphony. Scraps are all that are left to me of that
time. The brassy glint of a soundless trumpet at Massey Hall,
players blowing and bowing and plucking to the dim roar of
blood in my ears. The galleries were only footfalls and whispers,
the restaurants a clatter of dishes, water splashing in glasses,
waiters' shirt cuffs and dextrous hands. Walking the streets I
caught glimpses of myself in shop windows that brought me up
short. Rooted to the sidewalk I stared at a dishevelled stranger, his
dull eyes mounted in a setting of puffy, darkened flesh; a cigarette
smoking between the fingers of a limp hand dangling at his side, a
vee of belly bursting where the bottom button of his shirt had
popped. I grinned and he grinned back.

I stopped going out and kept to my hotel room. That was how

I developed my interest in *Dr. Friggenstein's Finishing School for Wayward Misses* — or, to speak more precisely, grew to admire one of the misses of that film, Maria. In all, I saw the movie three times. It played regularly on the "adult channel" provided for hotel guests.

Victoria spoiled my first viewing of *Finishing School* by lying in bed flipping through the pages of *Toronto Life* and making tart comments about the supposedly salacious hi-jinks taking place on-screen. She could not be convinced my interest was anthropological and not lecherous. The next two times I plotted to be alone in order to enjoy undisturbed a conventional fantasy apparently so unremarkable that it had found its way on to the bill of fare of an economy family hotel. While Victoria was off at the Eaton Centre Cineplex admiring the latest offerings of the masters of European film, I was staring at democratic erotica, seeking a way out of my dilemma.

What is *Dr. Friggenstein's Finishing School for Wayward Misses* (special X) all about, that it should have so completely captivated my attention? The travails of a headmaster in a girls' finishing school. Not just any finishing school, but a Swiss finishing school. Great pains are taken to establish the location of the doctor's academy in Switzerland, presumably because that country adds a sophisticated, international tone to the goings-on. So between frequent bouts of bum-paddling, simulated heterosexual intercourse, and outbreaks of sapphism in the student body, there are interludes of majestic alpine scenery pirated from travelogues shot many, many years ago during the garish birthpangs of Technicolor. Our convictions about Dr. Friggenstein's nationality are further reinforced by having him dressed in national costume. He is also apt to remark, without provocation, "The Swiss air is so stimulating!" and leer.

The moral of the film is apparently spare the rod and spoil the miss. Dr. Friggenstein is always turning one of his female pupils over his knees and paddling her bare behind because she is naughty. These spankings always excite warm feelings in both parties and produce predictable results. And so it goes for the first fifteen minutes, a dreary succession of ghastly moans and groans and grunts of unearthly pleasure, a sad parade of abused flesh.

But then an interesting twist. Dr. Friggenstein is indeed a firm disciplinarian, but all his strenuous efforts cannot stamp out the most serious breach of school rules: nude roller derby. No sooner does Dr. Friggenstein lay his weary head on his pillow than his cultivated young ladies creep from their beds for a little roller-skating, *au naturel*. It is never made clear why his charges are so intent on this form of recreation but intent they are. He cannot eradicate it.

Their unspeakable crime is nightly enacted in a dingy hall that looks suspiciously unlike a Swiss chalet and a good deal like the sort of fraternal hall one finds in small towns all over North America. There are even lighter-colored, plaque-shaped spots evident on the dirty imitation-pine panelling of the walls that suggest awards hastily removed before the cameras rolled.

Round and round the women unsteadily go, wheels clattering gloomily in the empty hall. The naked daughters of Philadelphia socialites, Roman marchesas, and British earls are shaky on their skates. Anxiety at falling and being hurt strips their faces of the last illusion of youthfulness, as the removal of school uniforms destroyed the last poor deception they were nymphets. Legs straddled far apart to maintain an uncertain balance, their vulnerable-looking pudenda are paraded past the camera. Breasts droop and bobble, and several women display the kind of stretch marks associated with childbearing. There is a good deal of timorous flailing about at one another, a burlesque of violence that does little to enliven this sad and creaky carousel of ersatz savagery. Everyone is plainly scared of upsetting herself and getting a nasty knock, scrape, or floor burn.

My eyes are always riveted on Maria.

I first noticed her earlier in the film because of the indifferent manner in which she counterfeited sexual ecstasy while simulating coitus with Dr. Friggenstein. The other women were eager, if bad, actresses. They bucked their hips and shuddered and gasped and ran their tongues voraciously around their lips and thrashed about spastically, all the while uttering cries of encouragement and utter abandon. Maria, however, at the supposed critical moment, allowed a look to pass over her face that suggested a twinge of neuralgia rather than unutterable delight. This cheered me. A guerrilla fighter in Gomorrah? I wondered how she had managed to carry off this remarkable, listless insubordination in the face of the tyranny of common taste. Why had this rebel been allowed in the film at all?

At that point I knew. Because she was the only one who could roller-skate. Beautifully. How easily she whirled through the naked herd with a graceful carelessness that provoked in my mind pictures of an innocent past: roller-skate keys and shaded sidewalks in happy subdivisions, lemonade and scraped knees.

Here, I felt, was a kindred spirit. I felt compelled to view the film again to search for further impertinences. When I studied her performance I found them. How had I missed on a first viewing the contemptuous lassitude with which she bared her buttocks for paddling? Or the barely perceptible wink of the left eye that followed her profession of abject terror at the outrageous size of Herr Doktor's manhood? And always, in every species of sexual encounter, she offered the voyeur nothing more than a mild furrowing of the brow, a curl of the upper lip, and a lazy roll of the eyes to register her orgasm, .01 on the Richter scale. It was a performance that lifted my spirits as nothing else had in months.

Two days before we left Toronto, Victoria told me she wanted to become pregnant. She had thought about the matter long and hard. We had agreed before we married that we wanted children. What did I think? Was now the time?

I said: "What about Greece?"

She said: "You don't want anything to do with Greece."

I realized that at that moment our marriage had entered a new stage. I was drinking Scotch out of the toothbrush glass. I took a swallow and then said I thought a baby was a fine idea.

Victoria told me that she believed my state owed something to the way we lived, in the pitch and toss of freedom. A child might be an anchor to keep us off the rocks.

I said: "Don't we do anything for love any more?"

I flick on the interior light of the Fiat and color the dot which signifies The Palisades on the map. Red dots appear at intervals along the length of 8th Street, like beads on a necklace. Scarlet for absence. She isn't here either.

EIGHT

My car wouldn't start this morning. I thought it needed a boost but the pimply thug dispatched by the towing company to galvanize the frozen corpse back to life rendered a dissenting diagnosis. "Sounds to me like your starter. Nothing I can do," he said, unclipping the jumper cables. "This baby's tits up. You want her pulled somewheres?"

I can't find Victoria without a car. I need wheels.

Naturally I thought of Benny. His is a three-car family: BMW, Land Rover, Pinto. And I knew where I could find him at lunchtime because Benny is a creature of habit. When he and I were locked in mortal combat over custody of Balzac, we always disengaged at twelve o'clock sharp so Benny could lunch at The Beef Dip.

The Beef Dip, contrary to the associations the name evokes in my mind, is not a Texas cow-wallow but a restaurant that specializes in roast beef sandwiches which "beg to be dunked in a one-of-a-kind gravy dip that smacks of all the goodness in the great outdoors". Lining up there at lunch-time to wait for a table, I found its rustic interior leading me into a reverie. There were kerosene lanterns dangling from rough-hewn rafters, swinging doors leading to the kitchens, and plenty of cute signs in evidence enjoining gentlemen to remove spurs and shooting irons at the door. I was hitching up my pants and running a cool eye over the crowd tying on the feed-bag in hopes of spotting my old trail boss, Sam Waters, when a little filly sashayed up and asked: "Table for one, sir?"

I told her no, that I was with the Benny Ferguson party. This got me led directly to a table where Benny was seated with two other men. As we approached I could hear one of Benny's pals loudly airing an opinion.

"They've got to raise admission standards to Law School," he said, "or ten years down the road there'll be an oversupply you won't believe. Even now I've got articling students begging for a place. It's going to get cut-throat if something isn't done."

His companion mumbled something I took to be discreet assent. This one was a tiny, perfect lawyer. He was plump, and despite going bald on top, he clung to the fashions of his youth. A fringe of long, lank locks tumbled over his collar. He looked the way I imagine a hobbit would look.

"It's the women," resumed the loud one. "There's too many of them entering the profession. Rats scrambling on a sinking ship. The trouble with women is they destroy the prestige of any profession they get into in any numbers — teaching, nursing, social work . . ." He faltered when he realized he'd lost Benjamin's attention. Benny was watching me hover by their table and, from the look in his eye, was preparing to repel all boarders.

"Benny," I cried, edging into a shallower orbit and dismissing the hostess with a nod, "what a pleasant coincidence! Mind if I join you?"

"Sorry, Ed, too bad. Working lunch."

His lawyer friends glanced at each other. It was clear this was news to them.

I pretended to have misunderstood amid the restaurant noise what he'd said. "Great! Glad to." I addressed Benny's luncheon companions. "Let me introduce myself. Just call me Ed. I'm an old friend of Benny's. We were roomies, as a matter of fact." I extended my hand in turn to the advocate of quotas and Frodo. As I did, I made my opening move in a play for the empty chair beside Benny. I tried to insinuate myself between the back of Benny's chair and the pole with a horse-collar hung on it. Benny planted his feet firmly and dug in. I squirmed. Not an inch of give.

"Les Silver," said the misogynist. "Harry Supra," said the other.

"You see, Ed," said Benny through clenched teeth, leaning back, hard, "we'd love to have you join us. But client confidentiality — "

"Hey, don't I know it? No problem, Benno. Loose lips sink ships, right? Mum's the word." I sucked in my breath and wriggled until I felt one buttock squeezed against the peeled-log pillar. Leverage. Archimedes was right about that: with the proper leverage you can move the world. I proceeded to lever with my pelvis, short, strong, thrusting movements. Benny continued to stubbornly resist. He braced his arms against the table, which was conveniently, for him, bolted to the floor. The post began to creak rhythmically to my thrusting and the ice to tinkle in the water glasses.

"Benny, if you could just pull forward a smidgeon . . ." I coaxed, flexing my haunches and hips with greater authority. Both of the lawyers opposite were now steadying coffee cups rattling in saucers, eyes widening.

"What the hell do you want?" Benny cried. His voice was blurred by rage. "What the fuck do you want?"

I pointed, answered meekly. "If you could just pull up a teensy bit, Ben, so I could wriggle over there — "

"Not *that*, goddamn it! What're you after now? *What do you want, you son of a bitch!*"

I ceased struggling with his chair-back. Benny's friends stirred uneasily in their places. A knife blade rang faintly, nervously, against the base of a water glass. Neither one of them appeared to be enjoying his lunch.

"All right then," I said quietly. "I want a favor, Benny."

"Get out from behind me. *Get out!*"

I did. Benny impatiently rammed back his chair, stood up, flung down the napkin he'd balled up in his fist. "First, I'll apologize for him," he announced to his friends, "because he doesn't have the sense to do it himself. And then I'll take him to the cocktail lounge so you can finish your lunch in peace. Have the waiter send in the tab to me. I'll get this one. It's the least I can do."

The two barristers stared at me. "I've been disappointed in love," I explained. "It's affected me."

"Shut up and get moving." Benny motioned me to lead.

As we wended our way among tables and diners, Benny kept feeding his shrill patter into my right ear. "What's the matter with you, for chrissakes? Couldn't wait to see me this morning? Well, he didn't believe it for a second. Are you insane? Is that why you're persecuting me?"

I wasn't following any of this. "What are you talking about? I'm not persecuting you."

"If you're not, it's the best goddamn imitation of persecution I've seen. You're sick. You ought to see somebody."

The Ember Room was graced by a natural-gas fireplace flaring variegated jets of flame. A number of people basked in its hiss and livid glow. I chose a remote, unpopulated corner of the room where we ordered drinks.

"I'll give you fair warning," said Benny. "He's considering going to the police."

"What are you babbling about? And who is considering going to the police?"

"You know who."

"Riddle me, riddle dee. I haven't the faintest."

"Your friend Tom Rollins. The talk-show guy. He got your letter this morning and he phoned me as soon as he read it. Not that he was taken in by it. He just wanted to know if I knew anyone who might be using my firm's stationery and forging my name to juvenile letters."

I sipped my drink. "My dear Benny, the mystery deepens. Elucidate your raving."

"Just one more letter and he goes to the police. I hope the fuck he does. He says he gets a lot of mail from disturbed individuals, but nothing quite like yours."

I was surprised. All those letters of admonishment I'd written to The Beast in the past weeks must have taken root in the thin and stony soil of his mind. Interesting. I hadn't thought they were having any effect.

"Am I to understand you suggested to this person that I and some lunatic at large were one and the same? Benny, Benny, Benny. Ed smells slander and a generous settlement."

I was ignored. "Let me give you some advice, Ed. I don't know how much of my stationery you got your hands on, or even how you got it. But here's a word to the wise — burn whatever you have left. Just to rid yourself of temptation." Benny paused to shake the ice in his glass before proceeding to dispense more counsel. "And another thing, don't ever sign my name to another letter if you know what's good for you. Rollins and I have your signature now, or rather your forgery of my signature. We've got you by the balls, Ed." Benny smiled, swelling with confidence. Power, as it had in the old days, was invigorating him. "You see, the first letter you wrote I couldn't very well ask the Telethon people to return, and I couldn't take action on it. So I had to ignore it. But this is a different matter. This time you committed a forgery. Big mistake."

Benny had a point. Unlike the first letter, the second was not foolproof. But then the first letter was pure inspiration, a flash of genius. Something given to one once in a career. Nobody would have dared set the law on me because it would have been much too embarrassing for those concerned.

You see, a short time after I'd pinched Benny's lovely parchmenty stationery, advertisements began to appear on my TV announcing an upcoming, locally produced Telethon to raise money for crippled children. The ads made me think of Randy.

When I was growing up, Randy lived several blocks down from my house in a split-level painted a brilliant turquoise. Not only was he confined to a wheelchair, he was also retarded. From what wasting illness he suffered, or had suffered, I don't know. But I remember dangling, shrunken legs, and strange, curling hands whose fingers actually touched the insides of his wrists.

Randy was the only child of an optometrist and his wife. During the summer the wife used to place Randy on the sidewalk outside their home for hours on end. Our suburb was a new development, all brightly painted houses and spindly trees that didn't offer a scrap of shade. Neighbors wondered about Randy's being left unprotected under a hot sun like that without even a hat. When someone mentioned this to his mother, she said, "Randy likes it outside." Later it was said the optometrist didn't know what his wife did when he was at the office.

Randy spent his afternoons in a painful progress up and down his block. His withered hands couldn't grip the wheel of his chair to turn them, but by holding an old broomstick in the crooks of his arms he could pole himself up the sidewalk, inch by inch, like a bargeman driving his boat slowly upriver against the current. With infinite patience, in a kind of blind questing, he toiled away under a fierce summer sun, making his torturous epic journeys.

He both terrified and fascinated me. I hated to confront him face to face on the sidewalk. His head would loll loosely from side to side and he would part his lips in the grim reflexive smile that is meant to ingratiate and ward off possible harm.

When I was in the religious stage of childhood, Randy presented me with a problem. Sunday school taught me that I should make friends of the afflicted, that I ought to visit the sick. But I didn't want to, not if they were like Randy. In any case, the authors of my Sunday school magazines apparently had no acquaintance with kids like Randy. Their stories were illustrated with colored pictures of radiantly healthy children visiting other children in hospitals, children who may have had a touch of tonsillitis but who looked not a whit different from their visitors, except that they were lying in bed, rosy-cheeked. They invariably assembled model airplanes on the bedclothes. Fat chance of doing that with Randy.

I never did steel myself to speak to him, nor did I ever do any of those small Christian kindnesses Mrs. Hoffner, our Sunday school teacher, urged on us. I was afraid of him; Randy was a sign of the perils of life, and it was best to keep my distance. So I was glad to be relieved of my religious problem after he was injured by the dog, and the Children's Aid Society, claiming neglect, had him removed from his parents' care. Randy disappeared and I had no longer to suffer childish scruples as I watched him crawl along the sidewalk, or feel him as a constant reproach to my charity.

It was a passing stray that attacked him. His mother had left him alone and unattended while she went to have her hair done. Perhaps the animal was aroused by the strange, creeping chair, or thought that the feeble, contorted human with the stick meant it some harm.

The boy's screaming, people said later, was horrible. I can well imagine how those screams of terror, those screams of helpless rage, sounded on our ordinary street of bright, new houses. He was bitten once on his flaccid, curved hand boneless as a seal flipper, once on his wasted thigh.

I never thought of Randy after he was taken away from the optometrist and his wife. That is, until two years later when my mother mentioned she ought to send his parents a sympathy card. Randy had died of a respiratory illness. She added: ''I don't care what anybody says, they let that kind die in those places.''

For two weeks afterwards I had the same dream. I dreamed of a black dog with eyes hot as red coals, and a stick striking weakly, tip tap tip tap, all around its dancing legs. Who was in the chair, Randy or me, I never knew. Because all I could see was the stick and the nimble dancing dog, its blackness, its red eyes.

Which is a confused way of beginning to explain why I did what I did when the advertisements began. I wrote a cheque, of course, not a very large one because I didn't have much. I wondered what else could be done and I thought of Benny.

I fed a sheet of the letterhead of Fitch, Carstairs, Levine, and Lemieux into my Olivetti and pounded out my announcement to the organizers of the upcoming Telethon. With it was a challenge to be read aloud at the beginning of the 48-hour fund-raiser. This was exuberantly enunciated by the sincere and quite-honestly-moved master of ceremonies. Still fresh as a daisy, perky, full of zip, and as yet unrumpled, he gave it his all.

''Who says lawyers don't have hearts?'' he bellowed to the cameras. ''Who says it? The guys down at Fitch, Carstairs,

Levine, and Lemieux have 'em. They went to the bottom line to prove they have 'em." He ferociously waved my letter as evidence. "I've got a note right here from a Mr. Benjamin Ferguson written on behalf of all the boys at Fitch, Carstairs and whatchamacallit, and they pledge *two thousand bucks in aid of crippled kiddies!*" He waited for the figure to sink into the collective mind of his audience before continuing his paean of praise. "Not only that, but Mr. Ferguson challenges all other legal firms in this wonderful, crazy, generous city to match or better that! Yes, match or better it! And the judges! Mr. Ferguson doesn't want to forget the judges! Dig down deep under those robes, your honors! Ha ha! Just a little humor. Seeing as I got to be in traffic court Wednesday. No, I tell a lie. I perjured myself. Just kidding, folks." Suddenly he assumed a different demeanor, became earnest, sincere. "Seriously though," he said, lowering his voice, drooping his eyebrows, "I've worked a lot of generous cities, but this city has a special, generous spirit. What a challenge to meet. What a cause. Handicapped kiddies. So I'd like to dedicate my first song of the Telethon to all the lawyers listening and watching, because, all kidding aside, we all know they're great guys. It's a little number called 'Climb Every Mountain'. Just remember, no one ever stands so tall as when they stoop to help a child. Come on, you legal eagles, help those kids climb their mountains!"

Then he proceeded to belt out "Climb Every Mountain" with agonized contortions of the body, succeeded by a more placid rendering of "Dream the Impossible Dream".

That afternoon the legal community forked over $26,800.

"Benny," I said, "all this talk of letters and forgery is making me fear for your feeble reason. I repeat: I know nothing of any letters. A letter to a talk-show host? A further letter . . ." I hesitated, "to Telethon people? Whatever is Telethon? A world, a civilization, far, far beyond our galaxy?" I pitched my eyes upward as if studying the uncharted emptiness of space.

"You're so fucking cute I could just puke. And wipe that shit-eating grin off your face. Have you any idea the grief, let alone the bread, that little practical joke of yours cost me? No, I bet you don't. My father-in-law's partners wanted my balls for bookends after I had to tell them some maniac had the firm's stationery. By some quirk of logic they held *me* responsible.''

''It's the unsavory company you keep, Benny. Chartered accountants, real estate agents, stockbrokers, politicians in embryo. Your betters quite naturally doubt your character.''

Benny forged on with his litany of sorrows, unheeding. ''Those old sons of bitches made me pay fifteen hundred bucks of the pledge out of my own pocket. Janice's dad kicked in the difference and agreed to pay for the printing of new stationery to get Fitch and Levine off my back. They were particularly pissed, those two, Fitch and Levine.''

A harrowed look came over his face. He took a long swallow of Scotch. ''You singlehandedly wiped out my skiing holiday to Banff, you jerk. But that wasn't the worst. Fitch made me phone every goddamn hostile, irate lawyer in town to try and explain the public challenge to match or better our firm's contribution. *And* the fucking judges. They were spitting blood, standing on their dignity. Old Monkman, who it seems I have to appear before every second week now, didn't believe me. I know he didn't. He hasn't ruled in my favor in months now. I couldn't get a word in edgewise with him. Kept calling me a buffoon with no regard for the credibility of the profession, or respect for his office.''

If I had a short memory I might have felt sorry for Benny at that moment. But that bastard had screwed me more than once in the past. The summer of 1968, unknown to me, he stashed a half-kilo of grass in my suitcase when we returned from a weekend spent in Minneapolis/St. Paul catching a Twins' home stand. In 1968 a person could go to jail for a very long time for a half-ki. Benny always maintained there had been nothing to worry about — that I looked 4-H enough not to be bothered at the border. The son of a bitch.

I splayed my fingers across my chest. ''And you believe that I, Ed, am the author of your misfortunes?'' I often talk like this to Benny. That is, I adopt a declamatory style with a whiff about it of the nineteenth century and the Old Bailey. Lawyers today lack the elegance and eloquence which were once their chief distinction and ornament. Lo, the glory has departed.

"You're fucking right, asshole. But better you put it this way: I *know* you are. I've got the goddamn proof. That's why ever since the mail was delivered this morning it's suddenly in your interest to start paying me back the fifteen hundred bucks you owe me, prick."

"I see. So that's how it is."

"That's how it is." Benny was enormously pleased with himself. He tickled and teased his ice cubes with his swizzle stick. "The shoe pinches now it's on the other foot, doesn't it?"

Benny is a poor winner and an obscene gloater. I thought for a time, taking rapid, peckish sips of my Scotch. "Let me make sure I understand you completely," I said. "Your overheated imagination has cooked up a scenario in which I scribble, then fire off nasty notes which embarrass, confound, and otherwise make your existence miserable. Is that correct so far?"

"You got it."

"And you are convinced you have proof? This proof being a signature on a letter, said signature on said letter to be analysed presumably by a handwriting expert and pronounced my very own, bearing the characteristic and unmistakable penmanship of Ed?"

"Right again."

"Let us hypothesize, Benny," I invited. "Let us deduce the character from the deed. Let me ask you this: Would the unprincipled creature who would descend to such low, mean, cunning tricks be likely to incriminate himself by signing such a letter?"

Benny squinted, an involuntary reaction to the birth of painful thoughts. "What're you getting at?"

"Or would he be more likely," I proposed, "to prowl the beer parlors of 20th Street and find there some drunken destitute with broken shoes and a dewdrop hung upon the end of his nose who would gladly sign his own death warrant for a five-spot? Let alone sign Benjamin R. Ferguson with a flourish at the bottom of an empty page."

"You didn't."

"Of course I didn't. That's what I've been saying all along."
But I smiled as if I had.

"That's your handwriting."

"Let me assure you that it isn't."

"You fucking creep."

"And I'm quite satisfied, Benny, that you won't risk discovering whether it is my handwriting or not."

All I'd have had to do was stick Benny in a sleigh, redden his nose a bit, and I'd have had the very picture of Bonaparte hightailing it out of the suburbs of burning Moscow. Defeat writ large.

"So," I said, "with these little misunderstandings cleared away I think we can proceed to a happier topic. How would you like to lend me your car?"

"You're insane."

I explained to him that I wouldn't have dared ask for such a favor except in the most extraordinary circumstances. I did my best to make clear to him why I felt I had to find Victoria and how I intended to do it. I also pointed out that public transportation and taxis were obviously unsuited to my purpose.

Benny sat with a glacial air throughout my speech.

"As you can see, I've got to get my hands on a car right away and find her. So naturally I thought of you."

"Goddamn it, doesn't anybody who ever crossed your path get a moment's peace? Who the hell do you think you are, coming to me and asking for a car? After what you did?"

"It's not who I am, it's who you are. You're a man with three vehicles."

"Rent a car, asshole. Talk to Avis, not me."

"I can't rent one. I forgot to renew my driver's licence. They won't rent me a car."

"Jesus, isn't that typical. No driver's licence."

"Victoria used to do all those sorts of things. I lost the habit. It slipped my mind. So hang me. I'm guilty."

"You expect me to loan you my BMW, which you will probably promptly total, and I'll find myself with no insurance because the prick driving my car had no licence? Dream on, dreamer. No fucking way."

"I'm not asking for the BMW. Give me Janice's Pinto. Or your Land Rover."

"No."

"I need a car, Benny."

"No way."

"I'll leave you alone for the rest of my life. I swear."

"Do everybody a favor. Leave us all alone. Or at least leave poor Victoria alone for a start."

"Don't you listen? I told you she wanted to talk to me."

"Note the past tense. *Wanted.* She's doing a lot to attract your attention now, isn't she?"

"I let her down. I didn't listen."

"So what's new? I've watched you operate for years. It's the story of your life."

"Listen to me, Benny, I've only got so much patience."

He interrupted me, leaned abruptly across the table, pushed his face into mine. "No, you listen to me," he said harshly, "because I've only got so much time and you've had all of it you're ever going to get. You've just run out of my time, Ed. We're finished. I don't want to ever see you again. Understand?"

I didn't answer.

"But I've got some parting words of wisdom," he said. "I'm going to tell you something, you son of a bitch, that you don't seem to be able to figure out for yourself. Have you looked in a mirror lately? You look like shit. I'll bet you aren't eating and I'll bet you aren't sleeping."

He happened to be right on both those counts.

"You're running all over goddamn town like a chicken with its head cut off looking for somebody who doesn't want to be found. You're going down a bad road, man. You get yourself physically run down you've got no resistance to these emotional upsets. You blow things out of proportion at the best of times. Anybody has dealings with you knows that much. You better stop it right now or it'll be last time all over again. My advice to you is stay out of everybody else's life and take care of your own. Get some sleep. Eat something.''

"What do you mean, last time?''

"You know what I mean. Fifth floor, University Hospital.''

"You don't know anything about last time. What do you know about last time?''

"I know enough to know you were in a bad way, man.''

"You don't know anything.''

"I went to visit you.''

"Like hell you did.''

"I *saw* you, Ed. Sitting in the day room like an old man in this plaid housecoat and a pair of carpet slippers two sizes too big. Don't tell me what I saw.''

"You never saw anything.''

"Jesus Christ, they had you so doped you didn't know who you were, or where you were. You were a fucking mess, man. Staring at this TV screen, lighting one cigarette off another, your pyjama flies open and your dork hanging out. You didn't even know you were hanging a rat. I had to cover you up. That's where you were at. I didn't think you were coming back to the land of the living.''

"Shut up.''

"Don't let that happen again, Ed. Take care of yourself.''

"You fucking prick. Give me a goddamn car.''

"Ed, nobody but nobody in their right mind is going to give you a car.''

He stood up and put some money on the table. "If you're crying,'' he said, "you better get a hold of yourself. The waitress is coming to clear the table.'' Then he went out.

The more I think about it, the more I see that Benny's position is essentially correct. None of those people I know, those people I marched with, for whose children Victoria and I bought silver christening mugs, whose furniture I helped move into successively larger and more gracious homes, will lend me a car. In the last ten years I've proved myself a bad risk, a man on the margin, a doubtful character.

On the other hand I have a carrot to dangle before Rubacek's nose. He wants something from me. Nobody else does.

I find his telephone number on the class list. We exchange pleasantries. I ask if he has a car. He does. A '71 Grand Prix, he tells me.

"I think we can make a deal," I say.

NINE

Rubacek hurried right over. He was here by three o'clock, almost ready to do my bidding. However, he drew the line at loaning me his car outright. Instead, he offered to chauffeur me wherever I wanted to go. Nobody, it seems, touches his purple Grand Prix but Stanley. In the end his persistence paid off on all counts. He drove the car and I agreed to help him with his book.

From the beginning Rubacek had been only looking for a collaborator. When the first session of COCWE was concluded, he had stridden up to me at the front of the classroom and said: "I'm in the market for a writing pro. Maybe you're interested? I mean, you're the only reason I signed up for this bullshit — that is so's I could make contact with a writing pro. You could help with like the grammar, you know? That's all. I don't want the style changed. Keep how I think about feelings and life just how I wrote her down here." An authoritative, spatulate forefinger emphatically tapped the bundle of dirty paper trussed up in cord.

Stanley takes neither a polite nor an impolite no for an answer. In the weeks following he proved practically impossible to dodge. Fleeing down hallways in the Extension Division I could hear the steel clickers on Rubacek's shoe heels ringing in pursuit, his voice pitched high in entreaty. "Perfessor! Perfessor! Wait up!"

Too often overtaken, I tried to vary my escape routes. One week I beat him around a turn in the stairs and, momentarily out of his ken, ducked into a washroom. There I waited a decent interval, seated in a stall, pants hung around my ankles. I was not discovered. After the next class I hid again, admiring my guile and my fat white shins blazing in the light of the overhead fluorescent tubing. Foreshortened by my perspective they looked like Ionian pillars.

But Rubacek, losing sight of his prey, had doubled back. The door of the washroom banged open, eased itself shut with a pneumatic sigh; familiar-sounding heels rang on the floor. He entered the neighboring stall.

"I recognized your shoes," he said, striking up a conversation. "I trained myself to be like observant. It's the only way to survive some places."

"Who is this?" I said, attempting to alter my voice.

"Stanley, perfessor."

It was hopeless. "Don't call me that. I'm not a professor."

"You're the boss."

The gravid feeling I had nursed through two hours of class had withered in my bowels due to his neighborly proximity, making me petulant. "What do you want, Rubacek?" I asked sharply. I felt self-conscious, too, throwing my voice over a cubicle partition. The tiles, the mirrors, the porcelain emptiness magnified our voices eerily.

"I was wondering, maybe you give some more consideration to my proposition what I made last week?"

"No."

"You can't ask me to go better'n 60-40."

"I'm not asking you to do anything, Stanley."

"After all, 60-40 is fair. It's only fair I should get extra for, what you call, the trouble I put in it. Heart and soul is what I mean. All you got to do is grammar, spelling, and like punctuation."

"I don't have time. I have other commitments."

"What's this commitments? Don't have time? You don't want a piece of action might go Book-of-the-Month Club? Get serious."

"I am serious. I'm a very serious person."

A pause. "You got paper on your side?"

"What?"

"Over there. You got paper? The thing is empty here."

I passed the necessary under the partition.

"Thanks. Take my word. You can't lose. Let's say 60-40 and 10 per cent of — what you call — subsidiary rights. Outside of movie and TV. I got to have artistic control over stuff in that respect because of . . . well, you know, personal type of thing, image questions. And your name goes on the book cover, too. Right under mine and in a little smaller type, so it'll be Stanley Rubacek with — and then your name, see?"

The peculiar thing is that all that time Rubacek was hounding me I never once inquired what his book was about. I suppose the explanation is that I just wasn't interested. He had never dropped any hints in class about it; in fact, Stanley had insulted the other members of COCWE mightily by a blunt refusal to read from his manuscript. "No offence to nobody in particular, or general," he had said, "but I feel maybe I got a top seller here and I don't want my best concepts lifted."

I had a vague notion it might be a work of science fiction. I say this because I think I recall Rubacek toting a paperback copy of *Dune* to class which he read with no apparent attempt at conceal-ment when Dr. Vlady favored us with an instalment from his novel. Not very strong evidence certainly, but somehow, over time, it grew to the status of a conviction. A conviction which, of course, was erroneous.

Actually I should have known better. For one thing Stanley doesn't resemble a bit any of the aficionados of S-F I've known. I mean, there's no battery of colored pens clipped in his shirt pocket. Nor is he weird in the other acceptable way. All S-F types who've crossed my path have fallen into two categories. They look either like astronauts or like Frank Zappa.

Rubacek, on the other hand, is the boy who occupied a seat at the back of your grade ten classroom with monumental indifference, met twenty years later. The baby-face voted cutest at the pyjama parties of 1964-65 has, with time and the acquisition of a poorly fitting upper plate, taken on the mildly ugly look of a chow. His hair is thinning, too, and to compensate, Stanley has swept a mousy-blond wing of hair from the left side of his head up and over the dome of his skull. Pink scalp shows between its strands.

His body, however, shows no middle-aged sag, no flabby thickening. It is energetic, hard, heavily muscled. It has been cared for. He looks a little odd, as if time had attacked him only from the shoulders up.

Stanley Rubacek produces the impression of a man who has never recovered from early vanity. Which is all to the good, since his self-absorption keeps him from inquiring too closely into my affairs. After I had explained that we were undertaking a search for my wife, and that she might be registered in a hotel under an assumed name, he only asked: "Is she shacked up with some guy?" When I told him no, he didn't ask anything more. That apparently satisfied his curiosity.

By four o'clock we'd completed the details of our bargain, shifted my box of survival gear from the moribund Fiat to the Grand Prix, and were tooling through Quadrant 1 in search of my wife. Stanley drove with special care. His mouth prim, he navigated the length of 8th Street, weaving the car from lane to lane. We headed east this time. The car was filled with the artificial scent of pine forest. Once he firmly reprimanded me for dropping ashes from my cigarette on the floor.

I sat huddled in my parka against the door. It had been a long time since I'd been chauffeured, been a passenger, not since the second year of our marriage when Victoria's father gave us a 1965 Ford Galaxie. I hadn't wanted to accept the car but Victoria had prevailed. She said her father couldn't understand how a married couple could ride bicycles.

As a matter of principle I refused to drive the car. Still, on hot summer evenings it used to carry us out of the sweltering city and into the country. Victoria loved the twilight fields, loved them in that hour when the sky goes slaty and the new grain suddenly looks greener, luminously greener, than ever it does in the sun, and rolls in the evening breeze like a jade sea. We drove with the windows down, a tepid roar of wind keeping us silent, snapping my shirt collar, whipping our hair, filling the car with the nostalgic smell of possible rain.

I watched the darkness concentrate first in the land, then in the sky. When it was truly night, Victoria would switch the head-lights on and drive a little farther, then reluctantly turn the car around in the middle of a deserted road, where we'd discover a great yellow July moon risen at our backs.

What do I want to say to her, after all? To tell her to choose happiness? Victoria always believed in it above all else. Yes, for her there should be no more compromises. I want to tell her that.

Suddenly Rubacek said: "*Society's Revenge: The Stanley Rubacek Story.* How's that for a title?"

"What?"

I was taken aback. This was entirely unexpected. "Don't tell me this book is your goddamn memoirs?"

"The story of my life. It has an uplift angle. Quite upbeat. How a man came back from hell."

I was suddenly worried. "Just what kind of hell are we talking about, Stanley?"

"Incarceration."

"Prison? You mean prison?"

"Yeah."

"Well."

"I knew you'd understand," said Rubacek, "being a writer, being educated. Most wouldn't. Some don't understand society's responsibility for a case like me. I mean, I see this book as my way of getting back some of what society took from me, you know? Not that money could ever repay me. But look at that Norman Mailer character. What'd he make on that book about Gilmore? Same topic basically as my book. What'd he make, I ask you?"

I declined to volunteer a guesstimate of Mailer's gross on Gilmore.

"Did you read that?" asked Stanley. "How'd he know Gilmore was thinking that and then he was thinking this? He don't *know* that. I thought that was some kind of nerve. The guy is dead and Mailer says Gilmore thought about pussy, pardon my French. But Gilmore can't argue back for himself, can he? He can't say, pussy my eye!"

"Good point."

Rubacek was just getting warmed up on the topic of authorial outrages. "Yeah, well, Mailer's book was shit but that one by the Frenchman with the butterfly tattoos was worst. What a bunch of bullshit. And they went and made a movie about him. Steve McQueen and that scrawny guy was in it, what's his name."

"Dustin Hoffman?"

"Yeah him. Was he blown off the screen or was he blown off the screen by big Steve? I guess he was." Rubacek allowed himself a mournful pause in his monologue. "There was a loss to the industry. I loved that man in *Bullitt*. And in *The Great Escape*? Simply outstanding. That was a movie. Steve and Charlie Bronson in the same picture. They ought to have charged double price." He shook his head. "That Bronson has a physique. Unreal. How old is he now? He's got to be fifty. Fifty and a physique like that. Shows what you can do, eh?"

I nodded agreement. What had Stanley been in for? How did one go about raising the question of what he had been in for?

Meanwhile Rubacek was free-associating. The question came out of the blue. "If you was to get some actor to portray your life in like a drama or movie or television special, whatever, who'd you pick?"

"I don't have the faintest idea, Stanley."

"Come on, *think*."

As five o'clock approached, the traffic had grown heavier. It crawled or halted in sluggish response to the change in the signals. The light was almost gone, the snow turned to pewter.

"Well?" demanded Rubacek.

"Charles Laughton."

I don't believe he caught the name. In any case the question was posed merely to provide himself with an opportunity. He continued to ramble.

"My all-time five to represent me would be like: Numero uno, Charlie Bronson. A close second, Steve McQueen. Then Clint Eastwood. Number four, Burt Reynolds. Fifth, Elvis. Surprised?"

"Should I be?"

"You didn't notice nothing funny about the list?"

I didn't reply.

Rubacek smiled. "Can't guess, eh? Well, they're in reverse order of handsomest. Like you'd figure I'd want the handsomest guy to play me. Like Elvis was the best-looking and then Burt, but they're number five and number four. But I figure I've got to play rugged, so I go with Charlie Bronson."

"Makes sense."

"Of course, McQueen was blond, like me."

"Makes sense, too."

"Anyway, I don't see how *Society's Revenge: The Stanley Rubacek Story* can miss," he said. "It's a very popular subject, crime."

"True."

"No offence to you, perfessor, but the guy I'd really like to have helped me on *The Stanley Rubacek Story* is the little jam tart used to be on Merv Griffin all the time years ago. The guy with a voice like Porky Pig without the stutter."

"Truman Capote?"

"Right. That's him."

"He could be difficult to persuade. You wouldn't get Mr. Capote for a couple of rides in a '71 purple Grand Prix."

"Well, yeah, didn't I guess. I like the one he done, *Cold Blood*. They made a movie out of that starring Robert Blake of *Baretta* fame. That's a guy with a good bod, that Robert Blake. And as I said, the book was no slouch either. It was pretty good how it went into the criminal mind and explains how a bad home life and a lack of a structured environment and all that can lead to crime. A structured environment is so important. What do you think?"

"I suppose it is. If your parole officer says so."

"A lot of my problems," Stanley said, "stemmed from having a lack of a structured environment in my formative years."

"Ah."

"So that's why I write every day. To build dedication. The way I look at it, it's like a muscle. You build dedication up like a muscle — by exercising it. What do you think of that one?"

"Very good."

"I put that one in *The Stanley Rubacek Story*, although I thought maybe I should send it to *Reader's Digest* for 'Quotable Quotes'. What do you think?"

"I don't know, Stanley."

"Jesus, I get a kick out of Q.Q. When I was incarcerated I thought up hundreds of sayings like that, and I sent a lot to *R.D.* But they never took any."

I unscrewed the cap of my thermos. "Your return address may have influenced editorial decisions." I took a drink of cold, bitter coffee and rum, then offered it to Stanley.

"What's that?"

"Rum and coffee."

"Not when I'm driving."

"Sound policy."

I drank again. We drove on.

At last it was truly night. The sky was a shiny, bituminous black. On the other side of the boulevard the cars advanced towards the river, metallic skins glittering, headlight beams skating on their sleek surfaces. Everyone in full flight for home. I was gripped by conventional nostalgia.

"I think you and me are hitting it off," observed Stanley. "Myself, I like a high grade of company." He reflected a moment. "I put that down to my intelligent quotient. They tested it, you know. They said I got no . . ." he hesitated, recalling the phrase, " 'impediment to success'."

"Great. Glad to hear it."

"You know what your intelligent quotient is?"

"No."

"They told me what mine is. Wanna guess?"

"No."

"How come?"

"I don't care to."

"Why?"

"Because if I guess too low you'll be insulted. If I guess too high you'll be embarrassed to say it's lower. That's why."

"Not me. Go on, guess."

"Fuck off, Stanley."

"Okay, you win. It's 125." He enunciated the numerals very carefully, one, two, five. Like Mission Control, Houston. "But they said they could be off ten points. Like on a good day I might have scored higher. Which means I could be 135.'' One, three, five.

He waited for comment. I offered none. Finally he said: ''Any idea what genius is?''

''The infinite capacity for taking pains?''

''No, I mean like how many points.''

''No idea.''

''140.'' One, four, zero. Another pause to allow me to voice the obvious inference. I didn't.

''I'm only five points short,'' he said at last.

''It must be discouraging, missing by so little.''

''I don't think about it,'' said Stanley.

''Still,'' I said.

''If you want to know,'' he said, ''I got in a lot of trouble in jail because of my intelligent quotient. I found it hard to relate to a lot of the guys in there. We weren't wired for one another. Not like you and me. We get along because our intelligent quotients resemble each other. I'd guess you were about 135 too,'' he said judiciously.

''Stanley, you're making me blush.''

''No, I mean it. I been studying you. You're at least 135 — maybe higher. That ain't nothing to sneeze at.''

''Well, Stanley, you've got a nice intelligence quotient yourself.''

''I don't think about it. Really, what's a high intelligent quotient.''

I pointed. ''Next right. Up there. The Travelinn.''

''Believe me,'' said Stanley, beginning to wrestle the wheel, ''*The Stanley Rubacek Story* got to be a success. On account of compatibility. Ours I mean.''

''Not to mention a combined I.Q. of two, seven, zero,'' I said, bouncing on my seat as Rubacek took the Travelinn speed bump a little too impetuously.

Rubacek is asleep in my bed. And I sit at the kitchen table, an insomniac. It's three o'clock in the morning. I'll give him another three hours of oblivion and then roust him out. After all, it was his idea to sleep here to ensure an early start in the morning, not mine. I've got to watch that bastard or he'll take me over.

One thing is certain. I'm not going to get any shut-eye tonight. That's a forlorn hope.

This happens whenever I get worried. I inherited insomnia from my old man. I wonder if he is still sitting up half the night fretting about his angina. It was his angina pectoris that scared him out of his business and led him to retire at fifty-nine. The doctor gave him a whole list of do's and don'ts. Don't walk in the wind, he told him. "Ed," Pop said to me, "how do you not walk in the wind in this part of the world?" So he packed up and left for Texas after a winter of sitting up nights at the kitchen table drinking mugs of cocoa and eating buttered soda crackers.

That winter my mother was always phoning me in tears. "He's not himself, Eddy. All he talks about is regrets. 'Why didn't I take more holidays?' he asks me. 'What'd I knock myself out for? For this thing in my chest, doesn't let me sleep?' "

Yet now that he's retired he seems happy enough. Is he? I think so. He sends me snapshots every several months, plays whist at the Snowbirds' Socials, eats potato salad and cold cuts every day. "It's like a picnic," he wrote in one of his letters. "Every day a picnic."

I feel like shit. Too much booze and too little sleep. It's the same every time. After a couple of hours' hard drinking my body revolts and the booze starts sweating out of me. My shirt's soaked through. I ought to put the Scotch back in the cupboard so I don't finish off the bottle. I won't, though. Put it back, that is.

I cool my burning face by laying one cheek, then the other, on the Arborite top of my kitchen table. A childhood stratagem remembered from the hottest summer days. Then there's the notorious all-body cool. I used to get a slap when my mother caught me clasping our Frigidaire in an embrace, pudgy body pressed to the cool, smooth surface, marring it with sweat.

It's so quiet I can hear the fridge making its trickling sounds, like a stream running under ice.

How long can a person go completely without sleep? When I was getting sick, I went for weeks on just a few hours a night. But I did sleep. Some.

Three or four days without sleep? Could a person last that long? Sleep deprivation is the preferred method of secret police all over the world. Keep the prisoner awake around the clock. Make him stand with his arms extended at shoulder height.

I stand up and try it. Time passes. It begins to hurt, high in the sockets of the shoulders, deep beneath the blades of the back. Now the sweat pops. I watch the second hand crawling around the face of the clock on the wall. Arms vibrating with effort, I tell myself I'll hold the position until 3:30 a.m., exactly. Like Stanley says, you build dedication up like a muscle, by exercising it.

TEN

On my map Quadrant 2 is a rectangle cast in red ink, a rectangle that bites an elbow out of the river and boxes the downtown. Now at seven-thirty in the morning I see it risen in relief like a bar graph plotted against a black sky, see it with the hallucinatory lucidity produced by sleeplessness. The high-rises, brightly striated with electric light, stand shoulder to shoulder and shimmer.

The bridge Rubacek and I are crossing is tilted like a man in bed, one end resting slightly higher than the other, head pillowed on the river bluffs of the western bank, the bluffs I haunted in my illness. Down this gentle incline Stanley's Grand Prix smoothly slips. At the bottom of the grade his foot stutters on the brake; he deftly switches lanes and merges his car with the traffic rushing into an underpass below the bridge. The inside of the car fills with the noise of engines echoing under the concrete arches and grey concave belly above, then the reverberations suddenly die behind us. To our left the white skin of the river flashes through gaps in a parapet of snow pushed up by snow ploughs and glazed blue by street lights. As the car accelerates into the long curve that climbs the river bank a new angle of vision shows me a cloud of stars. The road suddenly levels, the stars and their furious white light disappear as quickly as they sprang into view.

The car comes to a halt at a stop sign. Ahead of us there is the long canyon of a city street. Traffic lights blink green, amber, red, and the infrequent pedestrian fractures the beams of car headlights with scissoring legs as he hurries across an intersection.

"You ought to eat breakfast," says Rubacek reproachfully. "It's the most important meal of the day."

He has been harping on this theme since six-thirty. I don't answer him. I'm learning that a man who has come back from hell, a man trying to build a successful life, is a righteous pain in the ass.

Rubacek starts the car away from the stop sign. "And that cereal you got," he continues, "that Cocoa Puffs, that stuff is like eating sugar. Why'nt you buy some eggs and have a nice slice of whole wheat and a little orange juice instead of them Cocoa Puffs?"

"You don't want to eat my Cocoa Puffs, don't eat my Cocoa Puffs."

"There wasn't nothing else, was there? I didn't see nothing else to eat."

"There was a can of Mini Raviolis. Why didn't you eat that, Rubacek?"

"That's as bad as Cocoa Puffs. Maybe worst."

Car exhaust lies knee-deep at the intersections. It creeps uncertainly this way and that, nuzzling the ground, fraying at the edges.

"Look," I say, "if you eat anything with a glass of milk it's nutritious. You could eat the goddamn cardboard box the Cocoa Puffs came in and a pint of milk would make it a nutritious meal. You had milk, didn't you?"

"You need fibre. There's no fibre to speak of in Cocoa Puffs or Mini Raviolis."

"I don't suffer that complaint myself. I don't need fibre. I'm regular as regular can be. You could set your watch by me."

Rubacek deftly switches subjects. "I bet you don't get no exercise neither," he accuses.

"No, I don't. And I don't want any either, thank you very much. Especially if by exercise you mean that gruesome display I was treated to this morning. What in hell were you doing, Rubacek?"

"Five-BX. It's scientific."

"You tell that to old McMurtry downstairs. You tell him it's scientific when he complains about your heavy-hoofed prancing shaking the plaster loose from his ceiling. It's an old building and he's an old man. My intention is peaceful co-existence with my neighbors, Rubacek. Try and keep that in mind."

"You're getting to a stage in life when you might be thinking about tuning up the bod. An ounce of prevention is like a pound of cure. Right?"

"I'm also getting to a stage in this conversation when I might be thinking about homicide." Oops. Bad word, homicide, given present company.

Rubacek continues unperturbed. "Stress and overweight. Double threat. All the magazines say so."

"All right, I didn't eat breakfast because I'm dieting. Now if you'd shut up we'd take care of the stress business and both of us could be gladdened by my vastly improved prospects for longevity."

"We could do calisthenics together in the morning. It makes it easier for the beginner to get started, having a friend encourage him. Gets to be a routine. You want to do it?"

"You won't be around long enough for it to become habit-forming, you and I capering in unison. Forget it."

"There's lot of programs on the TV could keep you active and trim after I go."

"No."

"I can't understand how an intelligent person — "

"Probable quotient, 135."

"How an intelligent person who knows all about heart disease and like that wants to kill himself."

"You're a smoker, Rubacek. You aren't lily pure."

"I'm stopping first day of March. I wrote a promise to my diary. No more foreign substances in my body. I done enough of that in my time. It leads to nothing but trouble."

Promise to his diary. Who writes promises to their diaries? And why does my path have always to run across these types?

"I like that. No more foreign substances. What's that supposed to mean? What's a foreign substance, Stanley? No more

Brie? No more Camembert, Vienna sausages, Perrier?''

"Jesus, look who didn't get no sleep. Look who got out the wrong side of the bed. You know what I mean. Like drugs and alcohol. What you call — foreign substances.''

"I didn't get out of the wrong side of the bed because I couldn't. Somebody was in it.''

"You offered.''

"And another thing, Rubacek, if you want to be a writer strive for precision of expression. Avoid clichés.''

"Like what?''

"Like 'foreign substances' or, 'breakfast is the most important meal of the day'.''

"Well, isn't it?''

"Isn't what?''

"Isn't it the most important meal of the day?''

"Shut the fuck up, Rubacek.''

A block further down the street I can see the King Edward Hotel, all dirty-red-brick charm and tea-cosy respectability. Its lounge was the favorite after-work watering hole of Victoria and her girlfriends. Earlier this morning, when Rubacek and I divided between us the downtown hotels we would scout, I made certain that it was on my list. I am hopeful that familiarity may have drawn Victoria to the premises. On the other hand she may have steered clear of any place where she might bump into friends.

I spot an empty parking space across the street from the King Edward and direct Stanley to it. He swings the car to the curb and cuts the engine in front of a delicatessen with mahogany-colored sausage coils hung in the window. The sight makes me regret my uneaten breakfast. The cooling motor ticks in the cold and I feel a recurrence of the anomie that often accompanies exhaustion. This great heaviness of body and spirit, this piercing sense of dissociation, has been alternating with peaks of restlessness and irritability since four o'clock this morning. I dry-scrub my face with my hands, roll the muscles of my neck under the balls of my thumbs, light a cigarette.

"We're looking for a blue Volkswagen with a busted fender,'' says Stanley. I glance at him as I shake a match out. He isn't asking a question but rather preparing the ground for something else.

"Yes," I say. Rubacek is staring straight ahead through the windshield. My eyes follow his. What's caught his attention? I see nothing particularly arresting. Two women hurry down the sidewalk. Hips swinging under bulky coats, they occasionally punctuate their long-striding march by a skip and a hop that indicate the cold has stung them into a desperate trot. One of them has a rugby scarf pinned to the lower half of her face with a mittened hand. Canadian purdah.

I turn back to Rubacek and realize his attention is not being held by this scene. He's merely avoiding looking me in the face. "I was thinking last night that I could be getting myself into bad trouble helping you," he observes.

"You were, were you?"

"I don't ask you why you want to find her or nothing like that," continues Rubacek in apologetic tones, "but I'd appreciate some idea of what you're going to do with her when you get her."

"I don't know what you're trying to get at, Rubacek. I told you before, I want to talk to her."

"Begging my pardon all to hell," he says, "but that's what my old man used to tell my old lady from the doorstep when she locked him out—all he wanted to do was talk to her. Lots of guys say that. It's mostly a different story if they get inside. And if you don't mind me saying so, you're going to one hell of a lot of trouble for a little conversation."

"Meaning what, Stanley?"

"Meaning I don't want no part of, what you call, a domestic dispute. If you're going to talk to her by hand I don't want no part of it. I can't afford to get mixed up in that kind of thing. Even if my book was to suffer," he adds weightily.

"For Christ's sake, Rubacek," I exclaim, aghast, "are you suggesting I'm going to beat her up? Is that what you're suggesting?"

For the first time Rubacek turns his shallow, pale eyes on me.

"I'm not suggesting diddly squat, perfessor. I'm asking."

"I don't strike women, Stanley. You're talking to a civilized man."

Claims to civilization don't appear to cut any ice with Rubacek. "Excuse me for mentioning it, perfessor, but you don't look real civilized. In fact, you kind of put me in mind of Alley Oop or like that. You got the look of a guy might take a lady for a drag by the hair and so on."

I lean forward and crook my neck at the rear-view mirror. He's right. Two piggish inflamed eyes squint out of pouches of flesh, a dirty, raspish stubble makes my jaws heavy and brutal. I barely have time to take in this dark, sinister image when it begins to dissolve in the warm mist of my breath; blotches of vapor spread like a blight and consume my face. I fall back against the seat and say the one thing I suspect will convince him. "My wife's pregnant, Stanley. I'm not going to start knocking her around when she's pregnant. Do you think I want to hurt my kid?"

The King Edward Parkade is stacked beside the hotel in four levels. Climbing the stairs to the second of these allows me to experience what exercise in these temperatures can do. Breathing through my mouth makes my teeth ache and fills my lungs with a parching coldness. My heart jolts under my parka. I stop to cough. Too many cigarettes, too fat.

I cling to the railing collecting my breath. There is frost on the steel and the cold creeps into the fingers of my glove like a stain. The entire stairway is exposed to the wind and is treacherous with ice. A floor below I slipped and damn near broke my neck on a patch of glassy, yellow ice left by a pissing drunk. Now a biting, twisting wind is burning my face and moulding my trousers to my legs.

I pat my parka and hear the comforting jingle of car keys. Already numb with cold I congratulate myself for persuading Rubacek to give me his second set so I can return to the car for fortifying nips of coffee and rum. Without alcohol and caffeine I'd be a goner before noon.

The cold sets me moving again before my heart quiets; it is climb or freeze. A dozen more steps bring me to the second level of the parkade. I peer into a low-roofed cavern stinking of gas, dripped oil, and automobile exhaust where the parked cars wait like livestock in their stalls. As I walk among them panting, looking for a blue Volkswagen with a dented fender, I pat their cold flanks, sweep off bits of snow, rub away frost. Up and down the still ranks I go, swivelling my head from side to side as I search, my feet loud and abrupt under the low roof. Every few minutes cars arrive or depart while I briskly march through clouds of exhaust kindled by the embers of tail-lights, or lit in the sanctifying white blaze of headlights. So prophets once must have moved, wrapped in glorious effulgences.

As I step along I make a note to clean myself up. Benny criticized my unwholesome appearance yesterday and now Rubacek has done the same today. And I must admit that not only was the glimpse I caught of myself in the rear-view mirror unflattering, it was unsettling. Victoria would be most displeased if I were to present myself and plead my case looking like this. She cannot abide slovenliness.

Neither, apparently, can Rubacek. When I woke him this morning I saw that a lot of the junk I had scattered on the floor of my bedroom had been shovelled into a closet, and my books were stacked on my dresser top, a sheet of Kleenex marking my place in each. And he made the bed up very precisely, corners squared, blankets drawn drumskin-taut. I suppose they teach them that in prison.

Somehow I'm not entirely easy with Stanley. I don't exactly trust him. By that I don't mean I expect him to steal from me, or offer me violence. No. It's his attitude I distrust, his dead certainty that what he wants he'll get. He ought to have been my father's son. They'd have understood each other.

If Pop had said: "Dress to impress. Dress for success" to Rubacek as he did to me six years ago, Stanley would have had some idea of what he was trying to tell him, would have nodded enthusiastically in agreement with this sibylline message. I just went off to the job interview at the TV station knowing I was all

wrong in that godawful suit Pop had bought me. If I'd worn it
with confidence I might have had a chance. I might have projected
the image of a son of the soil. But all I could think of was how I
must look like Andy Devine. That's a difference between Rubacek
and me — the proper mental attitude.

I see it as a curse that I can understand so completely some
people, and others not at all. It keeps me off-balance. For instance,
why can't I find Victoria? After all these years I ought to be able
to guess what she'll do, but obviously I can't.

I have no idea what she'll decide about the baby. There's no
doubt that her desire for a child is strong, that she's a woman of
warm feelings. But I cannot also deny that Victoria has a strong
instinct for self-preservation, a will bent to assure her own
happiness. She will withhold herself just short of love if necessary.
And I'm not criticizing her, not at all. Weak people are no help to
anyone, are they?

At first I thought she had been hard when I went to pieces after
we returned from Toronto. I had expected her to follow me, to
cajole me, when I walked out of the kitchen and into the spare
room she had christened my "study". She did neither. She let
me go.

Maybe she'd decided that I was past helping, that if I could,
I needed to save myself. Perhaps she was right, because when I
walked through that door some part of me still saw it as a game in
which we were both participants. I still depended on her to draw
me back out of myself, to force me to continue. I was like a man
who can lean far back from the face of the cliff and surrender
himself to vertigo because he trusts the rope and the one who
anchors him. Victoria didn't plead with me. She let the rope go.

My "study". I had never wanted this study she created for me,
and had no notion of what I was expected to do in it. Certainly
nothing like what I did. But a husband happily lodged in his study
was one of those eccentric and implacable notions Victoria brought
to our marriage. I suppose I was meant to sit in there and write, or
tie flies, or carve duck decoys, or scratch the ears of a springer
spaniel — that is, conform to some manly configuration.

Instead, when I finally did enter I slammed the study door behind me, broke the light bulb so I wouldn't be tempted to switch it on, and fell on to the fold-away cot which had recently transformed the unused "study" into a "guest room". I stayed in there three days.

I can't remember what went on in that room, my inability being a consequence of shock treatments. There exists evidence of a kind, if I ever choose to consult it: the yellow sheets of paper I had clenched in my hands when I finally flung open the door and called for Victoria. She saved these to show to the doctors, and when they returned them to her she put them in the old jewellery box where all the documents (birth certificate, university degree, etc.) are kept which mark the milestones of my life. Some people might think this odd. I believe she put them there because she felt I ought to read them, although she never said as much. But by then they were part of a past I wanted to stay past.

Victoria never said much at all. She said that when I called to her I appeared incapable of crossing the threshold of the room. Standing just inside the door of my "study" I made an impulsive gesture of appeal and thrust out my arms, pieces of paper bristling from each fist, and said: "I've failed him. I'm afraid. I want a doctor."

I am climbing again. Three levels are behind me. The fourth, which is unroofed, lies under the dove-grey belly of a lightening sky. I emerge into weak sunlight and strong wind.

There are only five or six cars here on the roof; no one parks by choice in a place so unsheltered. Victoria's car is not among those scattered about.

I stand shivering on an asphalt surface striped with bold mustard lines, which are visible because the wind has swept the snow into a dune that rises up and curls over the eastern wall of the parkade. That's unsafe; at night a child could walk up it and over the edge.

I cross the roof, the tail of my nylon parka snapping at the backs of my knees in the wind. The snow of the dune is packed hard, easily capable of bearing even me. I edge up it, testing my weight as I go, rocking forward heel and toe until there is only air before me. Directly below, the street is still darkened by the shadows of buildings. In February the sun hugs the horizon in the way ancient seafarers kept to the coastline, sailing their ships in sight of land.

I remember Victoria shaving me before we left for the hospital. That is clear in my mind. The cream lay thick and smooth on my cheeks, white as the snow beneath my boots, but warm. She wanted me to be clean. I was in the bath. Victoria sat on the edge of the tub and sliced away the foam, dipped the safety razor in the cooling water, reaped another swath of soap and bristle, rinsed the blade with impatient shakes of her hand that shattered the surface of the water. Her other hand lay on the crown of my head, long, calm fingers steadying me. "It's all right," she said again and again. My arms lay heavy and lifeless in the tepid water. The soap on my cheeks was eroded by tears. The heat of her hand was salve.

If she is not here where I had expected her to be it may mean she has gone back to Peters. I'm not giving up. I want some sign from her before all this is over. I back down the drift very carefully, unwilling to turn my back on the broken arc of the city plumed with rising smoke.

ELEVEN

Is it possible that The Beast has saved my life? God, dropping off with the radio playing and the engine running. How long does it take someone to die of carbon monoxide poisoning? I couldn't have been asleep too long. I check my watch and find that it is eleven o'clock. It was no later than quarter to the hour when I parked.

I ought to be more careful. No, I *have* to be more careful when I'm this tired. I roll down my window an inch or two and let in an icy draft as a precaution. The morning sun glaring on the snowbanks burns my eyes, begins to incite a headache.

Was it a Pavlovian response on the part of my unconscious to The Beast's intro music that triggered me awake? I wouldn't want to feel that I owed him my life. Still, if it weren't for that blood-curdling tune I might have been found stretched out cold and blue.

I am sitting in Rubacek's car, on Anthony Peters's street. It is a fine old street, lavishly treed and lined with appropriately fine old houses which are within easy walking distance of the university. Professors' Row.

Directly across the street is Anthony's house. 918. I got the address from the book in the pay telephone booth. Fifteen minutes ago when I knocked at the door of 918 no one answered and I have decided to wait. His door-knocker is a brass lion head, the sort of thing Victoria would admire. Perhaps she even bought it, a garnish to domestic bliss. We never had the like.

I'm a little uneasy about having commandeered Rubacek's car.

However, it could hardly be considered theft if he gave me a set of
keys to it. Or could it? Anyway, I trust he'll be understanding
and not report it stolen. I suspect that ex-convicts have a disinclina-
tion to involve themselves with police under any circumstances
whatsoever. I devoutly hope so.

My speculations about Rubacek's probable course of action are
interrupted by The Beast. "Good morning one and all this frosty
February morn. My name is Tom Rollins and the program is 'A
Piece of Your Mind', the topical show that shuns no topic. Today
I have the very great pleasure of welcoming to our studios the
famous Californian clairvoyant Madame Sosostris."

I leave the radio on because I hope it will prevent me from
falling asleep again. The aimless, enthusiastic chatter continues,
Rollins pressing the woman on her claims to have extra-sensory
perception, and she assuring him that she does. "Experts" of
one kind or another are a staple of Rollins's show and this one
states that by tuning in to the "psychic emanations radiating from
someone's personal possession" she can draw a complete psychological profile of the object's owner. This gift, she wants everyone
to know, makes her an invaluable asset for a company choosing
among prospective personnel. She doesn't have to interview anyone,
merely fondle his lighter, or ring, or shoe perhaps. Also, Madame
Sosostris credits herself with being a "unique diagnostic tool in
the ever ongoing battle for mental health".

I am tired and I cannot bring my mind to fasten on the gibberish spilling from the radio. I wonder about Victoria's life in the
house across the street, her life with Anthony Peters. Has it
changed her?

It was about five years ago, some time after I was released from
hospital, that Victoria's and my life changed, that we began to
live differently. Until then Victoria had denied herself everything,
scrimping and saving for that trip to Greece we would never take.
Then I came apart and she had to bring us through all that.

When the pressure finally lifted, Victoria displayed the elation
of a survivor. She decided she was through with sacrifices. We
were going to have a baby and we were going to live a little, enjoy

ourselves. Greece was forgotten. She bought new clothes and
some jewellery, splurged on make-up. She enrolled in night classes,
threw herself into her work, joined a film society. She imagined us
on the move again.

While Victoria was occupied doing all this, I landed a job
teaching at the Community College and learned how to cook. In
no time at all I mastered pasta and proceeded to curries. On the
strength of my glamorous hobby we began to entertain in the
larger apartment we had rented.

Victoria seemed to want to be with people all the time. We saw
little of our old friends; she showed a preference for new faces,
people she'd met at work or at her night classes. Victoria was
excited by them because they saw qualities in her that had lain
undiscovered and dormant for years. She was a success again, as
she had been in high school. A promotion came at work and then
another. She was flying high, working and playing hard. I hosted
a Thanksgiving dinner for a dozen, a Hallowe'en costume party, a
Grey Cup party, then the Christmas season came. Her friends
began to get on my nerves. I asked myself if I was jealous. I
couldn't decide. The only thing I knew was that the amount of
smoke and noise these idiots made was appalling.

Victoria's soaring career prompted her to peer into the dark
nooks and crannies of mine.

"Somebody told me Cooper was looking for an administrative
assistant," she said to me one day.

"That's right."

"You should apply."

"Why?"

"There's room to move up in administration. There's nowhere
to go in teaching."

"Who wants to move?"

"God, Ed, you're twice as bright as Cooper."

"No argument there."

"Doesn't it bother you to see a man doing a job you could do
better?"

"I couldn't do it better."

"What do you mean?"

"I can't exude unction the way Cooper does. The balm that heals all wounds."

"I wish you wouldn't run away from a challenge."

"So said Lady Macbeth to her hubby."

"I can't stand to see you so aimless."

"I'm not aimless."

I didn't consider myself aimless. I was reading the *Journals* of Kierkegaard at work and Thomas Carlyle's *History of Frederick the Great* at home. Such books, like the prospect of death, concentrated the mind wonderfully.

Soon we were also at odds over the parties.

"Why can't we spend a little time alone?"

"By alone you mean that I should sit and watch you drink Scotch and read volume five of the life of some German despot."

"What the hell do you see in those people, Victoria?"

"I see my friends, Ed."

"God forbid that your husband should object to working his fingers to the bone feeding them."

"Don't start that. It's the *only* thing you do around here. You don't do laundry, you don't push a vacuum, you do nothing else."

"I'll do laundry."

"You'll do some hot hors d'oeuvres for Friday night after work. We're meeting here for drinks and then we're going out for dinner."

"Lawd be praise'! This ole house nigra doan have to serve Missy's dinner!"

"I'll be late. Give them drinks and hors d'oeuvres, Ed. *Hot* hors d'oeuvres."

They got hot hors d'oeuvres. Of course, they considered it a great joke and good, clean fun, but when Victoria came in and saw me she went pale with fury and then started to cry. I was moving among the crowd with a tray, wearing the cardboard bunny ears I'd made at work that afternoon. I was also naked except for the bathing trunks I'd pasted the cotton balls on to make a rabbit tail.

"Don't you have any pride!" she shouted. "You humiliate me and you humiliate yourself! In front of my friends!"

I'd gone too far again. The parties at our apartment stopped after that; Victoria met her friends elsewhere. I stayed home and read. We began to talk to each other as from a great distance. At times, though, we could still be surprised by happiness. I remember an afternoon I persuaded her to play hooky from work and we went to the racetrack, ate hot dogs, and made two-dollar bets. She was entranced by the gaiety and medieval splendor of the drivers' silks, the masked and blinkered horses and the flashing precision of their gaits. But even as I sat beside her and looked at her face lit with pleasure I remembered rumors of another man. Later that same year I joined her for ballroom-dancing lessons and we momentarily drew close in a staid, Viennese bourgeois intimacy that felt something like the beginning of a friendship.

But such pastimes could not heal our division. Success had returned to Victoria after an interval of some years. She had said to me once that she could not live without a sense of purpose and a sense of possibility. She had that sense of purpose in her work; now she was waiting on possibility.

Better not to think of that. Better to turn my attention to the radio, The Beast, and the clairvoyant from California who is finishing her explanation of how she determines a psychological profile from an object owned, or even merely touched, by the "subject of investigation".

"Amazing," says Tom when she has concluded. "As my listeners know, Madame Sosostris, I'm nothing more than a country boy, and country boys are by nature a suspicious lot. But who's to say? Stranger things have certainly happened and I wouldn't want to discredit anyone's claim to anything. We've got the Bermuda Triangle and all that craziness going on down there, and the evidence seems to point to spacemen having a hand in erecting the pyramids, and Uri Geller has been on Merv Griffin bending spoons with his mind. It seems to me that we have no idea of the ultimate potential of the human brain. All I say is: Who knows?"

Who knows indeed. And, as to bending spoons, Tom Rollins has bent one or two with his mind. Listening to him in the morning over Cocoa Puffs I've found that a number of tableware items have inexplicably contorted and twisted in my hands.

"What was it the great Bard said, Tom? There are more things in heaven and earth, Horace, than philosophy ever thought of," adds Madame.

"And that's likely true," says Tom, "but getting back to energy waves and personality and psychological analysis and so on. That really intrigues me. I wonder if you could give us an on-the-air demonstration? The other day I received a letter in the mail and I was wondering if you could profile the character of the man who sent it by immersing yourself in the energy waves of the envelope. And I say envelope because I don't want the contents of that letter to give you any clues."

Vague rustling of paper. "Well, Tom," says Madame Sosostris, "envelopes are particularly difficult because the sorting machines in post offices tend to rub off the energy waves."

"But could you try, Madame Sosostris?"

"Yes, Tom, I could. But without any guarantees as to complete, infallible, irrevocable accuracy."

"I understand, Madame. Nobody is asking you to do the impossible. Just let me pass the envelope over to you."

"Thank you, Tom."

An interval of expectant silence.

"Madame, are you getting anything?"

"Tom, the waves are very faint. I believe the postal machines have practically erased them. It's very difficult." Hesitation. "Maybe this is a friend of yours?"

"No," laughs The Beast, who finds the suggestion hilarious, "I'd hardly say that."

"Just as I thought. I had a sense of hostile emanations but they were quite feeble. They seem to be getting stronger now. Yes, I feel hostility coming off this envelope. Very definitely."

"Anything else?"

"A lot of hostility and . . ."

"Yes?"

"I'm not entirely one hundred per cent sure. Perhaps revenge?"

"I've got to admit it was that kind of letter."

"We're speaking about a very dark soul. The emanations are very, very black. This is a very vengeful person. Maybe even sick. Oh goodness, it's becoming overpowering! I feel like I'm choking!" A moment to recover, then, conversationally, "There's sure a lot of hate on this envelope."

"Male or female?"

"Could be either. Sex gender can't be determined from emanations."

"Oh."

"But I can say definitely that this human being's profile is sick and vengeful."

"Dangerous?"

"Could be if provoked. You can't be absolutely certain with this type of sick and vengeful person."

"Well, well," says The Beast, "this has all been very interesting and informative. As to the accuracy of Madame Sosostris's profile — why, I'll leave that up to the judgment of our listening audience. Yes, ladies and gentlemen, to you. Because the letter comes from an old friend of ours, the gentleman who regularly calls in to give yours truly, Tom Rollins, what for. How do I know it's him, you say? Well, Tom Rollins has his sources — sources which for the present shall have to remain confidential." The Beast decides to let Madame in on the private joke about the local maniac. "Maybe I ought to explain to Madame Sosostris. You see, Madame, I'm plagued by a man who imagines I've done him some wrong, or insulted him, or cast some kind of slur on his good name, or something of that kind. He regularly phones 'A Piece of Your Mind' — no matter what the day's topic is — and begins haranguing and harassing — "

"If I could just interrupt," says Madame Sosostris, "when I called this unfortunate individual sick, I should have been more specific and used the correct medical term. What I meant to say was that he is paranoid. There are very pronounced paranoid emanations coming from that envelope, believe you me. That guy is paranoid sick. A severe case."

"You don't have to sell me on that diagnosis, Madame. Paranoid is right. You wonder where these types get their strange notions. Over the past several months I don't know how many of my programs he's disrupted with his accusations and complaints. A real pain in the you-know-where. And now he's taken to writing letters to me. Very disturbing letters."

"It comes as no surprise to Madame Sosostris. Those are just about the darkest emanations I've felt in my entire clinical experience."

"Well, my experience with this individual has made me reflect. So it hasn't been altogether a write-off. In fact, I've found it quite thought-provoking. So much so I jotted down a few observations. That's why — right now — I'd like to take a moment to read an open letter addressed to this gentleman — and I use the word loosely. I sure hope he's listening."

The Beast cleared his throat. "Dear Aggrieved," he read, "this letter to you is about democratic rights. As you know, my little program, 'A Piece of Your Mind', only exists because we in Canada enjoy Freedom of Speech. To me, Freedom of Speech, along with a number of other Freedoms, is our most precious possession, more precious even than the clean air we breathe and the clean water we drink. In Canada we're free to criticize our government in the coffee shop, or state our opinion about last night's controversial TV show, or discuss the book that's made it to number one on the best-seller list without fear of reprisal from the Thought Police. It's this kind of freedom that's made our nation healthy and I, for one, would be willing to die to defend your right to speak up for what you believe in.

"But freedom, Dear Aggrieved, isn't the same thing as licence. In Canada licence is curbed by rules called laws. Now I'm not saying you aren't free to criticize Tom Rollins or his program as strongly as you please. I've been in the public eye for a long time and I've come to learn to expect criticism. There's an old saying: The tallest tree in the forest catches the most wind. And you can bet I've caught plenty of wind in my day. If you remember, a while back I came out strongly for seat-belt legislation at a time when it was pretty darn unpopular to do so, and I made enemies by going against the grain. And I'd do it again because I believe that the life of one child saved is worth any number of enemies.

"But, Dear Aggrieved, remember this. The word Freedom infers fair play and fair play is just another way of saying rules and rules are laws and we have them in Canada, don't forget. Now you break those laws when you threaten me and forge another man's name to a document. That isn't Freedom of Speech. It's something else. It's licence.

"I know who you are, sir. Be assured I know who you are. And be assured that if I receive another letter like the one I received the other day I'll make it warm for you. Like you, I'm a citizen, and like you I have rights. I have the right to live without fear of threats. I can't bend to your will or allow myself to be pushed around. As an electronic journalist I have the duty to promote a free exchange of ideas and opinions. I like to think of myself as an ideas broker and I like to think of ideas as the fuel, the gas, of democracy. I can't allow myself to be muzzled, because if I did, one voice of our democracy would be stilled. And one voice stilled is one voice too many.

"I think it's clear to my listeners what I stand for, what I've always stood for. What you might stand for nobody knows. So I'm appealing to you, Dear Aggrieved, to join the majority. Try to do something positive like the rest of us poor slobs. Don't brood on imagined wrongs and imagined insults. Help make this a better world. Don't retribute, *contribute*! Yours respectfully, Tom Rollins."

There is a dramatic pause to allow this all to gel in our minds. Madame Sosostris breaks the spell. "Beautiful. Just beautiful. And so constructive."

"I don't know," says The Beast, "maybe I'm way out of line here but I felt it needed saying."

In the next fifty minutes The Beast was treated to a multitude of calls of congratulation and numerous requests for a copy of "Dear Aggrieved". It had struck a chord in the greater public. A grade seven social studies teacher informed The Beast she often required her class to listen to "A Piece of Your Mind" because it was "contemporary issues oriented". She also wondered if he could supply her with a hundred copies of "Dear Aggrieved" for distribution to her pupils. Cynicism, she said, was rampant in the eighties.

The market for Rollins's epistle to Ed was so bullish that towards the end of his program The Beast confessed himself delighted to announce that the owner of station CKKX had made an unprecedented management decision to print "Dear Aggrieved" as a community service and provide copies at "less than cost to any listener who so desired them".

All the heady applause given The Beast's excursion into *belles lettres* unhappily tended to cast Madame Sosostris and her considerable talents in the shade. From the sound of her voice I was pretty sure The Beast had another Dear Aggrieved on his hands. But Madame bravely soldiered on and the last words were hers as she shouted into the microphone her mailing address in Anaheim, California, and the information that: "Madame Sosostris is available for psychological profile constructions at an entirely nominal fee via the U.S. Mail for those who cannot attend my seminar at the Holiday Inn, 2:30 p.m., Saturday afternoon, registration fee twenty dollars only!"

Now I wonder if I haven't hallucinated all of this. I must have, because this very minute, through the windshield of Rubacek's Grand Prix, I am watching myself, yes me, Ed, waddling up the walk of 918. What a queer sensation it is, too. A little like knowing the dream you are dreaming is a dream. I hold on to that sensation, savoring it, before I realize I ought to be made afraid by what I'm seeing. After all, this isn't a dream, is it?

Christ, what a morning. I press my forehead against the cold plastic of the steering wheel, trying to force the image clear out the back of my head. It resists eviction. I still see myself, huffing up the walk, glistening snow hip-deep to either side of me.

I open my eyes wide and there I am again, mounting the steps of the house. Ed, or my *doppelganger*, is panting steam which flies over my shoulder like rags of cheesecloth. A tan duffel coat is stretched taut over my backside.

It's the tan duffel coat which causes me to reconsider. I don't own one. This hallucination has no consistency. The thought strikes me that I am not imagining the fat man inserting the key into the lock of 918. Is it possible? Is this Anthony Peters? A *fat* Anthony Peters?

Good Lord, he's got to weigh as much as I do. He's gross. He must have his pants tailored at Canada Tent and Awning Ltd.

The door closes. Gone. The heartening vision is gone.

Was what I saw Peters? I light a smoke, unscrew the thermos cap and have another drink. I'm staring, and the snowbanks begin to twitch and shiver under the noonday sun like the muscles under the coat of a sleeping animal. I look away, squeeze my eyes shut against the harsh light.

If that was Peters, Hideous Marsha kept a choice tidbit to herself. She never even so much as hinted at what Victoria's latest playmate weighed in at. Victoria springing out of the frying pan and into the fire. My wife wallowing on the couch of shame with Moby Dick. I have another strange thought: the baby may look like me.

I take another snort from the thermos to jolt the faculties. What are the symptoms of snow blindness? I'll run a quick check. Eyes open and forward. White snow, blue sky, black elms. All correct. It's got to be Peters.

I have to see him close up, in the flesh. The car door swings open. Cold air. A scurry across the street. My mitten buried in the yawning maw of the lion, I begin knocking, the frozen air rings. Jesus, it's cold. He takes his sweet time.

The door opens. It's the man I saw and he is *obese*. This is no insubstantial airy *doppelganger*, this is real live meat and suet. He's got ten to fifteen pounds on me, easy. The way I can tell is the eyes. He has those little white bumps just below the lower lid that are symptoms of massive cholesterol build-up. When I bury the needle on the scale I have those.

And he buys his clothes too small. We have an optimist here. The waistband on his trousers is doubled over on itself, burying his belt, and he had to have shoehorned himself into that blazer. God, the man is an oink.

"Yes?"

Here I am without a plan of attack. On a whim I've trotted up and pounded on the front door. Clear the head. You've got to wing it.

"Yes?" he inquires again.

"Is the lady of the house in?" Brilliant opener, dork.

"No."

"Any idea when she'll be back?"

Peters is scrutinizing me very closely. Studying my face in a searching way. "You're Ed, aren't you?" he says.

"Fuller Brush." Oh Jesus, Ed, what are you doing?

He laughs, takes it as a joke. "I recognize you from a wedding picture I saw at Victoria's. I was hoping we'd meet some time. Come in." He opens the door a little wider.

One more denial? No point really. Warm house air is mixing with the cold and forming a rolling bank of fog at the threshold. I rip it apart stepping inside.

"Let me take your things."

I divest myself of parka, scarf, mittens, overshoes. I'm beginning to sweat before I've struggled free of it all. In the sudden warmth of the house I feel a little giddy. Drunk? How much have I downed this morning? Can't remember.

Peters is making conversation. "I see you're adding a little winter insulation."

What the hell is he nattering on about? "Pardon?"

He illustrates by stroking his jaw with pudgy fingers. "The beard."

I realize he is referring to my unshaven state. "Right. Face fur." Free of my parka in the narrow confines of the hallway I also realize I smell. However, if Peters has caught a whiff of pong he doesn't let on.

"I'm just having lunch," he says. "Would you care to join me?"

By the look of butterball Peters, lunch is a euphemism for tucking into the hindquarters of the fatted calf.

"Pass. I'm dieting." To tell the truth I can't remember the last time I ate.

"As a matter of fact, so am I," he says tartly. The boy seems a little prickly about his weight.

I'm curious. "What diet has she got you on?" Victoria had me on them all at one time or another. Dr. Atkin's Diet Revolution, the Grapefruit Diet, Dr. Pritikin's Diet. I'm interested to hear what's current gospel.

"Victoria? You mean Victoria?"

"Yeah. How's she starving you? I was starved every way known to man and a few others besides."

"It was my idea. Free choice, really."

I bet, buster. Don't parade your balls back and forth before me, I think, as I trail him down an eggshell-white hallway. The hardwood floor is wax and light, Victoria's handiwork no doubt. The walls are lined with paintings hung gallery fashion. There must be forty or more suspended on fine brass chains fastened to a bar fixed just below the conjunction of ceiling and wall; the colors flicker at the corner of my eye as we pass along the corridor; scarlet, bold yellow, a passage of blue. Anthony is explaining. "My first real love. A year at art school taught me I'm not a painter. Collecting is my compensation. My little *gallery*." A sweeping gesture, deprecating emphasis. He halts our progress. "That works rather well, don't you think?"

"Works its little buns off."

This he doesn't appreciate. "I'd forgotten Victoria said you hadn't much interest in art," he says stiffly. "I'm boring you by pressing an enthusiasm."

"I don't think Victoria does me justice."

"You ought to be fair. She's rather an admirer."

"Of what in particular?"

"Your potential," he says, moving on.

I follow him into the kitchen. There's a breakfast nook with what looks like a bowl of cold soup on the counter. It appears I disturbed him crushing a lemon into it when I rang the doorbell.

"I'm fixing spinach borscht. Would you like some?"

"Is that a *cold* soup?"

"Yes."

"In February?"

"It's low on calories and *quite* tasty," he bridles. The guy is very sensitive. He slices a hard-boiled egg into the soup and ladles in some sour cream. "Do you think we might be permitted an indiscretion?" asks Anthony after a time. "I have quite a nice bottle of white we could have with the soup."

"Why, Mr. Peters," I say, "indiscreet is my middle name."

There is a great fuss of uncorking, a bowl of soup is pressed on me, and in a short time the two of us are face to face across the table, spooning up spinach borscht. It has a fine flavor, piquant, rich. I try to remember when I ate last.

"A poor effort," says Peters. "Winter vegetables."

"Au contraire, mon frère."

Anthony parts his lips and trickles a little wine between them. We have taken the measure of one another by now and we know we don't like each other. He has me pegged as a second-rate boor. I have him pegged as a second-rate snob. I've detected, as he's grown angry, that the slightest suggestion of an English accent has crept into his voice. That is his high-horse voice, the one he assumes to ride roughshod over the wretched, huddled masses. I know what I'm talking about because I do exactly the same thing, adopting a high-flown vocabulary of abuse when working over, say, Benny or the old girls who loitered in the china department. Unnerving, the similarity. I suspect Anthony Peters did graduate work in Britain, though. He has the look of one of those characters who come back to Canada and insist on playing cricket badly with West Indians and Pakistanis who know what they're doing.

Of course, all that would have a fatal attraction for Victoria. She likes her men distinctive.

Peters is talking to me. "Pardon?" I say.

"I said, I don't mean to pry, but is your visit business or social? The reason I ask is that Victoria's gone on retreat. If it's important, you'll find it difficult to get hold of her."

"I know. I talked to her a couple of days ago."

'Really?"

"Pre-retreat as it were."

"Yes, well we all feel the need to get away from it all from time to time."

"And nobody more so than pregnant women," I editorialize. That one stung. An angry flush climbs out of his collar. Apparently he doesn't like me having the lowdown, the poop, on him.

"My, hasn't she been the Chatty Cathy," he says.

I don't bother to correct the impression that this news came to me via Victoria. He doesn't need to know that it was Marsha who spilled the beans. I'll take whatever advantage I can gain over this guy.

"I also hear there are rumors of marriage in the air." I pour another glass of wine for myself, extend the bottle to Peters. He places his hand over the mouth of his glass. "No? Well, anyway, I want to apologize for dragging my feet over the divorce. It's made for a messy situation with the baby on the way. But that's all in the past, Anthony old man. Be assured I don't intend to cloud your happiness at a time like this. I'll do everything I can to expedite matters. We must think of the child." There, that put the bastard on the spot.

"You needn't concern yourself. The two of us will manage."

"You're forgetting baby," I say, wagging my index finger at him. "Victoria and Anthony and baby makes three."

"I wouldn't concern myself if I were you," he repeats.

"No? Why?"

"Circumstances may not allow her to carry it to term."

"What circumstances?"

"They're none of your business."

"Excuse me, they're *some* of my business. I mean, I am involved, aren't I? I'm the husband of the pregnant wife." Contemptible observation.

"All right, since you're rude enough to press for an answer to the obvious, I'll spell it out for you. At Victoria's age there is an increased risk to the mother's health. There's an increased risk of birth deformities and mental retardation. We've decided it would be prudent to terminate the pregnancy."

"We? You're sure it's we?"

"We've talked it over. Victoria's taken a few days to think about it. I'm confident she'll see my reasoning."

"Did you ever think you might reason too well? I mean, I don't want to sound melodramatic but this pregnancy of hers is a kind of minor miracle. Victoria doesn't get pregnant easily, take it from me. In fact, we didn't think she got pregnant at all. Then all of a sudden, bingo.''

Peters shrugs.

"Listen,'' I say, leaning urgently toward him, ''what would you say if I tell you Victoria has always wanted a child? Badly.''

"I'd say what I said to her when she told me she did. I'd say wonderful. So do I. We can adopt. In our particular case it's the sensible thing to do. I happen to believe it's much more important to provide for children who are already here than bring new ones into the world.''

Mr. Altruism. "And would this home for an unwanted waif, this Dickensian urchin, be provided before, or after, your book was finished?''

"My book?'' he says sharply.

I try to appeal to a sense of justice. "Come on, what do you say? Bend a little on this. So she wants a baby. Suffer a little inconvenience, why don't you?''

Peters lays his spoon down. "First, from what I've heard, you're in no position to lecture me on my treatment of Victoria. Second, suffering inconvenience has caused the break-up of more than one couple. You must understand I'm not denying her a child. I, however, don't put very great stock in the same primitive impulses you apparently do. This blood-of-my-blood, flesh-of-my-flesh business means nothing to me. A child is a child is a child. And they ought to make their appearance when both parents are heartfeltly ready to receive them. What's the cliché? Every child a wanted child? Whether you or I like it or don't like it, there's truth in that. Every child should be a wanted child. If thinking, intelligent people can order their lives in such a way as to make them full with achievement and accommodate children — everyone is the better and happier for it, children and parents. I think Victoria and I are capable of that. I think the conclusion she'll reach is certain. Up until now she's lived a rather messy life with you and I think she has come to appreciate the difference between then and now. She'll do what's sensible.''

"So you can finish your book."

"Ah yes, back to the book. Is this the point where I'm expected to apologize for wanting a stretch of time to work undisturbed and uninterrupted on my book? Well, I won't. No matter how self-indulgent it sounds to say it, I will. Upsets affect me more than they do other people. Even Victoria's absence these last few days has made it impossible for me to work. I can't concentrate, given the circumstances."

I make a tsk-tsk noise, tongue on teeth. He appears not to have heard it, carries on with his justification. "As I've told her, there'll be time for children later, but I have got to establish my reputation as a scholar soon. The sooner the better. The academic world isn't what it once was. Things have hardened considerably. There aren't many tenurable positions around. And it's not easy to move up in the ranks. Assistant professors don't get promoted just for occupying space behind a lectern.

"And it's not my intention to sit stalled in a provincial university. This book, if it's ready for publication in three or four years, will be the beginning of a reputation. I'll be in my early thirties, an obvious up-and-comer. A bankable commodity for any department in the country. Offers will be made on the strength of what I can be expected to do. I can get a position back east where there are passable galleries, a passable symphony, passable plays. I can go back to where someone understands what I'm talking about and everything doesn't have to be explained twice in conversation."

"There are more important things than a book," I say. It comes out unctuous, trite.

"That may depend on the quality of the book."

I don't like the sneering, pointedly personal tone of that. "What're you driving at, Peters?"

"You're not entitled to make judgments on my book. After all, you haven't read it. I, on the other hand . . ." He allows the sentence to wind down suggestively, dangles the unspoken under my nose like a carrot before a donkey. Although I can guess with a kind of sickening certainty what's coming, I ask for it anyway.

"Go on."

"I, on the other hand, have been treated to *Cool, Clear Waters*," he says.

I choke on a sudden overpowering rush of shame like a dog on a bone. How could I have been so foolish as to put that book in her hands? By mailing it to Victoria I had only meant to prove to her that I had a glimmering of steadfastness in my character, that I was capable of seeing something through to the end. The book was all the proof I had of good intentions. And Victoria had betrayed me, betrayed my inner life to this man sitting across the table from me. I can see the two of them reading aloud to one another selected passages, punctuating them with snorts of derisive glee.

I burn recalling certain incidents in my western. How easy for Peters to prompt disloyalty in Victoria after reading in mock-heroic tones, say — well, my bathroom scene.

Sam Waters is in a zinc bathtub in Topeka, sluicing and scrubbing a couple of acres of Kansas hardscrabble off his weary body, Stetson firmly settled on his head. There's a tinkling of rowels on Mexican spurs, a floorboard groans, and Ike Grainger's syphilis-ravaged face looms out of the steam that clouds the room. Ike has got Sam where he wants him, naked as a babe, prime for murder *à la Marat*. But Ike enjoys too much the anticipation of the kill, talks too much, blows too hard. Ike doesn't know Sam bathes with a Derringer under his hat, and before he can cock the hammer on his Colt Peacemaker, he takes a slug in the breastbone. He manages to squeeze only a single shot into the ceiling as a second bullet slams him through a window and flat on his back on the boardwalk.

Sam requests more hot water from the shaken barber. It's suddenly chilly, he says. There's a draft he hasn't noticed before.

Now what would Anthony Peters make of that?

Apparently quite a lot, to hear him talk. "I suppose I ought to be grateful to you for your charming tale," he says. "It was your manuscript that finally brought into sharp focus some of my speculations about the ideological assumptions underlying most of the popular fiction of the century. It was seminal in formulating the hypotheses for my work *Fantasies and Fasces: A Study of the Ideology of Popular Fiction in the Modern Age*."

I pour myself more wine and try to look blithe. The bottle is nearly empty. "No gratitude need be expressed," I say. "Myself and my charming tale are honored, to be sure." Peters, like many an academic, appears incapable of absorbing any sensory input when discussing his research. He continues, impervious to my poor jibe.

"The value of your little book is that it is an unconscious parody of the western; that is, a western novel without even the crude attempts at characterization and plot development that clutter the stark imaginings of the most heavy-handed practitioners of the genre. *Cool, Clear Waters* is a western without a superstructure. The foundation exists without the encumbrances of architecture, and in my case it was the foundation that was of interest. The view was absolutely unobstructed, no girders, no scaffolding, not even guy wires to hinder my examination. Once I'd studied it and isolated its characteristics, all other forms of contemporary popular fiction could be analysed in the light of my findings. My intuitive insights were confirmed. The ideologies of the western novel, the detective novel, the spy novel, and science fiction are basically the same."

"What the hell is this ideology you're talking about?"

"Fascism, or a variant of it. At the beginning of the century it would be most properly described as proto-fascistic — the kind of thing found in the work of Kipling. Most recent science fiction is clearly crypto-fascistic."

I was aghast. "Are you saying *Cool, Clear Waters* is fascistic? That my book is fascistic?"

"That is exactly what I am saying. Throughout the book there is an assumption of the ineffectuality of law as the supreme arbiter in society, as well as the exaltation of the Superman above law. There is an obvious concern for cultural and racial purity common to many fascist movements. The fear of miscegenation is implicit in Sam's decision not to marry the Indian maiden Morning Star — "

"He didn't marry her because he felt unworthy of her! That's why he didn't marry her!"

"And the celebration of the will to power? Sam's brownshirt

tactics in assuring the election of the Ox Butte newspaper editor
to Congress is accompanied by a transparent apologia for political terror in the ceremonialization of the cult of violence at
the post-election barn dance. Those torch-lit dancers are very
Nurembergian.''

"Are you talking about the saloon brawl? Is that it? The
cattlemen started it! What was Sam supposed to do?''

"Of course," says Peters charitably, "the postulating of the
ideology on your part was largely unconscious. The mythology of
the western was received by you in the fashion the ancient Greeks
received their notions about Olympus. In your case an unreflec-
tive mind and a personality vulnerable to the siren call of authority
combined to create a fascistic cartoon with a strong undertone of
sexual-power fantasy." He paused. "Do you read *Heavy Metal*?"

"No, I . . .''

"What I'm talking about is particularly evident in that magazine.
Changing mores have made the expression more explicit, but the
link between sexual fantasy and its expression in political primalism
has literary antecedents. In my first chapter, 'Hierarchy and
Elitism: The Worship of the Gun', I subject Kipling's *Kim* to a
close analysis. Perhaps you know that the book begins with the
boy Kim astride the cannon Zam-Zammah outside the museum in
Lahore? He is denying all the other boys, *native boys*, the right to
sit astride the gun too. In a single yet highly sophisticated and
complex image are coupled notions of racism, political potency,
and sexual potency. The massive gun barrel protruding from
between the adolescent boy's thighs is too obvious a symbol to
need explanation. But in a very neat coupling of associations, the
gun Zam-Zammah may be read as phallus, sceptre, firearm —
instrument of repression.''

I lay my head on the table. It was a very hot summer the
summer I read *Kim*. I kept the curtains drawn in my bedroom for
the sake of coolness even though my mother said it was bad for
my eyes. It was cooler still at the feet of the Himalayas, and cool
too in the high-roofed Wonder House at Lahore when I entered it
with the Lama.

"What's the matter?" demands Peters. Only such a flagrant display of inattention could have deflected him.

"Where's Victoria staying?"

"I don't know," he says, startled by my abruptness. I can see he is telling the truth.

"When is she going to be back?"

"I don't know that either."

I get to my feet.

"Where are you going?" he asks, rising too.

"I don't know."

TWELVE

I welcome the night, feeling its blackness steal into my skin, my eyes, feeling it invade me, push out the panic. It's seven o'clock and the only light in this room enters from outside, shed from a light standard on the street. Its greenish-yellow lamp hangs level with my apartment windows and throws long, contorted shadows about the room. They run up the walls and break in the corners, cross and recross in dim webs and spiky asterisks.

Marooned in a broad bar of darkness I stare at my naked feet. Crossed at the ankles and propped on top of the TV set they catch a shaft of sodium light and glow like phosphorus. I pant, sip rum and Coke. The ice jingles in my glass. My hand shakes from exhaustion. I am resting between sets.

The music stops. The needle tracks soundless in the grooves for a few moments. There is a click and the arm rises from the The Who album. In the sudden silence I strain to hear whether McMurtry may be lurking outside my door in the hallway. It was only five minutes ago he finally gave up ringing my doorbell, but that doesn't mean he still isn't out there, shuffling his slippers on the spot in a rage, mumbling and slipping his dentures up and down on shrunken gums. Plotting.

My head aches. I've really gone and done it this time, pissing McMurtry off. No doubt about it, he'll do his best to get me kicked out of here. He means business. One slip, that's all he was waiting for. It doesn't matter to him that ever since the incident with the car antenna I've bent over backward to mollify him.

Vindictive old fart. Mad old fart. Still, I don't take anything back. No quarter asked for, none given. A man can only take so much.

God, I'm hot. Running back and forth dodging him, depth-charging him, worked up quite a sweat, and turning down the thermostat after I finally did him in didn't affect the output of heat from the registers. In this building thermostats are purely ornamental. Tenants freeze and swelter together, as one man.

But this is ridiculous. Look how it's coming out of me. Stripped down to my jockey shorts and I'm still oozing sweat the way a warm cheese oozes grease. It's the booze, of course. I've put a lot of liquor away in the past few days and hooch always makes me sweat. Maybe I should shower. I can smell myself. Still, there's no one else around left to offend.

Not Rubacek anyway, who's disappeared. Just one more damn thing to worry about. After leaving Peters I spent this afternoon cruising Quadrant 2, looking for both of them, Victoria and Stanley. I turned up neither.

I've decided to admit the idea that it might be wise to be scared of Stanley. So now I'm scared of him. After all, what do I know about the man? Why was he in jail? He may be unpredictable, violent. One thing is certain. He's attached to his automobile and I took it away from him. I may find it difficult to convey to him my impulsive nature, to explain to him why I had to have his car.

To top it all off, the note. I pick it up from my lap. If I hold it directly over my head the paper catches the light from the street lamp and I can make it out. It shakes a little in my hand, makes a raspy sound like dry, insecty legs scratching and rubbing against one another.

> Dear Ed,
> I must see you. It's important. Drop by tomorrow.
> Marsha

That's all. No explanation, no hint of what it is that's so god-damn important. Finding that slipped under the door when I came home wasn't tonic for the nerves. What did it suggest? Good news? Bad news? *Why can't people explain themselves?*

I got no answer when I phoned her. It seems strange now to think that when I settled the receiver in its cradle I was overcome by a flash of virulent optimism, believing that maybe Victoria had contacted Marsha and that Hideous now knew where she was. Life bloomed. I poured myself a stiff drink and set "Sgt. Pepper's Lonely Hearts Club Band" to spinning on the turntable.

I was swaying to the music when the phone rang. It was McMurtry.

"Turn that goddamn noise down!"

I cocked an ear before answering. He had a point. It was much too loud. I was too strung-out, too hyper, to notice until my attention was drawn to it.

"Okey-doke. You got it. It won't happen again."

"It better not. What's going on up there? You having a *orgy*?" Pronounced with a hard g, as in *Porgy and Bess*.

I almost said, yes. I almost said come on up, all the girls are begging for a clean old man. They claim there's nothing nicer. What I did say was: "Er, not really."

"If you had a job you wouldn't have the energy for all that. Do an honest day's work and see how you'd feel."

I didn't reply. He waited for a bit. Then he said: "Not all of us appreciate that noise, you know. I don't know how they call that music. It's just noise. I don't know why I have to listen to it."

And I wondered why every morning I had to listen to the base sound of The Beast jibbering, rending his prophetic garments, and clanking his madman's manacles. And how many quiet Sunday evenings had been shattered by the quacking fulminations of Donald Duck rising up as McMurtry sat entranced by the *Wonderful World of Disney*? And his taste in music?

"Let's make a deal," I said, "you don't make me listen to Maestro Welk and I won't make you listen to The Fab Four."

"What?" Suddenly he's deaf.

"I said, I'm tired of hearing Lawrence Welk bellowing from the depths. Turn your goddamn TV down." I yelled into the receiver: "Wunnerful! Wunnerful! Let's half a warm hant, folks, for dose two cute kits, Bubby and Sizzy!"

"You're crazy," he said, obviously shocked. "You ought to be locked up."

"Well, I'm not. And until I am you'll just have to live with me."

"We'll see about that. After I call the owner of the building, we'll see. We'll see if I have to live with you or not. He's my late wife's cousin, you know."

Oh fuck. The best I managed to croak was, "Aw, go call your mother."

"Maybe the owner don't want no hummosexuals on the second floor," he said.

I hung up, went to the stereo, and took off The Beatles. I replaced them with Jefferson Airplane. What did I have to lose? Let's run the sixties up the flagpole and see who salutes, I said to myself. Mr. McMurtry, meet Gracie Slick. Grace, say hello to Mr. McMurtry. I twiddled the volume knob until the window frames were pulsing in and out in sync with the bass. Then I started to boogie. I boogied out to the kitchen and I boogied back, glass in hand. Gracie and I were singing about white rabbits at the top of our lungs. Underneath it all I heard, or thought I heard, a muted jangling, a dim but insistent noise that made me feel as if I had a tooth that wanted to ache. It made me nervous. I couldn't locate the source of the sound. Was it the phone, or my head?

My blood sang with adrenalin. I boogied. My shirt was a damp leech on by back. I stripped it off. I boogied. My pants chafed the inside of my thighs, dove up my ass. I cast them off. I boogied. The ringing stopped. A poltergeist began to knock on the floor. I tried to ignore it. I pranced and whirled and shimmied in my zebra-striped apartment. Sodium vapor light blazed on my pale, quivering skin, darkness scarred me. Thud, thud, thud went his broomstick. It was the febrile pulse of a small mammal, trapped. Vague panic thickened the passages in my heart and lungs.

"Quit it!" I shouted.

Thud, thud, thud.

"Shut the fuck up!"

I boogied toward the bedroom. It followed me, bumping after

my heels, knocking with a crazy, senile rage. I spun around and pranced back toward the kitchen. It came too, a cardiac murmur under the music. My heart kicked in my breast, the broomstick stuttered a millisecond later. "Shut up!"

Under the glossy green skin of the kitchen linoleum the sound was hollower. Thunk, thunk, thunk. I stood panting. Odd images formed in my mind. Ice; hot, wet membranes; snow; burning faces.

I didn't dance, I ran back to the living room. What I'd seen scared me. *Thud! Thud! Thud!* It was louder. I saw him. Saw the mad old face frosted with white stubble tilted to his ceiling, slack, limp lips fallen back from dentures all gummy pink and white, glistening with spittle. The thin arms, brown and shrunken in saggy shirt sleeves, pistoning the broomstick up and down with crazy energy. With every blow he grunts. The shock of it jolts a cloud of dandruff out of his hair.

Craziness underneath me. Stumbling, sweating, blind rage shuffling back and forth. He'd kill me if he could.

I squatted down, rested my hands on my knees, bent forward to bounce my voice on the floorboards. "No fucking way, McMurtry!" I shouted. "No fucking way I'm giving in this time!"

I began to bang my fist on the floor. I fell into the rhythm of his knocking. It had bored into my muscles. I thought: Maybe he isn't the only one who thinks I'm crazy. Was it like this last time, before Toronto? Is this how it starts?

The record stopped. My fist froze above my head, sweat ran into my eyes. McMurtry struck twice, then nothing. Silence. We waited on each other.

That's when I thought of him as a U-boat. I saw him hung down there, suspended, listening for me. A U-boat of sagging flesh, stale smells, and fragile bones was hunting me blind, hunting me with sonar, tracking me with the huge dishes of his hairy ears. Because he isn't deaf. I'd thought he was. But he isn't. *He just likes things loud.*

I could hear my heart drumming in the stillness. Heard the wind. Yes. Yes. He was waiting for me to make a move. I wiped my face with my hands, dried them on my thighs. Went up on tiptoe. Kill, or be killed. It was in the closet. I had to get to the closet.

I stepped. The floor creaked.

Bang! Bang! Bang! Bang! Under my feet. I jumped.

"Stop it! Stop it! Stop it!"

He did. Stillness. I took several deep breaths to collect myself. Calmness. Don't lose your head. He strikes at noise. He tracks with his ears. Weight distribution over a large area. The principle of the snowshoe. I lowered my perspiring body full length on the cold floor. My wet flesh stuck, squeaked derisively, as I began to crawl towards the closet, sponging up a month's dust and crud off the floor with my squashed belly. But it worked. No creaking boards, no groaning joists.

At intervals on my journey to the closet I paused, pressed my ear to the floor. The sounds I heard from below were aquatic, muffled. It was like holding my ear to an immense, spiralled conch. A great static rush in the head. When McMurtry moved I heard it as a chain reaction of rustlings, knockings, bumps. There was no doubt he was listening for me, casting back and forth for the telltale creak. I imagined him shuffling along, stopping, raising his broom to strike, hesitating, reconsidering, lowering the trembling handle.

I crawled on over the bosom of the cruel sea. My nostrils jetted along filaments of slut's wool, my sticky palms clutched the hardwood. Couldn't he hear my heart drumming on the floor? Couldn't he? Why didn't he strike?

I reached the closet, pried on the door. It swung open. I reached in, pawed through shoes, rubbers, tennis racquet. There. My fingers closed on the heavy, cold sphere, lifted it free. I rolled on my back, cradled it in the soft, yielding nest of my belly. Felt my muscles relax with relief, gratitude. Now I was armed. The hunted had become hunter.

The old shot. I've kept it with me more than fifteen years. It has moved whenever I have moved. Victoria always asked, "What use is it?"

I'd forgotten how it felt. A long time since I had it in my

hands. It isn't something one takes out and fondles, although there is pleasure to be taken in its shape, its weight, its steeliness. It felt good. It felt like power.

McMurtry was about to be depth-charged.

The scenario owed a lot to the sub-hunting movies of my youth. I could remember the depth-charges, the "ashcans" thrown high into the air, rolling end over end against a sky of maritime blue, falling with a heavy splash into the sea, there to explode and rattle the teeth of the sub's crew, flicker the lights, make the bulkheads reverberate with their crumps.

I was going to sink that old fart downstairs.

But first he had to be tracked and found. He was running on his batteries now, running silent, running deep. I wanted to lay the first one in right over his head, wallop his hull, pop his rivets, split a seam. Can-opener him.

Gingerly, I rolled over on to my side, cupped the shot in both hands, pressed my ear to the floor. Nothing. Nothing but the hum of vacancy, the hot shushing of blood rushing in my temple and jugular. I waited. My watch banged behind its glass face. Come on, move, you old son of a bitch! My heart sagged into my ribs, swollen and heavy with anticipation. The air tasted of dust. I realized my mouth hung open, dry. I was breathing through it.

Off in the distance, a sound. Faint shuffling. He was moving! I couldn't home in. Too indistinct. All I knew was that he was off to my right. Too chancy to unload; I wanted a direct hit. I waited, held my breath; a tear of sweat slid off my nose, splashed on the hardwood.

He coughed. Coughed again. I had him.

I stood up. Went tense. He was mine. I had him. There. Yes. Over there. Directly below the entrance to my kitchen, just left of the divider. Good.

I rolled the shot back on my fingers. Tucked it into the neck below my ear. It came back to me. You never forget.

From the hallway where I stood, across the living room to the spot I'd x'd in my mind was a fifteen-foot toss. I lifted my eyes, noted the height of the ceiling. I wanted to exploit maximum loft without hitting it. I was aiming to drop the shot in right over his head.

I'd have to dispense with the hop across the circle. The clumping would alert him. Just lean back, Ed, I said to myself. Extend the left arm, begin the put, transfer your weight from back to front leg, drive through, finish up on right leg, left cocked stylishly high, quivering. Follow the arc of the shot.

I took three deep breaths, pumped the shot with my fingers, gathered myself, let fly. "Uumph!"

Briefly the grey metal surface of the shot shone, lunar, reflecting the strong light of the street lamp outside my window. Then the small moon was gone, lost to sight as it tumbled down through shadow.

Kathunk! It bounced. *Bunk!* Bounced again. *Bunk! Bunk!* It made a ponderous rolling sound, gave a firm thud when it came to rest against the kitchen baseboard.

A shocked silence succeeded. To McMurtry it must have sounded as if I'd let loose the pulley rope and dropped a Steinway or a safe directly above him. Had plaster come down, had a light bulb danced, had he crapped his drawers?

He roared, a wounded, strangled roar. I ran, racing after the shot, bare feet slapping on the hardwood. I veered from side to side. *Thunk! Thunk! Thunk!* The broomstick rapped in my boiling wake. I skittered hard to port, snatched up the heavy ball, broke for the living room.

The noise of the broom was sharper there. *Bang! Bang! Bang!* Unload a quick one. I dipped my knees, lobbed the sphere underhand. It rose and fell in an elegant sine wave.

Kathunk! Bunk! Bunk! Bunk!

He bellowed. What? Stop? Surrender? No. No surrender. The broom had gone wild. Here, there, backward, forward. It made crazy scratching, knocking sounds that had me thinking of broken, bleeding fingernails, mashed knuckle bones, smothered screams. The noises of a man who wakes to find himself nailed in a casket. It sounded as if he was trying to break his way through the crust of the floor to get at me.

I puffed after the shot. It had rolled under the chesterfield. The knocking spattered all round me. I was shaking with fatigue, my fingers couldn't seem to close on the shot; it squirted out of my sweaty grasp. There, I had it. McMurtry was yelling. The knocks were getting louder. My head fell forward against the arm of the chesterfield. No sleep last night. Tired. I closed my eyes. But him? What about McMurtry? I saw him. He was wearing a U-boat commander's cap. Backwards, so that the peak wouldn't interfere with his use of the periscope.

Blood trickled out of the U-boat captain's mouth and ears. That deep the pressure was enormous. The shock of the depth charges exploding above him shook the hull. Bolts were shearing away, snapping with a ping, steel plates were warping and buckling, the sub groaned, its steel skeleton shivered. An eardrum broke, an eyeball bulged in a socket like a grape pinched to the point of exploding.

Thunk! Thunk! Thunk! He was tiring too. McMurtry was tiring. The blows did not follow one another as rapidly or sharply as before. He was straining. But this also made his pursuit of me seem more deliberate and ominous. The knocking was advancing across the floor toward me; the cold grey snout of the sub was snuffling me out.

I got slowly to my feet.

Thunk! Thunk! Thunk! Five feet, four feet, three feet. At two, I swung my arms above my head, both hands cupping the sphere. My back arched. I popped up on my toes, stood poised, slammed the shot down in front of my feet.

Kathunk! Kathunk! Bunk! Bunk!

I listened. There was a faint sound of crumbling, crackling, the dry whisper of falling dust. Silence.

"Surrender?" I called.

No answer. I waited, felt perspiration run out of my hair, noticed my body gleam wetly in the lamplight. Would the counter-attack come when I moved? I took a few steps, the floor creaked. Nothing. Had he gone deeper to avoid my barrage? Was he even now settling into the pliant ooze of the ocean floor? Had I made him run? Had I beat McMurtry?

I walked a little more, nerves filed raw, ready to jump out of my skin at the first thud. It didn't come. I bounced my weight up and down, listened to the cheerful donkeyish heehawing of the floor-boards. Still nothing. I jogged heavily to the kitchen. Silence. I did some jumping jacks.

Beaten?

The last test. I put The Who on the stereo in an attempt to raise him. Red flag for the bull. I lay down on the floor. It felt cool against my hot cheek. There was no knocking.

Had I won?

It doesn't feel as if I have. Halfway through the first side of the The Who album, just as I began to relax and bask in the glow of my moral victory, the doorbell sounded peremptorily. New tactics. It had to be McMurtry. The old campaigner had manoeuvred the scene of the battle on to my territory and taken away my power of retaliation.

It was a war of wills. I refused to go to the door. I simply sat and drank my rum and Coke and tried to ignore the plangent pealing of the door chimes. It was difficult. McMurtry persisted in pushing the button for a long time. I was considering hammering the plastic box that houses the chimes into splinters with my shot when he finally relented five minutes ago.

The The Who album is finished. All is quiet. Is he out there? I listen suspiciously for the small noises that would signal that McMurtry is prowling outside my door, hatching plots, brooding on rude revenge.

I can't help myself. "Are you out there?" I call in the direction of the door. I can see a squint of light from the hallway squeezed under it. My voice sounds all wrong. I am pleading. I try to correct my tone, make my voice throb with confidence, authority. "Are you there, McMurtry?"

I take my feet off the TV, hunch forward in my chair, wait. I feel vague shadows gathering about my shoulders.

"If you're out there, answer me." Nothing. "I know you're

out there, so you may as well admit it." Is he? "Come on, admit
it." I fall back in my chair, drain the weak mix of melted ice,
Coke, and rum into my mouth. I nervously chew the shrunken
ice cubes, grinding them with my molars. "I'm not fooled, you
know!" I shout. "I know you're out there!"

That he won't answer makes me more and more uneasy. I find
myself on my feet, rummaging in my records. I draw a disc out of
its jacket, blow the fluff off it, place it on the turntable. I am still
talking over my shoulder to the presence I feel at my door.

"You don't scare me any more," I say. "You can do what you
want. Piss on you." I hesitate. "McMurtry, quit fucking around,
eh? Answer me!"

The record begins to play. It's The Stones. Mick Jagger, still
going strong while I'm winding down. He's got years on me.
Jesus Christ, look at him. A rocker in his forties with the hairless,
scrawny body of a British punk raised on sugary, creamy tea,
Eccles cakes, lemon curd, jam tarts, custards. Soft, sweet, yielding
sexual foods that make the lips pout, make the skin go dead-
white, make androgyny bloom. The pasty, puddinged look of
English decadence. Toffee eater's mouth, hollowed cheeks like
he's sucking on something rich.

My idol. Or should I hate the bastard? What's he doing with
that body? Lean and famished-looking as a whippet. Mick's singing now. Can't you see him? Wagging his little tush, flaunting
and shaking his degenerate forty-year-old buns at screaming teenies.
Dirty, nasty boy. Unspeakable swine, I'm dying of envy.

The music pounds. I strike a favorite pose of Mick's, hand
perched on hipbone, elbow flaring, head held arrogantly high,
jaw thrust formidably forward in profile. A tubercular Mussolini.
Then I saunter mincingly to the kitchen and back, slightly knock-
kneed, kicking my heels out, swivelling my ample buttocks in
imitation of Jagger's insouciant manner.

I wail: "Start me up!" They're going crazy in the front row,
jumping up and down on the spot, breasts bobbling. I jackknife at
the waist, lean out over the stage, primly squeeze my knees
together, wag my forefinger naughtily at the munchkins vibrat-

ing like tuning forks. "You make a grown man crii-iiy!" I moan. They go nuts.

I retreat momentarily, prance spastically over to Keith, high-stepping it like the famed Lippizaner stallions of Vienna, veer back again toward my fans. My lips purse over the head of the microphone: "You make a grown man crii-iiy!"

"Mick! Mick! Mick!" they sob. My face is wet, my mouth is dry. I flounce around, offer them my back, wiggle my satin-swathed behind, cast a heavy-lidded glance over my left shoulder. They're mine. "You make a grown man crii-iiy."

When I spin to face them, I realize I don't feel all that well. The room shudders with heat and alcohol; I feel unsteady strutting about on a patchwork quilt of light and darkness. I stumble, thrust my hand forward against a wall to save myself. "You make a grown man crii-iiy!" My undershorts are soaked. I pick at them, pulling them loose from my skin.

But I'm possessed. It doesn't matter. I lift my hands over my head and begin to clap, pound my bare heels on the floor flamenco style. It feels good. I drive them down hard enough to make them ache. The right heel goes numb.

I'm whirling round and round, spinning, careening, smacking my palms together. The room blurs, light and darkness flash in my eyes, like flags unfurled and cracking in the wind.

"You make a grown man — "

It hurts. My elbow. I've fallen. Blood on my lip. I've bitten it. Legs don't work. Shaking. I ought to crawl. Where's that light come from? There's too much light. My eyes don't work in the light.

I glance up. The two figures in the open doorway are black cut-outs, target men on a police firing range. The shock of seeing them makes something suddenly hurt in my chest. It feels like a muscle has ripped.

"Who?" A whisper.

One of them flicks a light switch. It dazzles my eyes. I blink, squint. I'm grunting too, panting. What is this? I've been hit in the chest with a brick. It's smashed my sternum. I can't lift my head; I'm staring into a slippery pool of polished hardwood. I hear footsteps.

"Who?" I say.

Two pairs of shoes stop. "He's drunk," someone says. Then: "Can you hear me?"

I can't seem to talk. I reach for the shoe. It pulls back.

"There's plaster all over my apartment." McMurtry. I roll on to my back, press the pain in my chest with both hands, trying to hold it down, keep it from spreading. I look up two pairs of trouser legs; the faces hang over me. Rubacek and McMurtry.

Rubacek pitches his voice very high. "Can you hear me? Where's my car keys?"

McMurtry's feet give off an earthy odor. There's a pee stain the size of a quarter centred in the crotch of his pants. He stoops down. The pull of gravity makes the loose skin sag away from the skull. He looks like death.

"Go through his pockets," he says.

Rubacek shouts, "*Where's my fucking car keys?*"

I snatch at McMurtry's pant leg. He pulls back, totters, almost falls.

"My chest," I say. "It hurts."

"What?"

"He's drunk," says McMurtry disdainfully.

"He doesn't look too hot," says Rubacek.

"My chest. Please. It hurts."

"Now he's crying," says McMurtry. "Shame."

THIRTEEN

"Y ou're still in your hospital gown," observes the nurse.

I am sitting in a chair by the window, and balanced on my red, scurfy knees is the note pad I sent the candy-striper down to the tuck shop for several hours ago. I don't lift my eyes from it. I'm making a list. My pencil hovers above the page and then scratches down another name. *James Agee.*

"Dr. Keitel has signed your release. It's one-thirty now. You'll have to be out by two o'clock. All right?"

I don't answer. *Dan Blocker.*

"If you have nobody to pick you up I can call you a taxi from the nursing station," she offers. "Would you like me to call you a taxi?"

"No." *Elton John.*

Out of the corner of my eye I watch her step into the hallway and beckon. Her legs, encased in white hose, are muscular chalk. She and her superior confer. "What do you mean you don't think he's going to leave? He's been discharged. He's *got* to leave."

"Yes," agrees the nurse, "of course, he'll have to leave. But what if . . . ?"

"What if what?"

"What if he won't?" She's coaxed me two or three times to get dressed and I've ignored her. The nurse says that in her opinion I'm scared to leave the hospital.

She's right.

There I go, pressing too hard again. The lead has cut through the paper. *Mama Cass.*

181

"Well, damn it, give him fifteen minutes to make up his mind to get unscared. We've got a surgery to be admitted at two. If he isn't out of there by then, call me," she says grimly. "Where is he? In here?"

"Yes."

She pokes her head in the door. "Okay, get your pants on. Shore leave at two, sailor." She's gone, her passage marked by a starchy whisper of garments.

Elvis Presley, Roy Clark.

What the younger nurse said is true. I don't want to leave the hospital because I'm afraid. At first I was afraid to be here, and now I'm afraid not to be here. Because this is the place they have the tubes that go up your nose and into your veins to keep you alive. This is the place that doctors and nurses stand alert, ready to fire a stalled heart with jumper cables, or hook up a respirator to inflate and deflate weakened lungs.

I can't sleep. The first night, the day before yesterday, they gave me a strong sedative and a muscle relaxant, so I managed a little shut-eye. But I slept in fits and starts and could not stop myself from dreaming that it was my father who had had the heart attack. I would wake with a start, again and again, each time confused as to where I was, incapable of thinking anything but: He's dead. My father's dead.

Gradually I came to see this wasn't so. I remembered it wasn't Pop who had had the heart attack, but me. And then the truly awful realization took hold, that this was worse than the dream. Better Pop than me. Better anyone than me.

But slowly, gratefully, body and mind gave way to the drugs. Just at the moment the dream began again, I experienced a stab of recognition; I tried to fight free of it, knowing what was coming, but by then it was too late.

The dream was the same each time.

It is a murderously hot day in Texas. I'm sure it's Texas. My father is walking on the shoulder of a highway toting a gas can. My mother and I are sitting in the stalled car watching him approach. Behind him lie brown fields, a white sky.

My mother says, in a flat voice, "He doesn't look well. He's getting old."

"Not Pop. He looks like a million bucks."

I take my eyes from him for only a second, to light a cigarette. Mother screams.

My head jerks up. He's gone. Everything is gone. Pop, gas can, everything.

My mother shrieks, "The angels came! The angels snatched your daddy away!"

The white Texas sky is full of fire, fire twisting and shaking and leaping. Why doesn't anyone else pay it any mind? Cars continue to tear by us, in monotonous succession, with a whine and sizzle of tires barely audible above the windy roar of flame lapping at our roof and the broken sounds of my mother's grief.

I'd rather make this list than think of that.

Arthur Ashe.

Last night the duty nurse caught me talking to the other patient in my room, the stroke victim they moved to neurology this morning, Mr. Beattie, a gentleman my father's age. He was brought in sunk in a coma, breathing deeply, pinkish eyelids fluttering, beaky nose tilted at the ceiling. For nearly sixteen hours he never moved.

About two o'clock this morning I heard myself speaking to Mr. Beattie. I had made an unconscious shift from thinking to talking. I was aware of the low murmur of words in the room and that brought me up short. I paused and listened intently. The ward was heavy with a suppressed kind of quiet, different from true stillness. Far off down the corridor I could hear an old woman faintly calling, "Nursie! Nursie!" She'd been doing that off and on for most of the night.

I started to talk again. I don't know how long I'd been speaking to Mr. Beattie when he gave me a fright. Suddenly his long, bony hand sprang off the bedclothes and gripped the railing on his bed so violently that the bars shook with the vehemence of his grip.

I broke off, waited. There was nothing else. He didn't move

again. The hand clung fiercely to the bar, the knobbed arthritic fingers I'd noticed earlier in the day twisted clumsily around the chrome. I thought he might be waiting too, waiting for the sound of my voice before he summoned his strength to pull himself upright.

I raised myself up on my elbow and continued. "Ain't this a solemn night a-layin' on our backs admirin' them stars? Ain't it still? And looky at that town up high on that black hill, just looky at them bully winder lights! Lord, looky at the lights on that hill, Jim!"

The nurse in the doorway behind me said: "Is there something the matter with Mr. Beattie?"

I threw a look over my shoulder. I couldn't make out her face because she stood solid and dark against the soft night lamps of the corridor. They outlined her figure in an aura of ragged, spiky light.

I didn't know what to say. The best I could manage was, "I think he moved."

She went past me to his bedside.

"His hand," I said, pointing.

She prised his fingers loose with some difficulty. "There," she said, "there, Mr. Beattie." The nurse forced it down along his side, stuffed it like wadding between his hip and the bars.

She turned to me. "Can you sleep?" she asked. "Do you want something more to help you sleep?"

"No," I said, "I can sleep." I was afraid of the dreams of the night before.

"Try not to pay him any attention. They often talk gibberish," she explained to me. "Try and ignore him if you can."

She left our room. I listened for the squeak of her crepe soles to fade away. When they did I propped myself back up. "Listen to that water," I went on, "ain't it soft? Cain't you smell the mud in the river? Ain't it good?"

And up, up from the pale coverlet the thin arm levitated, up through the darkness it rose, until his fingers found the uppermost bar and closed gently.

Peter Sellers? He must have had the first one before he was forty-five.

My list is lengthening. I didn't know I'd squirrelled away in my mind such a dreary roll call of trivia. There are a lot of them, aren't there? Famous People Aged Forty-Five and Younger Stricken With Heart Attacks. I actually scribbled that heading at the top of the page. It's a sign of mild shock, I suppose, doing this. Keeps control of my thoughts though, focusses them. The word *stricken* is an indication of my state of mind. I wouldn't normally use such a word. Hate it in headlines and news reports: Family Stricken With Grief.

A really surprising number of the famous are stricken, which leads me to wonder how many ordinary folk of the same age must have keeled over, unremarked, because of defective pumps. People I wouldn't hear about because their coronaries aren't news. It's apparently not as unusual to have a heart attack at thirty-one as I once would have thought.

I catch myself listening to it now. If you're really worried about the condition of your heart, there's no need to fiddle for a pulse. It'll interrupt a conversation. Take my word for it. It'll thump so loudly for attention you won't hear a word being said to you; sitting on a hard chair you can feel it chock-chocking in your buttocks. I've learned all this in the past thirty-six hours.

I've been waiting for a warning twinge. This morning, after my third EKG since I was admitted two nights ago, I caught myself shuffling down the corridor, leaning on the railing bolted to the wall, taking it easy. I sometimes even have a picture of my heart in my mind — tender, bruised, the tissues empurpled and livid with strain.

I'm a maniac. Whatever possessed me? I know better. A sedentary fat man shouldn't leap around his living room in a frenzy. A sleepless, stressed, sedentary fat man especially shouldn't leap around his living room in a frenzy. Top it off with the blood-pressure problem you've had since you were twenty-five, Ed, and your stupidity stretches the bounds of credulity. Not to mention the liquor. You've read about the strain alcohol puts on the heart, how it constricts arteries, restricts the easy functioning of valves. Christ.

The pain. It felt as if a wedge were being pounded into my breastbone with a mallet, as if I were splitting. I sat up, it didn't help. I lay down, it didn't help. I groaned, it didn't help. I gave up groaning, no change.

And all the while Rubacek kept asking me what was the matter. I hated him. Couldn't he see what was the matter? There I was, lying on the floor, clasping my chest, twisting from side to side. Did he expect me to say it?

The view from a stretcher is ceiling. The ambulance attendants and Stanley struggled with their burden down two flights of stairs; there is no elevator in the Twin Spruce Apartments. Turnings in the stairway were difficult to navigate. I was bumped, tipped, jogged, cursed. My eyes fixed, I watched the ceiling tilt and slide. Whenever McMurtry came too near me I yelled. He trotted alongside the stretcher with my clothes bundled under one arm.

"Keep away from me, you goddamn vulture!" I shouted. Apartment doors opened. I heard a baby crying.

McMurtry kept plucking at the coarse blanket that covered me. I slapped at his palsied hand, raged whenever his avid face lurched into my field of vision. "Bugger off!" He was trembling with the horrible happiness that overtakes some of the old when they see a member of a younger generation seriously ill. On such occasions they are full of self-congratulation and flash the cheerful grimace of the survivor, the smile of the man found in a lifeboat with the dead stacked up all around him.

Rubacek was managing one of the stretcher poles at my head. I could hear him explaining my behavior to the ambulance attendants. His theory was that it resulted from mixing drugs and booze.

"I seen it before," he grunted. "Bad news mixing tranks and booze. Some guys flip right out, go ape-shit. Now I don't take nothing myself in that line, not even an aspirin, say. Keep the system clean."

It wasn't tranks and booze. McMurtry was trying to draw the

blanket over my face. That was what had me bellowing. I wasn't dead yet.

The younger of the nurses is back at the door. "You're in luck," she says. "Your brother is here. He says not to worry about a taxi, he'll get you home."

"My brother?"

She steps aside and Rubacek sidles into the room. He looks sheepish. "Hi, Ed," he says.

"Hi, Stan. How's Mom and Dad?"

"All right," he mumbles, casting down his eyes.

"Stan lives with my parents," I explain to the nurse. "He can't hold a job."

"I'll leave now," she says pointedly, "so you can change into your street clothes."

When the door closes I scold Rubacek. "What do you think you're doing, telling people you're my brother?"

He shrugs. "I know these hospitals. They won't tell you nothing unless you're like a blood relative."

"And just what the hell did you need to know, Stanley?"

"Well, Jesus, I was worried, right? You looked like death warmed over by the time we got you here and into emergency."

"What do you expect? I was having a heart attack."

Stanley shakes his head. "You weren't neither, Ed. And you know it."

"What!"

"Come on, Dr. Keitel talked to you this morning and he told you same thing he told me. You wasn't having no heart attack."

"I sure as hell was! Keitel! Keitel! So you've been talking to him, have you?"

"Yeah. That's right, Dr. Keitel."

"Dr. Keitel? The bone through his nose didn't cause you second thoughts? Keitel a doctor? The man's idea of medical diagnosis is to split open a pullet with a hatchet under a full moon and peer into its steamy entrails while he hops around the patient on one foot awaiting revelation. We're talking witch doctor here. We're talking graduate of Haiti's ivy league, Voodoo U.''

Stanley chuckles.

"*Literally! Literally!* I'm speaking *literally!*"

"Get off it, Ed. The man's an important cardiacologist.''

"Cardy*quack*ologist!'' I shout. "That's what he is. Cardy-*quack*ologist!''

"Sssh! This is a hospital,'' warns Stanley. "And you're getting excited.'' He opens the closet door and hands me my pants. "Here, put these on.''

I carry on, my voice reduced to a vehement whisper. "Yeah, well, let Oogooboogoo Keitel have the kind of pain in the brisket that I had. You saw how I was. Let *him* have the goddamn excruciating pain in his chest and see if he doesn't say it's a heart attack,'' I mutter, struggling into my trousers.

"Dr. Keitel says it was muscle spasms. Brought on by tension.'' Stanley passes me a wrinkled shirt.

"Muscle spasms!'' I throw up my hands in disgust, the shirt sleeves flap. "So he gave you that little song and dance too, did he? What do you expect? That he's going to tell the truth? Tell a thirty-one-year-old his heart's ready to go? Make him worry so that it poops out sooner than it would have otherwise? Listen, Stanley, they tell you what they think is good for you.''

"He says your EKGs are fine.''

"I heard it. I heard it all.''

"The other doctor agrees.''

"Who? The skinny one?''

"Yeah.''

"When didn't they ever agree? The whole medical profession is a network of pathological cronyism. When they graduate from medical school they swear a secret blood oath of mutual protection and kiss each other on the cheeks. Compared with them the Mafia is a loose organization of snitches and squealers.''

"Your shoes,'' says Stanley.

As I bend over to tie my laces the blood rushes into my head, my temples feel swollen. Is it an elaborate hoax? Is Rubacek also in on the plan to keep the truth about my precarious condition from me? I sneak a sly glance at his face.

"Dr. Keitel says your blood pressure is up," Stanley informs me, "but I explained you're experiencing some inter-personal problems."

"Did you mention Victoria to him? Did you? Answer me, Rubacek."

"Sort of."

I throw back my head and groan, "Lord, stay my hand."

Stanley is unconcerned by this breach of privacy. "Somebody called Marsha phoned. I told her you was in the hospital."

"Phoned? Phoned where?"

"Our place."

"It isn't our place. It's *my* place."

"Maybe not for long," says Rubacek. "That old guy had me down to see what you done to his apartment the other night. You knocked plaster off his ceiling. Believe me, he's bugged."

"So he's bugged."

"You ought to be nice to him. He can make trouble. I played him a couple of games of rummy and sweet-talked him and said you'd be glad to make him a reimbursement. I explained . . . you know . . . about your wife running away and being pregnant and like that. Maybe it helped. He said he'd consider your offer."

Not only has Stanley been fraternizing with the enemy, he also has been bearing tales.

"You explained about my wife? You don't know anything about my wife to explain. Quit explaining my situation to people, Rubacek. Understand? As to my offer, he's got nothing to consider. I didn't make him any offer."

Rubacek shrugged. "Save yourself some trouble. Give him a few bucks. He told me he's saving for a trip to see his daughter. What the hell?"

"The road to hell is paved by compromise. Some people can't appreciate principles." Anyway, I've already paid that old ogre thirty bucks and what did it get me? Public electronic abuse.

Rubacek opens the door, ushers me into the hallway. We make

our way amid gurneys, trolleys, wheelchairs, creeping patients. I'm leaving the hospital. I don't want to. How did this happen?

"That Marsha a girlfriend?" asks Rubacek.

"No."

"She seemed real worried about you. Wanted to know if it was serious."

"What did you tell her?"

"I said no. Said you were in for a rest."

"What a diplomat."

"She said something about a wedding."

"So that's it." Trust Hideous Marsha. "That's what she's worried about. That I'll be in Boot Hill before the glorious day dawns."

"You got her in trouble, Ed?"

"Rest your evil little mind, Stanley."

We continue down the hallway in silence, turn right, enter the waiting room, where a woman wearing a corsage sits at an information desk. Descending a ramp we arrive at the hospital entrance. Only now do I realize I haven't a coat. When McMurtry bundled up my clothes my parka was forgotten and left behind in my apartment.

Stanley suggests I wait by the door. He'll warm the car up and bring it around to the entrance. I watch him cross the road to the parking lot, straddle-legged on the ice. Where the glass of the door meets the metal frame the pane is scalloped with frost, finely veined like feathers. I watch Stanley start the car in the parking lot. It'll be some time before it's warm enough for a man in shirt sleeves.

I turn away from the door just as a middle-aged man and woman come down the ramp. He wears a shabby overcoat and an unfashionable suit. Her brand-new plaid housecoat and fuzzy pink slippers mark her as a patient. Her thin hair lies flattened on her scalp, the skin of her face is ravaged with milky splotches.

When the man catches sight of me he hesitates, as if considering going back, so I turn politely away, only to discover their reflections in the glass of the door. Encouraged by my back, they huddle in a corner by a direct-line phone to a taxicab company. It's obvious they've come here seeking privacy, to talk. The woman must be on a general ward.

I try to look through the glass, past their reflections, to concentrate on the exhaust of Rubacek's car unravelling in the wind like the strands of a thick, white hawser. But my eyes keep snagging on the figures in the glass.

I see the woman. She is speaking very quickly. The only word that is clear is the man's name. She says it emphatically and distinctly. "John," she says. And again, "John," and once more, "John."

"The tickets," I catch him saying. He keeps mentioning tickets.

I reach out and flake a crescent of ice with my thumbnail. I wish they would go away.

I hear him say it again. "Tickets." Followed by the wet, flabby sounds of spilling sorrow. Crying, he bows slightly and fumbles in his pockets for a handkerchief, a Kleenex, something.

The woman wraps him in the plaid arms of her housecoat.

"Tickets," he says loudly. "I have the tickets."

Her face is the color of cream. Her eyes, wide and dark with knowledge, stare. I thrust the door open. It is a way of making the eyes disappear. Stepping outside is like wading into a cold lake; my skin flinches, my shoulders lift in my thin shirt. There is a taste of chilled metal in my mouth. I run. Halfway to the car I remember my heart.

FOURTEEN

W hile I, sweating and shaking, struggle up the narrow goat-track strewn with stones the color and size of loaves of bread dough, I can hear someone calling my name. It can't be Victoria because she has gone ahead of me, up there, and this voice is coming from another place, far off.

My face is stiffened by sunburn and dust. Behind me the untroubled sea stretches out to meet a sky that drips down into it like thin blue paint, running and blurring the horizon line. The shrubs and grasses and little gnarled trees on the hillside are dry, scorched, bitterly aromatic; they make the air hot and piquant. It stings my nostrils the way the feverish noise of flying insects stings my ears when they whir and click their wings in the molten light.

I hear my name again and am suddenly awake in my bedroom, awake in weak, northern sunshine.

"Ed, how do you spell perpetrator?"

Dazed, I roll on my side to consult the alarm clock. After so much sleep my limbs stir heavily between the sheets; there is a locus of lethargy in the small of my back. The clock says a quarter to three. When did I drop off again? An hour ago? Two?

"Hey, are you alive in there?" Rubacek is calling from the kitchen. Probably still grimly scribbling on those smudged sheets of foolscap spotted with erasure marks that resemble inky fingerprints.

"What do you want?" My mouth is parched and I feel feverish. Dog-like I paw at the stifling bedclothes with one foot, trying to drag them off me.

"How do you spell perpetrator? Is it e-r or is it o-r?"

"P-E-R-P-E-T-R-A-T-O-R," I shout.

God, how many hours have I been out? Last night I was in bed by nine, slept until ten this morning, rose, staggered to the bathroom, lurched back in here to collapse, insensible, until twelve, when Stanley served me a baloney and sweet pickle sandwich. It was his way of saying he forgave me for last night's contretemps. I don't feel particularly guilty, though. Stanley has a mind akin to certain faces, the kind that seem to invite a slap.

I was asleep again by one o'clock. I've logged sixteen or seventeen hours and I feel on the verge of nodding off again. A consequence of the heart?

"You going to get up now, or what?" he calls, voice pitched to carry down the block.

"Not just yet."

Disapproving silence. "You ought to get up, Ed."

"Why?"

"It's a sign of depression, not getting out of bed."

"Well, so maybe I'm depressed."

"That's why you ought to get up."

I attempt to correct Rubacek's logic. "It's not that I'm depressed because I don't get up, Stanley," I shout; "I don't get up *because* I'm depressed. Let's not confuse cause and effect, okay?"

"That's for sure, Ed. Now you get up and you'll feel one hundred per cent better."

I give it up and turn over on my left side. The heart starts trampolining on the mattress. Not good. I flop over on my back and wait for another sally from Rubacek. Nothing. He has obviously turned his attention back to his manuscript.

Where was I dreaming of? It must have been an island in the Aegean. A vision constructed from those travel brochures and books Victoria and I pored over in the early seventies, a vision tarted up with choice bits from *The Magus*. Yes, it had to have been Greece.

But why were we climbing in my dream? What were we climbing to? Monks. That was it. We were trying to reach the monastery on the brow of the hill.

In the beginning Victoria and I are standing on the packed sand of the beach. I am loaded with her cameras, and the straps have chafed my shoulders raw. I feel uncomfortable leaning back to look up at the cliff of crumbling grey rock from which snakish shrubs grow sinuously wherever they find a pocket of poor soil in which to anchor roots. The limbs of the bushes strain out of the shadow of the scarp, stretching to catch a bit of sun. The monastery squats at the top of this cliff, its white cupola glistening like a mound of sugar. Behind us the sea slops and creeps, sighing along the sand to wind warmly around our ankles.

We prepare to climb, but not up the rock face. With the capricious logic of dreams, the white dome has shifted to my right and somehow the sea has fallen far, far beneath where I stand with my ankles still wet with foam. Looking back I see waves chopping shoreward. They look like wrinkles in cellophane. I feel peculiar. Distances and perspectives have altered. I turn to comment on this to Victoria and discover she is moving up the slope. She is moving much too easily and nimbly. Ordinarily Victoria is clumsy and cautious. Now her toes jam into the loose soil, a flexible ankle boosts, a knee lifts, a haunch bulges, and she rises, rises.

I scramble after her, trying to pull myself up by clutching at bushes studded with thorns or dressed in sticky leaves that strip off in my hands. Victoria's camera cases swing back and forth, bunting my hips. The trail begins to twist around large outcroppings of rock which have burst out of the hillside like fractured bone through dirty skin. Victoria disappears again and again behind these boulders and I must trot to avoid losing sight of her altogether. With panic I realize that each brief moment I lose sight of her she miraculously covers incredible distances, distances beyond human capability. Each time her figure reappears it has dwindled, the intervening space between us produces arresting effects; now she shimmers behind a gauze of heat.

I can't follow any faster. There is the danger to my heart. My short spurts of running are strictly rationed, no unnecessary galloping.

I hurry around the base of a huge shattered stone, pawing and stumbling to catch a glimpse of a contracting figure that bobs, jerks, is gone. A few sobbing breaths before hustling into a quick march, then I break into a rolling half-run.

I call, "Victoria!" She doesn't hear, or pretends not to. The hillside has, in any case, grown noisier. Insects zither madly in the patchy grass, gusts of hot wind crackle and rattle in desiccated leaves and branches with a fiery sound, and when I call they snatch her name out of my mouth with a burning hand and cast it like a stone into the sea behind me, leaving my mouth gaping, mute.

After her. Faster. The heart, I remind myself. My back goes rigid in anticipation of the dreadful squeezing that will cause the heart to shed pain the way a sponge sheds water, a gush behind the breastbone.

Rest, I remind myself. But I can barely make her out now, only black stick legs and arms, a dot for a head, twitching up the hillside. Shrinking. She is not that small. This must be a distortion of air or altitude.

The hot air is beaten by bells. I swing around in confusion and stare down on a sea grown enormous. While I climbed, it crept around me; now it laps on three sides. A great briny-green gorget for the throat of the island. The bells cease. I look up. The white dome shimmers; inside, monks with grizzled beards and sweat on their faces stare up the bell tower. They can see stars.

The dot and the stick legs are gone. Victoria is lost. Hurry, I urge myself, beginning to climb. Hurry. *Hurry.*

And then came the voice that woke me. Voices? I sit up in bed and listen. There are two voices now. Rubacek is talking to someone. Someone has come into the apartment.

I ease myself quietly back down on the mattress and lie absolutely still and quiet. I have my suspicions it is old McMurtry out there and I don't want to draw any of his fire if I can avoid it.

They are keeping their voices low. No matter how hard I try, I can't make anything out of the subdued murmuring that floats to me from my living room. The conversation is certainly one I'm not meant to hear, maybe a discussion of my mental health. Or maybe they are bandying about figures for war reparations, assessing the damage I did the other night. They can amuse themselves as they wish. I couldn't care less.

I hear footsteps in the hallway. They're coming. Shit. I draw an arm over my face, commence to snore sonorously.

There is diffident knocking at the door. They wait for an answer, repeat the knocking. I bray, I flute, I strangle, I gargle for all I'm worth. Peeking under the crook of my arm I see the door inching open; a slab of Stanley's face is gradually revealed: strands of blond hair, eye, nose, bisected mouth. "Ed!" he stage-whispers. "*Ed!*"

I continue to lustily spew a geyser of noise at the ceiling. On a less raucous inhalation I hear Stanley scratching at the door with his fingernails, like a goddamn dog. "Ed!" he sings out. "Rise and shine! Wakey-wakey!"

It is perfectly clear there is no point in shamming anything short of a coma. Rubacek will persist.

"What do you want?" I snap, flinging my forearm off my face.

"You busy, Ed?"

"Jesus."

"You got a visitor, Ed."

"Tell him I'm not receiving. Tell him to go away."

"Ta-ra!" bugles Stanley and throws open my bedroom door with a ceremonial flourish. "Surprise!"

And who stands revealed? Not the hoary-headed and time-twisted old codger I expect, but Marsha, Hideous Marsha, looking like the last Romanov princess in an astrakhan pillbox hat.

"Surprised?" inquires Stanley hopefully.

"I said I don't want visitors. I don't feel so hot."

Hideous gives me the kind of smile that can strip varnish off old furniture and then turns to Rubacek. "Maybe I should speak to him alone, Stan."

"Try and get him to get up," pleads Stan. "I told him he's going to get depressed." Marsha nods knowingly and, reassured, Rubacek eases out of the room, closes the door softly behind him.

Marsha sits on the edge of my bed, plucks off her hat, and

bounces her hair around with the palm of her hand. "An interesting addition to your domestic scene, Ed. I trust your relationship with Conan the Barbarian is platonic?"

"What's it to you?"

"To me? Nothing. It's just difficult to keep abreast of developments in your life. You're so unpredictable."

"I'm not."

"I'm not, he says. Well, this is certainly a new one. And he is a lusciously proportioned number. Mr. Beefcake tells me that you've come away from your hospital stay with the novel idea you've had a coronary, all evidence to the contrary notwithstanding. Is that why you're still in bed in the middle of the afternoon?"

"It's none of your business what I'm doing in bed."

"And the heart attack?"

"I know what I felt. Doctors have been known to be wrong."

"Could it be," says Hideous, "that you're trying to lure Victoria back with this bogus affliction? You wouldn't be concocting one of your famous guilt numbers would you, Ed?"

"I'm sick."

"No argument here." Marsha knowingly taps her forehead with a lurid red fingernail.

An interesting notion, Marsha's. Would Victoria come back if she knew I was ill? Maybe. My eyes mist at the thought of Victoria back in charge. She'd put me on a program. There'd be a diet and exercise. In months she'd have me better than new, the heart as sound and solid as oak.

Marsha lights a cigarette, then looks around for a place to put the spent match. She finally reaches out and deposits it on the top of the dresser.

"Is that out?"

"You worry too much, Ed," she says. "And by the way, it's not necessary to keep the blankets clutched under your chin like that. I've been exposed to the sight of a man's nipples before."

"The reason I mention the match is I don't want burn marks on my furniture, thank you very much."

Marsha looks sceptically at my scarred and battered chest of drawers. Then she glances at the Allied Van Lines cardboard wardrobe. She points to it. "Like that priceless period piece?"

"I would prefer if you didn't smoke," I say on the spur of the moment. Just now I've decided to renounce cigarettes. They're bad for the heart.

"Sorry, Ed. I prefer the smell of tobacco smoke to the smell in this room. The air in here is fetid. The place smells of marsh gas."

"No one invited you to sample the air in this room."

"God," says Marsha, casting her eyes about the room, taking in the compost heap of soiled clothes in the corner; the mugs incubating scum in a finger of coffee; the water glasses with a milky rime in their bottom, the precipitate of evaporated Scotch, "when you determine to hit bottom, you *plunge*, don't you? When do you intend to shovel this place out?"

"Mind your own business."

"I am, in a way. I'm glad I dropped by," she sighs; "I didn't think you could be trusted."

"Trusted to do what?"

"Ed," says Marsha, "you're a pig. Where's your suit?"

"Trusted to do what?"

She's on her feet now, rummaging in my closet. "To make yourself presentable at my baby brother's wedding. That's what. Have you hung it up? Is it hung up at least?" she asks, zinging hangers along the bar.

"Get out of there. Take your hands off my personal stuff."

"God, is this it?" she asks, hauling out my ensemble and holding it at arm's length, a fisherman sizing up the catch.

"Yeah, that's my suit."

"When did you buy this — " she hesitates over the word deliberately, "*suit?*"

"1972."

"Ed, the pants are flared. There are buttons on the side pockets of the jacket. Is this a yoke at the back? More buttons," she mutters, discovering one on the breast pocket. "There are buttons all over this thing. What is this?"

"It's my security suit," I volunteer. "A nice number to wear to the midway. It's pickpocket-proof."

"Ed," says Marsha, "is this a cowboy suit?"

"Western wear."

"Oh my God," she says, "you were going to wear a cowboy suit to my brother's wedding?"

"It's conservatively styled," I remark. It is, too. My father bought me these duds when he arranged the job interview for his boy Ed with an old friend at the local TV station. The job was reading the farm news. I didn't get it.

"Look, Ed, Dale Evans might think your suit is a model of restraint — I don't. You aren't wearing it." She throws it across the foot of the bed. "God, I just knew to expect something like this."

"I've been thinking, Marsha, that this isn't such a hot idea anyway. Maybe we should forget it."

"My invitation was addressed to Ms. Marsha Sadler and guest. You're the guest. In a blue suit."

"Just a minute, Marsha, I — "

"Kramer's can do a made-to-measure in a week. I'll phone Irv and let him know you're coming in. They dress Dad — have for years — he'll get right on it if I call. *Dark blue*, Ed. Like for a funeral; I don't want you standing out in a crowd. And tell Irv a fine pinstripe, it'll make you look thinner."

"Go to hell. I'm not buying a new suit for the wedding of some brat I never even met."

"It's on me," says Marsha, abstracted. Her mind is already on something else. "I'll tell them to send me the bill. Don't worry your pretty little head about it." She crosses the room and flicks the ash off her cigarette into an empty glass on the windowsill. Suddenly she asks, "Can you dance?"

"What do you mean, can I dance?"

"Dance," she says tartly, "not boogie, *dance*. Waltz, foxtrot, etc. I'm not spending the evening 'cutting a rug', as they so quaintly put it, with my uncles at this wedding. For this occasion you and I have eyes only for one another. My dance card is full. I'm not going to stand for you sitting on your ass sucking back Chivas Regal while the geriatric cases show me a good time."

"I can dance."

"Don't lie to me. It's all right if you can't. I'll teach you."

"I can dance."

"Let's see."

"What?"

"Get up. Come on, right now."

"Not likely."

"Quit the shrinking-maiden bit. I just want to see if you can dance. Come on, it'll just take a minute." Saying this, she reaches down and rips the bedclothes off me like a magician whipping the tablecloth out from under the dishes. I am exposed.

"Jesus, you didn't even know if I had pyjama bottoms on!"

"Well, now I know. You do. Come on."

I swing my legs gingerly out of bed, sit up, dangle my feet.

"If you aren't the craziest bitch — "

Marsha reaches out, grasps my wrist, yanks me upright. "Waltz," she commands, assuming the position, one hand on my shoulder, right arm extended.

"I need music."

"Hum something."

I decide that the sooner I get this over with, the better. I percolate "The Tennessee Waltz" in my nasal passages and begin manoeuvring Marsha in the space between closet and bed. The soles of my feet are moist; they stick to the floor.

"Who's this Rubacek," she asks, "and where did you find him?"

Who is Rubacek? It is a slightly more intriguing question than I once would have suspected, particularly when viewed in the feeble, flickering light of last night's little flare-up. A combustion ignited because he wouldn't shut up about my heart attack.

"Ed," he said, "why don't you believe me? You didn't have no heart attack. It was what you call spasms."

"Spasms my ass."

"You didn't have no heart attack, Ed."

"Who are you to say? Are you a doctor? Answer me that? Are you a goddamn doctor?"

"No."

"Then shut up."

"Are you a doctor neither? No, you ain't. Don't tell me to shut up."

"I'll tell you whatever I want to tell you. Don't presume to give me orders in my own home. Shut up, Rubacek."

"You ain't a doctor. That's one thing you ain't."

"No, I'm not a doctor. And here's another thing I'm not. I'm not a thief." A dangerous sally perhaps. But my mouth has a habit of running away on me.

"What's that supposed to mean?"

"It's obvious, isn't it?"

"What's that supposed to mean?"

"Just a reference to what I presumed to be your professional capacity. Since we were discussing occupations."

"A man never escapes his past does he? Society won't let him forget what he was. They always throw it up in his face. Well, I paid my debt, Ed. I'm a straight arrow now."

"Excuse me. Let me correct myself. Another thing I'm not is an *ex-thief*."

Stanley looked highly uncomfortable. "I wasn't no thief."

"What then? An arsonist?"

"Get serious."

"A pimp?"

"They're scum."

"Not a wienie-wagger?"

"You watch it, Ed."

"Dear me, I appear to have exhausted my meagre store of underworld lore. Why don't you tell me your specialization, Stanley? I wait with bated breath."

Stanley cast his eyes desperately around the room.

"Come on, Rubacek."

"Bank robber," blurted out Stanley with a guilty hunch to his shoulders, averting his eyes. He was lying, that much was clear.

"Like Jesse James."

He was oblivious to the irony in my voice. He brightened. "Right," he said with conviction, "or John Dillinger." And he added, "You better be careful when you insult me, Ed. You don't know who you're fucking with."

But as to Marsha's question who Rubacek is, the simple answer must suffice. I break off humming and say, "He's in my writing class. An aspiring author."

"Is he living here now?"

"Overnight guest." I try whistling.

"He's not a little worked up over your mental state. He told me you were acting very strange last night, very difficult. Just now he asked me if I'd stay with you while he slipped out to get some clean clothes. He doesn't think you should be left alone."

This news makes me break stride. "What?"

"Foxtrot," orders Marsha.

I begin to trot. A salacious dance. It is producing a lazy, wobbly tumescence. I wonder if she is aware of it gently butting her pelvis. Marsha is fragrant with eau de cologne.

"He's worried about you getting depressed. He thinks you ought to be kept occupied."

"What's this? Did you two have a summit conference?"

"Just bits and pieces on the phone the other day when I tried to get hold of you. A short chat in the living room when I came just now. Stan believes you should be writing. It would keep you from becoming depressed."

"Not that I have anything to be depressed about."

"You didn't have a heart attack. They wouldn't let you out of the hospital this soon if you had. The doctors would be liable, or culpable, or whatever the word is. Anyway, people your age don't have heart attacks."

"Jim Morrison did."

"That was drugs."

"I don't take care of myself either."

"You don't take drugs."

"But I don't live right," I say, struggling to make my point. As the soles of my feet dry, I am able to embellish my performance with some fancy footwork. Marsha does not respond to my lead. She steers like one of those rogue shopping carts with one wheel askew. I relent and go back to the meat-and-potatoes stuff.

"So what? Nobody lives right," says Marsha. "Waltz." And the band strikes up, or rather Marsha strikes up, an appropriate tune in my ear. We dance on in the fading gimcrack light of a winter's afternoon.

FIFTEEN

Some men might have settled
for less. I set my heart on a coal-black tux, as glossy and satiny-
looking as a long-playing record. A blue suit may be classy in an
understated way, but the man who squires Marsha ought to part
the shabby sea of festive hoi polloi like Moses. Not that I put her
to the expense of made-to-measure evening dress — after all, one
ought not to forget who one is or who is footing the bill — but I
did lay hands on a slightly used rental item, the last occupant of
which had been built along similar lines to me. Peering at myself
in Kramer's mirror, clad in the habiliments of Hollywood, I
thought I detected a marked resemblance to the youthful Orson
Welles and was sold on the spot. A tuck here, the stitching eased
there, and Kramer assured me it would fit like a glove. All
alterations guaranteed to be completed in two days.

However, this morning's journey to the tailor's proved to be
unexpectedly dangerous. I'll remember to avoid buses in future.
Rubacek ought to have driven me but didn't. He had to keep to
the apartment to prepare his surprise — a place for me to work, to
write. Naturally I thought he was refusing because he was unwilling to interrupt the transports of composition. For the past two
days he has kept hard at his ratty manuscript for as long as eighteen
hours at a stretch, scrawling page after page with concentrated
fury before lapsing into a recuperative trance in which he bemus-
edly produces telegraphic noises by clicking his pen against his
front teeth. Waking in the middle of the night I discover light
leaking into my bedroom through the seams of my badly hung

door and know that Rubacek is at his station, tapping out his cryptic code. An SOS to the Muse: Rubacek at work.

Now I am supposedly at work too, seated here at this unsteady table, Venus Velvet HB in hand and a few creased sheets of yellow scrap paper spread out before me. I suppose I ought not to have dug these pages out of the jewellery box where they have lain untroubled and untroubling all this time. I had a feeling of vague apprehension when I sorted them out from the diplomas, degrees, and confirmation and baptismal certificates. But I thought it would be easier to show these to Rubacek than to fill pages at his command. Stanley expects to see something at the end of the day, and these stark black sentences are capable of persuading him I'm writing, keeping the fell lion of depression at bay by brandishing words as if they were a whip, a chair.

I haven't yet brought myself to read any of it. I remind myself that I was crazy when I wrote these pages, that it was these pages I held in my hand when I came out of the dark room and said to Victoria, "I've failed him. I'm afraid. I want a doctor."

Maybe it's the difficulties with my heart that have sapped my will to resist Rubacek. Maybe I want to be looked after. This afternoon I hurried home from the bus stop, frightened, hoping only that I would find him at home so I would not be alone. He was here. He'd made everything ready for me. This card table was in place in the living room, chair facing the window. He had borrowed it from McMurtry, with whom he is apparently on good terms, even though Stanley inhabits the enemy's camp. On the table were sharpened pencils and pads of paper, yellow and white. He'd even scraped the ice from the window so I would have an unimpeded view of the snow-burdened boughs of the spruces and the sparrows scattered among the green needles.

"She's all set, Ed," he said.

So here I sit on a collapsible chair, unable to write, or even to read what is in front of me. I know, however, that it is the epigraph of my crazy manuscript printed in huge, spidery, insane-looking letters that can't be ignored: The concluding words of *The Adventures of Huckleberry Finn*.

If I'd a' knowed what a trouble it was to make a book I wouldn't a' tackled it, and ain't a-going to no more. But I reckon I got to to light out for the territory ahead of the rest, because Aunt Sally she's going to adopt me and sivilize me, and I can't stand it. I been there before.

So far that's as much as I've been able to bring myself to read. I just sit here patiently, because doing so keeps Stanley from harassing me. From here I can see him sprawled all over the kitchen table. It took me a while to place where I'd seen that odd, contorted posture before, that gawky attitude he assumes when writing. And then I remembered. Elementary school. Memories of row upon row of little kids, cheeks almost touching notebooks, eyes cast in a sidelong squint that follows bunched, crabbed fingers driving a pencil between pale-blue lines. That's the way Rubacek writes, like a child. One shoulder thrust up, legs nervously jigging under the table.

I only wish I'd had as much time to study Bill Sadler as I've had to study Rubacek. I find Sadler more interesting. But this morning all I was granted was a glimpse or two from a bus window. I spotted him when the driver parked at the stop in front of the Army & Navy to wait for transfers. I had impatiently cast a glance over my shoulder to see if buses number seven and number nine were rolling up behind us when Bill caught my eye as he placidly plodded through a confused crowd of people scuttling about on the sidewalk, hurrying to catch buses.

Unlike the old days, he wasn't toting a placard but wearing a sandwich board of thick plywood over the kind of dark car-coat immigrants prefer as winter wear. The wind was gusting and the board, which hung to his knees, acted as a sail. Every few moments he locked his knees and jittered along, leaning back against the blast. The board blanketing his chest had a Bible text painted in red: "Be sober, be vigilant; because your adversary the devil, as a roaring lion, walketh about, seeking whom he may devour:" I Peter 5:8.

Above the board his face was a little thinner than I remembered it, the cheeks a trifle hollowed, mouth pinched, and skin mottled pink and blue by the terrible cold. He walked on through the crowds with a kind of hopeless doggedness, walked unseeing past the store windows filled with bankruptcy trash and impossible, failed fashions.

I gave up my seat to get a look at whatever was written on the plank on his back. The crowd on the sidewalk had thrust Sadler over to the curb and so close to the bus that from my angle, from where I was standing, I could only see the top of his head bobbing along, hair neatly trimmed, the teeth marks of a wet comb frozen in his hair.

I decided to get off the bus, to speak to him. I groped forward against the current of boarding passengers, muttering as I did, "Excuse me. Please. Excuse me." I popped up on tiptoes to follow the bobbing head, shoved ruthlessly past those who showed no inclination to give way.

All passengers boarded, the bus suddenly started with a jerk. I snatched the overhead bar to keep from crashing backward. At precisely the moment I threw up my arm two things happened. Bill Sadler swerved away from the curb, and I felt a mild pinch of pain in my chest. The sign on his back said: "And they worshipped the dragon which gave power unto the beast: and they worshipped the beast, saying, Who is like unto the beast? who is able to make war with him?" Revelations 13:4.

There was a strange tickling all down the inside of my arm and a sense of fullness, of mild discomfort, in my chest. I cast my eyes over the bus for an unoccupied seat. There were none. I decided on the spot that there would be no more bus rides for Ed. I'm not about to die lying in melted snow and gum wrappers in the aisle of a bus, supine at the feet of strangers.

I wonder what Bill would think if he knew I'd read his counsel, seen his message? I believe he is only warning us all out of a sense of duty, not out of love. He expects nothing to come of it. That's obvious in the way he joylessly trudges.

What would it be like to carry in one's head Bill Sadler's particular visions? Visions of scarlet priapic devils, of dragons with green leathern scales and curled, cumbersome claws. But maybe that's not it at all. Maybe for Bill the dragon is simply sin. I don't know. Still, I think he senses the ether pregnant with blood and blazing brimstone ready to rain down on our heads. What would it be like to be under conviction, to be slain by the spirit, to be sober and vigilant, to leave messages?

Bill and I leaving messages. Because I'm sure that in these pages I wrote in the bad time, in that dusky room, there was some kind of message, either to myself, or to Victoria, or to both of us. It's just that I don't remember what it was. But it is here, before me, ready to witness if I allow it.

I begin at the beginning with a surprise, the name of an old friend.

Sam Waters swung down off his horse and looped the reins around the hitching post. Then, as he did in all inhabited places, all civilized places, he unbuttoned his canvas duster and tucked its long skirts behind his holsters to give himself free play with his Colts. He took this precaution even though the street was empty on a November morning, or almost so. A farmer in baggy pants anchored by galluses was loading a wagon in front of a dry-goods store. His woman held the team of mules, her eyes following Sam from under a limp sunbonnet the way they might have followed a tumbleweed blown down the street.

The street was empty, lonely-empty in the way of a Kansas railhead town in late autumn, when the saloon pianos don't tinkle and the Texas trail hands are nothing more than a bad memory of broken glass, shot up signs, and blood in the sawdust on bar floors. Even the whores had thinned their ranks, climbing back on trains bound for Chicago toting pigskin portmanteaus bursting with feminine fripperies that were part of their stock in trade. They travelled their wares like Eastern drummers, chasing business. In the white clapboard houses of Chicago in the slow times of early afternoon when the wind keened off the Lake and the fresh snow in the streets below their windows was turning grey with chimney soot, the girls would discuss who smelled worse, the cowboys who drove the cattle, or the meatpackers who slaughtered them.

Sam Waters shivered and hunched his shoulders in that deserted street. A cold wind smelling faintly of snow and dust was blowing off the northern plain.

His belly was near as empty as that Kansas street, and now he saw there was no grub to be had here. At the far end of the prospect he had been able to read the sign as plainly as if it had been his hand in front of his face. EATS, it had declared in huge letters outlined in gilt. But now he made out a smaller, clumsily printed sign propped in the window. Closed For The Duration and Repairs, it said. Sam took the duration to mean the absence of wranglers from the Nueces country who were willing to pay a silver dollar for corn-pone, coffee, steak, and pan gravy made by somebody other than a trail cookie called Bones or One-Eyed Jack. In fact, directly under EATS the owner boasted, WOMAN IN THE KITCHEN, CHANGE AS GOOD AS A REST, BOYS.

This is it, then. This is Sam Waters's first appearance. One thing at least is cleared up. Three years after I had written this I sat down to write again in that other bad time shortly after Victoria left me. And Sam had sprung on to the page without hesitation, without my taking thought. I had described it to myself as a case of automatic handwriting. That was how it felt, I felt something had taken possession of me. I didn't realize I was writing about a man I knew. Sam Waters hadn't been obliterated by electricity, by shock treatment. He had just gone deeper into me, into hiding.

What I am reading has to be the final copy. There are no alterations, no scratchings out, nothing added. The drafts which I scribbled in solitude, day after day, are gone, destroyed. I can only guess what was in them, for what I finally arrived at has the appearance of being willed, of being strait-jacketed into a familiar pattern. This is the cherished western of my childhood, homage

to the cold-eyed hero. And despite the ironic winks to myself in
the prose, I must have followed Sam Waters without hesitation
when he turned away from the hash house and crossed the street
to the Diamond Saloon.

When Sam leaned into the swinging doors of the saloon he
did so sideways, leading with his left shoulder. Ever since he
had taken a slug in Wichita strolling into a bar, shoulders
square to the door, he had preferred to pare down the size of
the target he presented whenever he eased himself into any
place where rotgut and gunpowder were mixed.

There wasn't much doing in the Diamond Saloon at that
hour. Not a single riding boot was propped on the brass rail
of the fifty-foot bar. Only three people were there: a barkeep
with a face the color of old ashes who glanced up from
wiping out a shot glass; a fancy lady in a low-bodiced dress
worked with jet beads who was dealing a hand of solitaire on
to green baize; and a barfly pushing dirt around with a
broom in hope of earning his first drink of the day.

Sam walked to the bar. His spurs sounded loud as church-
bells in the hollow quiet.

"What's your pleasure, mister?"

"Beer."

The bartender drew it. "You look like you come a ways."

"Far enough."

"That'll be a nickel to oblige. Some pays before service. I
seen you warn't sich, though."

Sam fished in his waistcoat, put the coin carefully on the
countertop. Out of the corner of his eye he was watching
the barfly sidling up to him. You never knew. He might be
laying for you. He might be somebody's brother.

"Darn'd if I hain't done," the juicehead informed the
barkeep.

"Corners too?"

"I allow so."

Sam watched the man beside him as his drink was poured

out. Younger than Sam expected, not above thirty-five, he was got up in a long grey coat, broken shoes, and pants stiff with mud. Under a week of ginger stubble his skin was the color of buttermilk. He had bad teeth. When he smiled he looked like the keyboard of an old whorehouse piano.

The drunk had trouble getting the first one of the day to his mouth. If it had been a glass of cream instead of whiskey he'd have been lapping butter when he got it to his lips. But he got a bit noisily down, licked his wrist clean of slops and turned to Sam. "A fambly weakness," he explained. "Pop was jest sich as me. Always a-havin' tremors and visions when he went to a-drinkin'. Often I rec'lect how he'd scare up the Angel of Death when in a parlous state."

Waters nodded and looked in his glass. His neighbor gave off a thin, tired stench.

"Oh," he said, "I know what you're a-thinkin': You're a-thinkin' I hain't fittin' for conversation. You're a-thinkin' you'd like as soon shake hands with a hog as me." The man leaned closer and said confidentially, "I warn't always as you see me now, pore and pitiful. I warn't always a-smashed to flinders. It was the war between the States done me down. I come here to Kansas in Territory days afore the War. Even then every kind of fool was set on a-killin' one t'other. Jayhawkers and Kickapoo Rangers and Doniphan Tigers a-murderin' and a-burnin': Missouri men a-shootin' fools so's they could keep a-holt their niggers, and John Brown a-murderin' Pottawatomi innocents to make them lose a-holt their niggers. Sure as God made little green apples they was jest a-gittin' primed for the big blow-out, and I seed it so from the beginnin'. Jest ast me."

Sam did not oblige him by asking.

"And then it come, jest as I knowed she would," he continued. "Well, sir, a frien' of mine writes me a letter to Kansas. He was a-raisin' a reg'ment fur Jeff Davis and the Good Ole Cause. This frien', he had his heart a-set on a plume and bein' a Colonel. 'The South needs her sons in her hour of travail,' he writes, 'and I call on you to join with the Flower of Chivalry and scotch the Serpent of Tyranny.' And I done so 'cuz I was right partial to that man and never could stand agin what he wanted. So I a-joined and me and a passel of other fools marched arter him and he was kilt at Vicksburg a-ridin' back 'n forth in the enemy fire, his hair a-blowin' ever' which way, a-wavin' his sword and a-singin' out, 'Give Us Liberty or Give Us Death' and Death obliged and fetched him off his horse, a Yankee minie ball plumb dead center in the head, and he was done in and stretched out cold and white as alabarster.''

''If he's botherin' you,'' said the bartender to Sam, ''give him a shove with your boot.''

''I was a-took captive at Vicksburg,'' said the barfly, ''and my health and spirits was a-broke in a Yankee jail and this here is my fate.'' His hand steady now, he finished off his drink and pushed it toward the barman in a way that suggested he expected it filled again.

''Don't go shovin' at me. You had your drink.''

''This territory has a-changed,'' said the barfly. ''It went civilized and nat'ral good manners went by the by. And me as dry as a powder horn.''

''Fill it up,'' said Sam, putting money down.

''Thanks aplenty.'' The man thrust his face closer to Sam's, covered his mouth with a grimy hand and whispered, ''That one back there,'' he said, motioning with his head to the woman dealing cards, ''is a dollar. But I kin rec'mend better. There's a high yaller girl I know'll do it fur two bits. I'll take you 'long to her direckly fur a nickel, mister.''

''Obliged, but I'll pass,'' said Sam, draining his glass and turning to the door.

''I know this here town,'' the man called out after him, ''I know this here territory. You want sump'n, a woman, or any sich thing, jest ast fur me. Ever'body a-knows me. I kin scare up a good time. Ever'body knows me. Jest ast arter Huck Finn.''

SIXTEEN

"Are you sure, are you positive you haven't heard anything from Anthony Peters? Are you absolutely certain, Marsha?"

When Marsha thrusts up the bar, the row of little muscles that lie between her breasts and her collarbone leap exuberantly under the skin. "Gruunph!" The metal plates clink.

"We had a deal, Marsha," I remind her. She is lying on a long, narrow padded bench upholstered in black vinyl. Bolted to its head is a chrome-plated rack.

"Whoosh! Whoosh!" goes Marsha, hyperventilating. Her lips are puckered in a crinkled white o. Her face is flushed and sweaty, loose strands of hair adhere damply to her jawline. She tenses, heaves again. "Grrnph!"

"Remember we had a deal, Marsha," I repeat for emphasis. I am dismayed to find she is producing mildly erotic sensations in me, lying there on her back, legs splayed out on either side of the bench, bare feet planted in the nap of the carpet. She is dressed in a white body-stocking over which she has pulled a blue bikini bottom. When she jerks the bar off her chest her pelvis tilts upward and her buttocks snap off the vinyl, making an unsticking sound like adhesive tape being pulled loose. I can see the vague swirls of darkness on the body-stocking that mark her nipples.

"I think you know where she is," I say, taking off my parka and slinging it over my arm. Here in the steamy exercise room of Marsha's apartment building the temperature is kept at a level sufficient to produce heatstroke. I had the misfortune to buzz her

213

just as she was off to her daily work-out. The sacred ritual apparently cannot be postponed, so here I am.

"Whoosh! Whoosh!"

This is the perfect setting for a revival of the myth of Sisyphus. The glum smell of effort that produces little reward pervades it. The sour failed dreams of weight loss, flat tummies, firm thighs, haunt the room. Off in a corner a grey-haired retiree pedalling morosely on a stationary bicycle might be the fabled Greek himself, condemned to the present age's equivalent of boulder-rolling up mountain slopes. The old boy's gristly legs are doodled all over with bright blue veins.

Marsha interrupts these thoughts by settling the barbells in the rack above her head with a clank. She sits up, twists her torso to give me a view of her back, tenses her muscles, and forces back her shoulders. "Can you see definition in my back?" she asks.

"Pardon?"

"My muscles, do they stand out? Are they well-defined? I always check for myself in the bathroom mirror but I can't tell if it's just shadows or real definition. The light is so poor."

I study the crescent of fast-fading Arizona tan, the toffee-colored skin revealed by the low-scooped back of her body-stocking. "Why don't you answer me?" I demand. "Does Peters know where she is?"

"No he doesn't. I told you that already." She wriggles her shoulders. "How are my delts?"

I don't even know what they are. "Lovely. What did he say to you?"

"He hasn't heard from her," says Marsha, uncoiling her body and beginning to pat her arms dry with a towel, "and quite frankly I think he's come to the end of his patience. He doesn't care for emotional blackmail. It's gone too far now. Victoria has badly misjudged Anthony. She ought to have acted like an adult."

"How does an adult act in these circumstances?"

"Not a surprising question from you."

"What do you mean?"

"Well, in your case you might refrain from prowling the streets looking for her. That'd be a start."

"I have." I don't explain that this is not by choice. Rubacek won't let me have the car because I don't have a driver's licence — a piece of criminal sophistry on his part — and I can't get him to leave his writing. He claims his memoir is on the verge of completion; it's a question of mere hours. "This is the big push, Ed," he tells me. "Do or die."

"I am glad to hear it. And to see you've finally crawled out of that grungy apartment. What's-his-name must be thrilled."

"Rubacek."

"Yes. Stanley, isn't it? Is he still cluttering up the premises?"

"Yes."

"What interesting little friends you make."

"He's no friend of mine. He's driving me nuts. He *drove* me out of my apartment. And he's *driving* me nuts. When he's not reminding me not to be depressed he's asking me how to spell words that don't belong in the English language."

"Throw him out."

"It's not that easy. I've hinted rather strongly a number of times he should get out but he says he couldn't leave me when I'm depressed like this. If I did anything foolish he'd feel responsible, he says. I can't make him go." This is not entirely the truth. I could make anybody go. Let's face it, I've never had any problem driving people away. But just at the moment I can't summon up the necessary will and energy, and to tell the truth, this heart condition is never out of my mind. I think I'd be afraid to stay alone. Rubacek is better than nothing. I've made him memorize the phone numbers of all the ambulance services in town.

"Maybe Stanley is your karma," says Marsha with a wicked smile. "He who imposes shall be imposed upon."

"Marsha, I'm constantly amazed at your compassion and depth of understanding."

"Lighten up, Ed. You keep trying this hard to win some sympathy and you're going to start believing you're as badly off as you pretend to be. I'm warning you — it's a dangerous game you're playing. I was talking to Benny and he sees you're developing problems too."

"Sees what? What does that son of a bitch see? Go on, say it.

There's too many walnuts showing in the fruitcake. Is that what he was getting at?''

"Let's just say this business about your heart isn't healthy. We both agree on that. It's obvious there's nothing wrong with your heart. If there was, you wouldn't have been let out of the hospital."

"I'll let you know I have a history of high blood pressure."

"You've got a history of crawling around inside your own head. That's what you've got a history of. Everybody who knows you knows your history."

"All right, so you're the expert. Go on, what's my history?''

"Let's just leave it at that."

"You ought to review your own history, Marsha. Studded as it is with successes."

"What do you mean?''

"Let's just leave it at that."

"Oh, gamesmanship. All right. Okay, Ed. If you *have* to hear it. You want to know what everybody knows? This is what everybody knows. You're a fuck-up, an infantile jerk. We've always been embarrassed for you, the way you act. What did you need? A telegram informing you Victoria was missing in action? Do you think she was only gone when you separated? She was gone years before that. Believe me, people are losing patience with you.

"And you, did you behave with any kind of dignity, any kind of sense? No way. When she was running around with Harold you spied on them. And what're you doing now? Running around spying on her again. Phoning people. Hassling Anthony, hassling me. Why do you do this? Because you're lonely? Because you want a woman? Go find yourself a woman. They're out there. Haven't you heard? There's a selection. You're allowed more than one a lifetime."

I sit down beside her. She gives off a mingled scent of baby oil, fabric softener, sweat. It is very pleasant. "What do you call this thing?"

"A bench press."

We sit silent for a time. The old man is still pedalling. The bicycle tire whines against the resistance roller.

"I don't want another woman," I say.

Marsha shakes her head as if she can't believe what she's hearing.

"You know where she is, don't you?" I ask.

"Christ." Marsha props her elbow on her knee, forehead in her palm. "What is it? What is it you miss so much? She ought to bottle and sell it."

"Could it be that we were both misfits? Is that how we got together? It's the only explanation I can see." This is a genuine question. Such an idea had never occurred to me before. Is Victoria a misfit too?

"I never thought of her that way," says Marsha. "No, I don't think so."

"She must have been a misfit in some way nobody recognized," I say, unwilling to abandon the notion. "The reason I say this is I've never had any success with women. Absolutely none. Then Victoria comes along. I just wouldn't give up. Finally she went out with me. To hear Dick Gregory."

"A real fairy-tale," says Marsha.

"I've never really understood my complete lack of success with women. I mean *complete*. There are guys as fat as me that women like, and guys as opinionated, and guys as neurotic. Granted I'm all three, but the overwhelming abhorrence with which the opposite sex regards me is a bit of a puzzle. It's not entirely fair. I mean, Benny charms them out of the trees and it's obvious he's a moral idiot and sexual criminal. I was a virgin when I got married. Well, not exactly a virgin when I got married, what I mean to say is I was a virgin until I met Victoria.

"Ed," whispers Marsha, nudging me, "he's eavesdropping."

He is too, the old coot. I stare at him until he guiltily resumes pedalling.

"Wouldn't you say that was rather remarkable?" I continue. "Finding a male virgin of my advanced age? I mean, when free love was the orthodoxy?"

"Maybe you were fastidious."

"Wendy offered. Remember her? One of Benny's. But that was revenge. He'd dumped her. I considered it seriously before refusing."

"I get a queer feeling when you talk about what happened back then," says Marsha. "It's like listening to a documentary or something. It's as if it never really involved you. It's as if you Rip Van Winkled out, woke up ten years later, and got all your information from old newspapers. Where the hell were you?"

I shrug.

This seems, unaccountably, to make Marsha angry. "Nobody felt comfortable around you, everybody felt you were judging them, even poor Victoria, who was so patiently and pathetically waiting for you to join the human race. Do you have any idea how good the rest of us felt believing we weren't going to end up like the walking dead all around us? Do you? And then this messy shlub, this twenty-two-year-old zombie, would shuffle into the room and piss on our parade. Do you know what I remember best about you? There were six of us sitting around talking about Gandhi and passive resistance and all that crap and you piped up and said that Gandhi had advocated, in his early days, that the Hindus slaughter the sacred cows and begin to eat beef. He believed that beef-eating was the source of British strength. That to beat the English you had to out-eat the English. It had nothing to do with what we were talking about."

"A little-known fact."

"It had nothing to do with the man he became."

"Do you have any idea what *you* all sounded like? You weren't really talking about Gandhi. You didn't give a shit what Gandhi thought. You wanted to convince yourself that if he were alive he'd have been sitting in that circle, passing the roach and being self-righteous."

"Bill had you pegged. Terminal narcissism. He said you'd book yourself into Carnegie Hall some day and buy an audience for your final rant."

"I'd have had to get in line for a booking behind him."

"He was an idealist, Ed. Not a cheap cynic."

"He was the goddamn Ayatollah Khomeini then and he's the goddamn Ayatollah Khomeini now."

"He was an idealist, Ed."

I don't answer. She can have that much. After a bit she offers, "What he is now I can't say."

I can see Bill Sadler walking down 3rd Avenue, clasping the sheet of plywood tightly to his chest. He should look crazy. The disturbing thing is that he looks perfectly sane and probably is. Clinically speaking.

"Yeah, well . . . "

Marsha stands. "I don't want to talk about Bill any more," she says. "I don't like marching over old ground. Let's go upstairs and have a drink to the realists."

There it is, that peculiar tension, awkwardness, that can surprise two people who had never intended such a thing to happen.

I run my hands down my pants creases. "I won't bother you any longer."

"Come along," she says, "I'll take a quick shower and you can make us some drinks. I've got those powdered mixes. You can have whatever you like."

"No, I'd better go."

"You can have whatever you like, Ed."

"No."

That's the end of it. Her face displays neither anger nor disappointment. I have, with a twist of perspective, become once again a fat man of limited qualities. "Suit yourself," she says.

I show the taxi driver the money and the map with its numbered quadrants, o's, red lines. "I've got thirty-five dollars," I explain. My finger runs up 22nd Street on the map. "I want you to pull into every motel along here until the meter hits thirty-five bucks. When it hits thirty-five bucks, stop the cab and let me out. Okay?"

"Just let you out wherever?"

"That's right."

"You don't know where you're going?"

"That's right."

"You mind if I ask for the money first?"

Returning to my apartment exhausted, I find all the lights are burning but the place has an air of vacancy. While hanging up my parka I call out to Stanley and get no answer. I walk through empty rooms that have been cleaned, tidied. The dishes have been done. My bed is made. My dirty clothes have been picked off the floor and stowed in the laundry hamper.

In the living room I spy a stale package of cigarettes I'd left on the top of the TV days ago. Lighting one, I break another of my recent resolutions to preserve the tenuous health of my heart.

I sit down and close my eyes. The tobacco, very dry and strongly flavored by the plastic-tasting heat of the TV, snaps and sizzles faintly. The cigarette burns between my lips like a fuse. I think of the afternoon spent looking for Victoria. Images twitch behind my eyelids. Lamp standards jerk by, snow drifts, men in neutral-colored clothing stand in the windows of motel offices, hands in their pants pockets, shoulders rounded. Thirty-five dollars spent and a bus ride home. Another resolution broken.

I wonder where Stanley's gone. I have a feeling he mightn't be back. That would explain his putting the place right. The lights would have been left on as a welcome. He knows how I hate an empty, dark apartment.

If Rubacek had moved in with anything more than the shirt on his back I could confirm my suspicions by checking to see if anything is missing, by checking to see what he's taken with him, but he came with nothing.

I remember the manuscript of *Society's Revenge: The Stanley Rubacek Story*. Surely he wouldn't leave that behind.

It isn't on the kitchen table where he worked. The table has been cleared and cleaned. I can make out the wipe marks that have dried in dull, soapy streaks on its Arborite top. I search all the rooms, even going so far as to rummage in a linen closet, to go down on my hands and knees to peer under a bed. No manuscript. Stanley is definitely gone. What if I have another heart attack? I could die alone here and nobody would know.

It's in the fridge. With a bottle of ketchup resting on it like a paperweight. There's a note.

"I knew you couldn't miss it here!!! But seriously Ed don't

leave this on *ice* to long, okay??!! I'm dying to hear the *verdict*. (Bet you never expected to hear that one from an excon. Ha. Ha.)."

Cold has made the pages feel slippery and damp to the touch. He is coming back. I set the manuscript on the table, pour myself a drink, read the first page, reread it.

I finished the book in six hours. It is clear from this creaky melodrama that Stanley has never been a convict, likely never even committed a crime. However, it is equally clear that he has read a good many books about crime and criminals.

Yet he is not simply a liar. I once knew a girl like Stanley. She attended my junior high school. When she was twelve she suddenly announced she was Adolf Hitler's daughter, smuggled out of Germany at the end of the war. Her parents, her teachers, nobody could dissuade her from making her bizarre claims. She suffered for them. Teasing made her life hell; she lost her one friend, a girl almost as strange as herself. Unclever, plain, nearly ugly, she was still somebody, the daughter of modern Europe's greatest madman. She was Adolf Hitler's daughter. Even when somebody pointed out in 1962 that she was too young to have been born in 1945 she merely said, "I'm not thirteen, I'm seventeen."

She was taken to a psychiatrist. From that moment on she ceased saying she was Adolf Hitler's daughter. She began to say, very calmly, "My name is Eva Hitler." She began to sign test papers, essays, and letters with that name. When tormented past endurance she would cry: "I'm not responsible for what my father did! I was only a baby!"

After two years of this her family moved away. A report reached us in a couple of months that in her new home Eva Hitler was once more Doris Wright.

And so with Stanley, I suspect.

SEVENTEEN

"What the hell time is it?"

"Seven," says Rubacek, stepping into the apartment. He is pale and his eyes, which are bright with excitement, seem all the brighter because the flesh beneath them is darkened with fatigue.

"You could learn to ring the doorbell instead of hammering away like that. I've got trouble enough with my neighbors. What did you want to do, wake the whole goddamn building?"

"I found her," he says. "I found your wife."

Across the road lies the Skyways Motel. The airport is half a mile away. A descending jet fills the car with noise so that Rubacek has to raise his voice. He is explaining how he tracked down Victoria. "All night," he says, "I drove every place. You know? All around looking. And then I thought of the airport. The fucking airport. Airport equals hotels. Right? I seen it there, must've been 6 a.m. of the morning. A Volkswagen, I says to myself. Busted up? Blue? I even wrote down the licence number." He twists in the seat and fishes a slip of paper out of the change pocket of his jeans. "JRS 257," he reads. "That it?"

I'm very nervous and that makes me snappish. Rubacek wants to be praised. "I told you before, I don't know her goddamn licence number." Nevertheless, it is Victoria's car parked there in front of room 37, beginning to show its blue paint in the winter morning light.

Last night Rubacek had to strike a match to be sure. He has told me that several times.

"What time is it?"

"Nearly nine," says Stanley. I've kept us waiting here nearly forty minutes and Rubacek is growing a little impatient. "If she isn't up by now she ought to be."

"She likes to sleep late every chance she gets."

"Well, how long we got to sit here? Are you going over there or what?"

"You want to start the car and get some heat in here? I'm getting cold."

"I ain't got much gas. You ain't cold, you're just nervous. Lots of people feel cold when they're only nervous."

"I said I'm *cold.*"

"Bite my fucking head off." He turns the key, the motor whines into life.

A strong breeze is blowing, unusual for so early in the morning, and serpents of driven snow writhe on the black pavement. The wind has cleared the steadily brightening sky of cloud. The day will be sunny and cold. The spreading light gives me a sense of distance from all those things of the past few days. Victoria is close at hand now. A short walk across the road and I am in the thick of possibility, of opportunity.

Rubacek, however, has been steadily diminishing in this light, has shrunk to the size of an anecdote. Is this because we have come to an obvious parting of the ways and now return, each to our separate solitudes? I had better speak.

"I read your book," I say. His reaction is not what I thought it might be. I see he is, at the crux, afraid of discovery. "When? Last night?" he asks quickly, avoiding my eyes.

"Yes."

"I don't think you should think that's it. You know? I ain't sure. I don't think I've got it just right. It don't feel right to me."

"It's an interesting book, Stanley."

"I don't want that. I don't want an interesting book. I want a fucking monster book. I want—" he seems to lose the train of his thought, "I want — you know, my story to be told."

"I see."

"But if you think I got it . . ."

"You know best, Stanley. Your sense of what you want is better than mine."

"Maybe if I put the love interest in. I left it out."

"Perhaps."

"She was beautiful," says Stanley, "she lived only for me. But her family wouldn't let her associate with a known felon. If we'd been allowed to marry I might have reversed my life around."

I turn away and watch the snow creeping over the pavement. After a bit Stanley says, "Go on, Ed. Go on over there."

"Not just yet. She mightn't be up."

"Go on. I'll wait."

"No, I'll find my way home. You can leave."

"Sure?"

"Yeah."

"We'll talk about the book some more?"

"Sure," I say, opening the door. "We'll talk about the book some more, Stanley."

Trotting across the road, hunched sideways to keep my face averted from the wind, I'm nervous as a bridegroom. I'd have delayed this if I could. Suddenly I don't feel ready to face her.

I think, What pose should I assume confronting her? What mental attitude? Something Philip Marlowe-ish seems appropriate for a hard-bitten character who has tracked a wayward woman to a cheap motel on the edge of beyond, just short of nowhere. A place where some guy called Burt or Art or Frank discounts the price of an uneasy sleep if you intend to stay a week or more.

Rapping briskly on the door of room 37 makes my knuckles smart because they're cold. I'm sucking them peevishly when I realize there's a peephole in the door through which Victoria can peruse sex-slayers requesting admittance. Knuckle-sucking is not hard-boiled. Has she seen me?

Inside there are dim rustlings, silence. She is probably in bed. I strike the door sharply with the palm of my hand. "Victoria. It's me. It's all right."

"Who?" Evidently she isn't using the peephole. Her voice is muffled, flannel-mouthed.

"Me. It's me."

"Anthony?"

She sounds hopeful. It is an awful moment. Anthony. Loathsome, acorn-gobbling swine in the groves of academe. I steady myself against the doorframe. "Me, yes!" I shout. Not exactly a lie.

The bolt shoots back with a click, the chain rattles, and when the door opens I lurch in before Victoria can swing it shut again.

A small cry.

"It's Ed. It's me — Ed."

In the hiatus that marks my announcement I experience a piercing sensation, a feeling that on entering this room I have entered my past. Not déjà vu but a perception more definite, exact. The room smells of cigarette smoke and dirty underwear. None of the lights are turned on.

Our images in the large mirror on the dresser catch my eye. We move in it, vague shapes. The hood of my parka still drawn up, I am an awkward, dropsical monk of the Middle Ages, one of the fearful ones, burdened under his habit by chain mail. Victoria glimmers in the glass, skin-toned panties and bra dark against her dead-white winter flesh.

"Liar," she says vehemently. "Liar."

I walk past her to the bedside lamp and switch it on. In the brazen light she looks ill, jaundiced. Her hair hangs lank, greasy. She hugs her breasts as if trying to cage pain. "Fucking liar." I've never seen her like this.

The room is a mess. This isn't like Victoria. Half-empty Cokes standing on the dresser float shredding cigarette butts and burnt matches. A towel that has been used to sop up a spill of some kind lies sodden and twisted at the foot of the bed. In the middle of the room her suitcase lies split open like an overripe pod, bursting with rumpled, soiled clothing.

Suddenly I feel very afraid.

"Have you been eating, Victoria?" I ask, taking off my parka, trying to keep my voice level.

"Liar," she says dully, not bothering to look at me.

"I didn't say I was him." The room makes me edgy. I sat in

such a place, in the half-light of drawn curtains, closed doors, in used air.

"Do you know how long I've been waiting? And then I open the door and it isn't him. It's the fucking liar at the door." Her face has lost its yellowish cast; it's gone blindingly white. The contrast reveals traces of old lipstick on her mouth.

"Have you been out of this room at all, Victoria? Have you seen anybody?"

"I don't want to see you. Why don't you just get out?"

I try to explain. "You don't know how hard I've been looking for you. Everywhere. I want to make up for what I did in the restaurant. I've been sick with worry. I drove for days, looking. I—"

"Don't give me any of your crap," she says. "I know why you're here. Marsha sent you. He wouldn't come, so Marsha sent you."

"What do you mean, Marsha sent me? Marsha doesn't know you're here."

"Marsha sent you," Victoria says, "because he wouldn't come. And I told her not to tell you anything."

I take a moment to absorb this. "No," I say, "Marsha didn't tell me anything. I found you myself."

"The dirty liar is lying again." She covers her ears with her hands. "I'm not listening to any more lies."

"Stop it," I say, catching at her arms, trying to pull her hands down. "Listen to me, Victoria."

Speechless struggle, a rubbery twisting of arms. She wrenches loose from my grip. I see my finger marks livid as burns on her white skin. We stare at each other, breath ragged. Her face is a furious mask, eyes flat and black.

"Liar," she whispers hoarsely.

"Listen to me, Victoria."

This time she covers her ears and squeezes shut her eyes too.

In a hot rage I pull at her elbows. Flailing arms, hoarse breath that smells faintly of ether, tangled legs. We sway in a dance of contention. Her forehead burrowing and knocking against my breastbone is a dull pain.

Suddenly I remember the baby and break the circle of my arms, releasing her before she harms herself. "All right, *enough!*" I shout.

She's caught a fistful of hair at the side of my head. Hangs on it. All in a rush I feel like a man seized by a drowning swimmer. Her weight is suffocating.

"Stop it!" My palm twists and slides against her temple as I try to push the hard, obstinate skull away, try to break her hold. Reeling in a stumbling shuffle, off-balance, locked against one another, I slam into the bathroom door. The knob punches into the pad of yielding flesh over a kidney. I hang transfixed by a bright pain that daubs little blurred circles in my eyes. All I can manage to say is, "Please. Please let me go."

"Bastards," sobs Victoria.

I lurch off the door, really panicked now, trying to run away. Grunting under my burden I stagger across the floor. Two blows. Something sharp, hard, bites into the cartilage of my ear. The moonstone. She must be wearing her moonstone. My ear roars with sea noises. I wag my head madly, trying to shake her fist out of my hair. I can't breathe.

Wall to wall, corner to corner on trembling legs. Plunging against furniture. A chair topples, a Coke spills and rolls off the dresser to the floor.

Nails rake the skin under my eyes, scratching furrows of heat, tracks of smarting wetness. I snatch her wrist. "Victoria!"

"Sons of bitches. Sons of bitches."

Christ, she's trying to knee me. I twist my pelvis. She batters my hip. A hand grabs my collar, my shirt front spits buttons as cloth rips.

I've got both her hands. They flutter and flap as I squeeze her wrists. "Now," I say, "stop it!"

My right leg scoots out crazily, a muscle gives way in my groin with a wrench. Pitched sideways my head bounds off a corner of the dresser with a crack. I tumble to the carpet. A yard from my face the Coke bottle I stepped on is still spinning like a deranged compass needle. I'm afraid the pain will make me vomit.

There is always plenty of blood from a scalp wound; already I can feel it creeping out of my hairline and when I sit up it spills down my face.

The sight sobers and chastens Victoria. She sits down abruptly on the bed as if she's been slapped in the face. One of her bra straps has fallen in a loop down her arm and wisps of hair are plastered in the tears and sweat on her face, or tangled in saliva at the corners of her mouth. She brushes at them with a shaking hand.

I get to my feet and hobble to the bathroom, where I run cold water on the back of my neck and gently probe the lips of my wound with a finger. It's not very long or wide. In any case, the flow of blood has eased to a slow, steady seepage. I wad toilet paper onto the ache and stickiness and limp back to Victoria. She is stretched full length on the bed, a forearm thrown across her eyes.

"You all right?" she asks, hearing me. She doesn't move.

"Yeah."

"I thought I'd killed you."

"It wasn't for dint of trying," I say, and add, "I've hurt my leg." I move to the edge of the bed and sit down beside her to take the weight off it. Feeling the mattress sag, she removes her arm from her face. "Maybe you better lie down," she says, edging away, making room. "You don't look so hot. You're pale."

When I lower my head on the pillow I feel dizzy. The bed slowly wheels as it does when I'm drunk. The fit passes and I find myself concentrating on the comfortable closeness of another person's body, her breathing. How long has it been since I companionably shared a bed? A year and a half? Our silence lengthens. I hear water coursing in pipes, a car engine starting in the cold with a mechanical squeal of protest.

"Don't think it was you, Ed," she says at last. "It was things in general, coming to a head. Things have been too much lately. It wasn't really you."

"Oh, I suppose it was," I say. "More than you imagine."

"No." Victoria hesitates. "Marsha probably told you everything, didn't she?"

"Yes."

"Everything?"

"Yes."

"I thought so. Then you know. I asked her not to."

"Well, if you ask Marsha not to, she does. If you ask her to, she doesn't. It's the nature of the beast."

"I didn't have anybody else to talk to. She's got more heart than you give her credit for."

"Actually Marsha and I have grown to be friends, quite affectionate really. She bought me a tuxedo. I'm escorting her to her brother's wedding."

"Which brother? The skinny one? Danny?"

"I don't know *which* brother. *A* brother. There was a whole litter of them, wasn't there?"

"Yes. I think so." She rattles off names. "Kenneth, Danny, Paul. Robert?"

I shrug.

Victoria remains silent for a time. Her face in profile is stony, the lips compressed. "I don't know what to do," she says, eyes fixed on the ceiling. "I've thought and thought. But there doesn't seem to be any answer. I've just sat here and watched TV and smoked those goddamn cigarettes and bawled."

"If it's any use to you, I'm not going to give you any more trouble over the divorce. I've given up on that. You want to marry this guy, or whatever, marry him."

"The only thing I ever wanted," says Victoria, "was to feel that things could get better. I need to feel things getting better."

I could say we're old enough now not to count on much; our experience teaches us the contrary, but I don't. I'm turning into a diplomat. I don't say anything.

"He's got his good points. But he's selfish."

Nor do I question her as to what these alleged good points are. What I do say is, "You can't stay here forever. You have to make up your mind. And arrangements have to be made either way."

"I know all that."

"Then act on what you know. It's all you can do."

Victoria turns on her side. Her face looms near mine. The bones are more severe than I remember them. "What would you do, Ed? If you were in my place, what would you do?"

"Christ, Victoria, you know me. Who the hell knows what I'd do? I can only say what seems to make sense. Forget about, you know . . . That's a complication you don't need right now. If you want to make things start to work for you, maybe that's the only way to do it. In a year he could change his mind about a kid. But that's not for me to say, you know him better than I do. But be calculating for once. Neither you nor I were ever very calculating and look where it got us."

Victoria fumbles at the bedside table, locates a package of cigarettes and lights one. "Sometimes I think of myself at fifty," she says, expelling smoke. "I've never done very well making choices. It seems I can't trust myself — anyway the evidence suggests I can't. When I'm fifty the kid would still be with me — in some way. I don't want to be alone at fifty. Somehow I don't expect Anthony will be around when I'm fifty, I have that feeling now. He didn't come for me."

"Then come back to me. I'll be there at fifty. And so would the child. You can have us both."

"Ed," she asks, "why do you insist on this?"

I suppose there is no explanation that makes any abiding sense. But I try to offer one. "Because we made a stab at growing up together. We married too young and lived in such a way at the beginning that a part of me didn't develop, it withered like an unused limb. Responsibility, whatever word you want to call it. Anyway you supplied a crutch, Victoria, and I grew up the way I am. Without you all I can manage is to get by."

"And that's what I was? A crutch?"

I see I've made a mistake, explaining. "No, not just a crutch. The thing was you never showed any fear of life. You expected happiness. You were my courage."

"But not always enough." Victoria is thinking of my breakdown.

"No, not always enough. But as much — more — than anyone could be expected to give."

"When you went into that room and didn't come out I thought at first it was a trick. One of your games."

"Maybe it started that way."

"Marsha told me about this heart attack business. Are you looking for sympathy, or do you believe it?"

Do I? At one point I did. I'm not certain any more. "There's something wrong with me," I say.

"It's all in your imagination, Ed. You know that. And you know where your head can lead you."

"Do you mind if I turn this light off?" I ask. "My head is pounding and the light in my eyes makes it worse."

"Go ahead."

I pull the chain.

"I'm afraid, Ed," she says. "I'm afraid to live with regrets. I honestly don't know what to do."

"Yes," I say.

We lie in a queer, artificial dusk, side by side, untouching, like effigies of a medieval couple carved on a cathedral tomb. Thinking this, I cross one leg over the other. A knight depicted on his tomb with crossed legs, someone once told me, is a sign he had been on a crusade.

"I'm *tired*," Victoria suddenly exclaims.

I don't say anything in reply.

"You have no idea what this is like," she says. "How can I decide? I love him, Ed."

"Yes."

She says no more but cries quietly for a bit. Then her breathing grows regular, measured. She's fallen asleep.

When she wakes I feign sleep, listening to her careful, discreet movements as she gathers up her clothes and packs. When the door closes and I hear the Volkswagen start, I uncross my legs, which have begun to cramp.

EIGHTEEN

When Marsha picked me up for the wedding tonight, Stanley waved goodbye to us from my apartment door and shouted a request for me to bring him home a piece of wedding cake. He is staying on at my place to work on revisions to *The Stanley Rubacek Story* and gives no indication that he ever intends to leave.

I am wearing the tux this evening, but not even being dapper can lift my spirits. Ever since Victoria stole away from me in the motel four days ago, I've gone into a kind of slide. I keep mulling over all the mistakes I've made in the past, terrible, wounding mistakes. I am bitten again and again by regret.

It must be evident how I feel because earlier this evening Marsha chided me for looking glum. "Show a little enthusiasm, why don't you," she said. "You're at a wedding, not an autopsy."

So I've tried to lighten my mood for the dancing that is to come later. After all, that's why I'm here, for the dancing. But even drinking all those cocktails before dinner and nearly a bottle of wine with the meal hasn't seemed to work. I still feel awfully low.

There were a lot of speeches and toasts before, during, and after dinner, a veritable banquet of oratory. They're still going at it while the busboys clear the tables. It has all reminded me of my own wedding and has started me thinking of Victoria once more. So here I sit trying my best to get happy and to convince myself that all will be for the best.

The more I drink, the more moving I find the speeches. On

several occasions I have been brought to the point of tears and had to dab at my eyes with a napkin. Marsha took note of this and when the waiter came around with the brandy she put her hand over the mouth of my snifter and gave me a look that wasn't hard to interpret.

But at a wedding the love and good feeling present are contagious. I decided that Marsha ought to know I hold no ill-feeling towards her whatsoever. So I said: "Marsha, I know you lied to me all along about not knowing where Victoria was, right up to the last, but I forgive you. What's past is past."

She said: "I don't know what you're talking about, Ed, but you better straighten yourself up before the dancing starts."

It was then that I excused myself, ostensibly to visit the little boys' room. However, I went nowhere near any lavatory. Instead, I went downstairs to the hotel bar, quickly downed two doubles, and then hot-footed it back here. I've arrived just in time to catch one of the grizzled uncles making a speech full of advice for the newlyweds.

Right at the moment he is emphasizing that they should never go to bed angry with one another. That's worse than poison, he says. As he rambles on, bride and groom gaze up at him, necks twisted and patient smiles pasted on their faces.

As I listen to him speak I find myself growing agitated. What he is telling them is all very well, but surely he is failing to raise issues central to the survival of modern married life. This young man and woman ought to be warned!

As he finishes I find myself getting to my feet, ablaze with a sense of mission.

At first there is difficulty in getting the master of ceremonies to acknowledge me, and Marsha, tugging at my trouser leg, almost topples me over, but by exerting a considerable effort on both counts I manage to gain and hold the floor.

I begin in the customary way by extending my heartiest congratulations to Robert and his bride, whose name for the moment escapes me. Then I go on to say that I wish to offer a few cautionary notes to bride and groom as they embark on their voyage through life. I urge them to listen carefully to what I have to say because there is no teacher like failure. For the first time this evening I feel a little better because I can help these people, I can be useful. And for five or six minutes everything seems to me to go very well. There is absolute silence as I sketch the course of my own unhappy career in marriage and the various pitfalls into which Victoria and I tumbled. Yet somehow I feel my points will be lost on them if I fail to generalize. So I strike on another illustration. "Of course, Robert," I say, addressing the groom, "you already know something of the similar difficulties your sister Marsha found herself in, in respect to troubles of the kind I have been outlining."

"Who is that man?" says someone very loudly and rudely.

Another person calls out, "Sit down and shut up!"

I ignore these interruptions because of the importance of my message. I say that I know Marsha won't mind my touching upon certain aspects of her marriage because she knows that in the great experiment of life we are all workers in the same laboratory, and that whatever one researcher discovers he is honor bound to share with his fellows.

By the time I complete my review of Marsha's marriage there is a good deal of noise in the room and I am forced to hasten to a conclusion. Once more I am on the brink of tears. Turning to the bride and groom I throw open my arms and cry, "Embrace one another with courage. Search each other's hearts for hidden suffering and never flee what you discover! That's the ticket!"

I am a little surprised there is no applause when I take my seat. I thought that last bit might have moved them as much as it moved me, bringing tears to my eyes. There is no accounting for people's reactions.

Then two of Marsha's lubberly brothers latch on to my arms and begin to drag me towards the door. I appeal to Marsha but she averts her eyes. In the hotel corridor an altercation ensues; I receive a split lip and my lovely tuxedo gets ripped.

Now it's four in the morning and I'm sitting in a twenty-four-hour doughnut and coffee shop eating bismarcks. When the bank opens this morning I'm withdrawing all the money I have left in my account. I'm not even going back to the apartment for my clothes and the rest of my things. Stanley can have it all. Or the landlord.

I'm running away.

NINETEEN

Today was a stifling hot day, much hotter than a day in May ought to be. Now it's raining. I've flung wide all the windows of my basement suite and let my rooms fill with the nostalgic scent of wet grass and the sound of water running in the eaves.

The old woman upstairs must have gone to bed; I don't hear her moving around up there. She's a widow. I rent these rooms from her and give her a little something extra to do my shopping. I don't go out much because I'm pretty sure Victoria is looking for me. I feel that I should at least be in when she comes. She's probably terribly worried.

The old woman upstairs is a good cook. Last month, April, I paid her to bake me a dark-chocolate birthday cake. Last month I was thirty-two. We had a simple, quiet celebration. I went upstairs in the afternoon and we sat and ate cake and watched the soaps on TV.

I needed a clean break with the past. Things got out of hand. That's why I never went back to the apartment, just walked away from it all and let Stanley have it.

I disappeared. Goodbye to Benny, Marsha, Peters, COCWE, Victoria. A new, simpler life.

There are only two people from the past I've been in touch with, Mr. McMurtry and Tom. Courtesy of the radio, that is.

Lately I've thought Mr. McMurtry sounds enfeebled. I suppose it's because of Tom. He isn't as patient with him as he once was and Mr. McMurtry feels his displeasure, I can tell from his voice. It's not as robust as I remembered it; he's lost confidence. I thought I'd try and cheer him up, so I had the old woman buy a greeting card, but in the end I didn't send it. A disappeared man doesn't send greetings.

Tom, however, is doing wonderfully well. His star is rising. In just the last two months the station has given him another program in addition to his morning open-line show. It's a nightly five-minute spot that is a lead-in to the eleven o'clock news, editorials on questions of the day. Or, as Tom styles them, "Rollins Radiotorials". I never miss his show. It makes a welcome break in the long evenings. You see, I'm having trouble sleeping again.

Tonight Tom is discussing evolution. There's been another dust-up in the city school system and light needs to be shed on this delicate topic.

There are those of you who will disagree with me on this one, he says, *but I see Evolution as here to stay. You can't make Progress go away.*

I've always liked that soft, gentle sound, the sound of rain dropping mildly out of the sky. This rain will continue for hours.

Maybe the problem is that she's leaving it up to the others. I don't suppose any of them would be out tonight looking in a downpour. Well, maybe Stanley might. But not Benny. Or Marsha. And Victoria certainly shouldn't be, not when she's pregnant. And anyway, is there one of them who is capable of organizing a search on the scale I did? I mean a search with a map, and quadrants, and red circles, and all of that? It'll take them more than a few months to find me. I covered my tracks.

I should turn my radio up. Tom's voice seems to be fading in and out in the rain.

Several centuries ago, the famous British Prime Minister Disraeli — that's D-i-s-r-a-e-l-i, if you want to look it up — said in regard to the then controversial topic of evolution, "If it's a choice between the apes and the angels, then I'm on the side of the angels." I think he had a point. I'd like to agree with that great British statesman.

Of course, angels. When I was little, and afraid to go to sleep, my father used to say, "There's no need to worry, Ed. Your angel watches over you. God made the angels so they never need to sleep. He did that so you and me can."

It's not really that I'm afraid to sleep. It's this business of closing my eyes. When I do I see the strangest things.

Pop. He'll be getting his letters returned because I left no forwarding address. I haven't told him where I am because he might tell Victoria. I think she should work as hard finding me as I worked finding her.

So all those envelopes of Polaroids are being sent back to him. Sometimes when I close my eyes I see him sitting in his lawn chair under his striped awning. All the returned letters have blown in drifts around his knees. He looks as if he's sitting in a snowbank and I feel as if I'm watching him through a zoom lens. As I focus in on him, less and less of him fills more and more of the camera until there's only a big baseball cap, huge sunglasses, a plain of white face. And then I see frost on his lips and know that he's been frozen solid in my blizzard of returned letters.

The world is billions of years old and getting older by the minute. Now here's a thought I had. Maybe evolution, or whatever, is slowly turning Mr. Disraeli's apes into angels, but it's all being done so gradual we don't realize it. Wouldn't that be something quite unique? Stranger things have happened. Look at the platypus.

This is Tom Rollins, this May 23, asking all you good people to keep thinking about it.

I'm tired. Waiting is tiring. And then because I don't want to see things I have to keep my eyes open. The rain makes this hard. It can lull you. I wonder how long it will keep up. It's a fine thing this smell of drenched, yielding earth. If I could only close my eyes without seeing things I could sleep. And if I could sleep I know I'd soon be as right as rain. Right, right as rain.

But as soon as I close my eyes strange things begin to happen. Just now when I did for a moment, I heard footsteps and I thought it might be them. No, not exactly footsteps. It was the sound of naked feet shuffling in this room. I opened my eyes and saw nothing.

Now again. Who is that? That man standing there, face obscured in shadows. A big man, gentle on bootless feet, moving slowly through the room soft, soft.

"Do you hear the rain?" I ask him, now that I know who he

is. The kitchen light strikes his naked black feet. I can see a sliver of creamy sole, inky toes.

"You go to sleep," he says. "Right now."

I feel it coming. So simple and easy. And the last thing before I am pitched into sleep is the smell of wet, broken grass, and the rain's gentle thrumming in a room that waits on the promises of summer.